The Barbarian Geisha

Still trembling from the intensely personal
nature of her encounter with Nakano, Annabel
stared at the overlord in shock. She had not
known him long, and he seemed intent on
demonstrating his dominion over her. He had
forced her to strip and display her naked body
for his pleasure; he had allowed a stranger to
toy with her most intimate flesh; now he was
talking about training her.

She had no reason to trust him, yet once
that first kiss had sent shivers down her spine,
she had known beyond doubt there was a
deep, sexual bond between them.

The Barbarian Geisha
Charlotte Royal

BLACK LACE

Black Lace books contain sexual fantasies.
In real life, always practise safe sex.

This edition published in 2005 by
Black Lace
Thames Wharf Studios
Rainville Road
London W6 9HA

Originally published 1998

Copyright © Charlotte Royal 1998

The right of Charlotte Royal to be identified as the Author of
the Work has been asserted in accordance with the Copyright,
Designs and Patents Act 1988.

Typeset by SetSystems Ltd, Saffron Walden, Essex
Printed and bound by Mackays of Chatham PLC

ISBN 0 352 33267 0

Prologue

*I*n the aftermath of the storm the wind swept up the Izu peninsula from foreign quarters. Fresh, salty, unsettling, it blew in from the west, whipping up the white-crested combers that crashed on to the rocky shores of Japan.

Narrowing his eyes, a stocky peasant fisherman licked salt from his lips, clutched at his conical straw hat and pushed his way against the still-stiff breeze down on to the beach. He was not the first. The sweep of the sandy bay was dotted with tiny stooping figures, and more black dots searched along the rocky boulders that clung to the tips of the bay. The fisherman tensed, and then relaxed. No intruder was working the patch of shoreline that was his by tradition.

He went to his rickety shack first, to pick up some woven, circular baskets to hold what he might glean from the typhoon's leavings. Despite the storm damage to his shed and his squid nets, the old man was whistling through the gap in his front teeth as he collected his baskets and trotted down to the high water mark. After a storm like last night's, there was bound to be something good in the tangled piles of flotsam that now lay in heaped piles all along the shore.

It was still early, but the winter sun was hot on his back as he worked. He sifted methodically through the warm, slimy black line of wreckage, marvelling at how far the waves had rolled up the beach the night before. He put the soaking, silvery driftwood to one side, to be collected later for firewood. It was more important to deal with the tangled fronds of perishable seaweed first. He sorted the green salty ribbons into piles: the best would go to market, the rest could be eaten at home.

The fisherman's attention shifted away from seaweed for a moment as he turned over a pearly pink shell in his gnarled hands. He examined its fleshy intricate whorls. It was a particularly fine shell; perhaps he could sell it. He straightened up, meaning to put the shell to one side, and then he froze, all motion arrested, because he had seen a sinister shape in the tangle of high-water debris. The sun felt very hot on his head and the surf boomed in his ears as he strained his eyes towards the worrying, body-shaped mound.

He closed his eyes, swallowed hard and looked again. There was no mistake. It was almost concealed in the piles of seaweed and debris, but it was a body; a large, naked body. His heart crashed into his mouth and he took a step back. Inwardly he cursed his ill luck. A body on the beach might draw the attention of the terrifying lord of the province, the daimyo, with his razor-keen, bright swords. The old peasant's bones turned to water and he groaned softly as he thought of Lord Nakano. He looked around him cautiously. No one had noticed his find. Perhaps he could say nothing, allow the sea to reclaim the body at the next high tide and so keep him free of involvement.

His mouth was dry and his heart thudded dully. He knelt on the wet sand with knees that shook as they bent, and prayed as he never had before. The other black

2

dots on the beach worked their patches steadily under the clear blue bowl of the sky. The fisherman prayed harder. All he wanted was a quiet life. The seaweed before him steamed steadily as the heat of the sun grew, and the aromatic fishy reek that tingled in his nostrils seemed to clear his brain and help him to think.

He looked cautiously at the body. Only one out-stretched arm was clearly visible. The milky white fingers of the hand curled in the sand as if in supplication. He must cover it, so no one could see. He reached for his baskets of seaweed, and, careless of their worth at market, made to spread the vivid green fronds across the corpse. Then he stopped as the implications of what he was planning hit him. He swallowed hard. Could this be someone he knew? Could he leave an old friend to rot in the water? In the code of those who got their living by the sea, it was a serious offence to leave a fellow seaman's body to the nibbling fishes.

He reached out trembling, sun-darkened fingers to where the head must be. Softly he cleared away a twisted lump of bladderwrack, exposing the face, and then once more his heart burst into his throat and he heard himself making soft mewing noises of fear: a female, but not one he had ever seen before.

He shut his eyes and prayed hard into the darkness and the red specks that floated in it. He never wanted to open his eyes again. The corpse was nothing like the slender, dark-haired, almond-eyed people he had been used to all his life. Lying before him, skin glistening in the sunlight, was a pale milky body so foreign, so utterly bizarre in shape and form that it could only be some kind of supernatural creature.

His breath hissed between his teeth and he wailed softly. Only the terrible trembling that weakened his knees prevented him from getting up and running back to the familiar comfort of his home and his wife. He swallowed hard and wished that he were anywhere,

3

even in the prisons of the lord of the province, anywhere rather than sitting back on his heels on this gritty, sandy beach, within touching distance of the naked body of a dead sea nymph.

Time passed and the sun rose higher as he fought to control himself. The black figures of the villagers stayed mercifully distant. The breeze plucked at his kimono and tugged at the seaweed that covered the corpse. The fisherman's panic slowly cleared. The naked figure was not moving. He had that much comfort at least.

The wind was dying down, but it was still strong enough to lift more of the disturbed fronds of seaweed, flicking them away, exposing more of the naked body. Despite his fear, the fisherman began to register details. The skin of the sea goddess was an unearthly, pearly white. There was an iridescent pinkish blush to it, not unlike the shell he had paused to admire earlier. He thought of the gorgeous women, in the paintings he had masturbated over as a young man, clustered like flowers around the imperial court. This sea witch had finer, paler skin than the emperor's consorts.

He felt desire stir as the wind lifted a coil of emerald-green sea-grass in a teasing striptease, revealing more of her nudity. He sucked in his breath. Nipples! But such a colour as he had never seen before. Not chestnut, but a fine clear pink, like the double-flowered anemones that danced in the orchards. He licked his lips and couldn't help but wonder if her sex-lips were this desirable colour too. And the lips of her mouth? How would it be to kiss a pink-lipped woman of the underworld?

Above his head gulls screamed in the clear air. The breeze teasingly lifted a few more vivid fronds. The fisherman leaned forward as if in a dream and gently plucked at the leathery, dark strands of seaweed, revealing the secrets of the curvaceous nude white body that lay before him. He was mesmerised. A terrible fascination drew his eyes to her. He knew his danger well

4

enough. All sailors shivered at stories of the sexual prowess of the mermaids and demons that dwelt in the cobalt depths of the sea. He had been told enough about their dangers, but not enough about their beauty. This woman was beautiful enough to make him reckless, to risk death for.

He reached out one sunburned hand and began to smooth away the wisps of weed that covered the long pale body. Fine strands of gold silk coiled around his gnarled, knotted black fingers and he stroked them like one in a trance. He felt his heart lift at her beauty. Hair like gold spider webs! If he survived this encounter, he could spend what was left of his life writing poetry about her. He lifted the yellow threads and let them fall, hypnotised by the glittering lines of gold against the vivid blue sky. A moment of eternity went by before he turned his reverent attention to her face.

It too was pearl-white; an oval petal of ivory skin blossoming at the top of her swanlike neck. Her features were very distinct: strong slanting cheekbones, a curving determined mouth, an aristocratic, hawk-like nose, and dark brows curving over wide, deep-set eyes. The eyes were closed; thick silky lashes made sweet arcs below the lids. The fisherman touched the gold-tipped lashes with his trembling rough fingers, then traced the fine papery skin of the eyelid with one worshipping finger. How very black the sunburned skin of his hand looked against the ivory whiteness of her skin. And what curious eye arrangements sea nymphs had. Was it so she could see under water?

He imagined her wide-open eyes, her pale body shimmering in the emerald-green water, her hair trailing behind her in a rippling cloak, her breasts pointing towards him as, greatly daring, he swam towards her and took one eager pink nipple into his mouth. A deep sigh shuddered through his body as his imagination worked. His dark fingers moved down to stroke the pale

5

violet shadows that lay beneath her eyes. He shook as he touched her. Or she shook. A fine nervous tremor. He looked again. She was still. It could not be. He raised a dark finger and ran it gently over her full sensual lips.

The dark lashes trembled and then flew open. The fisherman fell back. Too far into the experience for fear now, he simply gaped at her incredible, commanding, round-like-a-ball eyes. They were blue! Blue like the sky at the peak of midsummer. Blue like ice when it sparkles under the sun. Blue like the sea when it foretells of deep oceans. And angry! The clear, unnatural blue of the irises burned with unrelenting anger around her pupils. The pupils themselves were glaring black pinpricks. She transfixed him with her merciless eyes and melted his heart with her anger. Unmanned, the old man bent forward and bowed low, laying his forehead on the sand, waiting for the blow that would dispatch him to join his ancestors.

He heard her naked body stirring on the sand next to him and felt hands in his hair, tugging his head up. She wanted him to face her. Weak with terror he lifted his head. He looked into the pits of her eyes. They gleamed like molten sapphire under the hot sun. Her pink lips moved underneath them. Despite his fear, the fisherman felt his penis stiffen at the blatant sensuality of those twisting lips. The rest of his body went limp and he longed for her to take him to her deep-sea lair and kill him with unnatural pleasures.

Through swooning half-closed eyes he saw her pale breasts gleaming in the sun. He saw her delicious pink-tipped nipples. A cloak of gold was floating all around her as her hair dried in the ever-increasing power of the sun. Mingled terror and exquisite pleasure rippled over the helpless fisherman. The milky form of the goddess bent low over him. The impossible blue eyes bored into his. Her fingers were sweet on him as they brushed across his shoulders. He was aware of her curving femininity. The reality of her touch was too much for him. He cried out and orgasmed. His cock jerked helplessly. His juices splattered through a gap in his rough, indigo-blue kimono and pattered on to the sand in front of him. Her hands let him go and he bent forward once more, shaking all over as he waited for sweet death.

But no death came. As his heart slowed, he felt only the hands in his hair once more and more musical noises as the pink lips writhed and twisted. The fisherman shuddered. His hands went protectively to his crotch. Fear had melted his brain. He could not understand what she wanted.

The mermaid pushed him aside impatiently and struggled to her feet. Her lips moved. She was shouting at him now, and the fisherman grovelled in the gritty sand. He felt small, his sunburned limbs powerless in the face of her superhuman white beauty. He sneaked a glance at her and buried his face in his hands again. She was terrible. She was like a white mountain with blue skies reflected in her eyes. But still no death came. And as he waited, and waited and waited again, listening to his heart booming over the surf, and the gulls screaming above him, he began to understand: she was no supernatural being, she was flesh and blood, just as he was.

Now he realised that her long slim limbs and her sharply ribbed thin body belonged to no superhuman denizen from the sea but to something infinitely more frightening: a gaijin – an outside person – a woman from the world outside Japan. He had heard garbled tales of such as her: fabulous women with round eyes – round like a ball! Although he'd seen them, it was still hard to believe. Yet here she was with her long pale limbs and her slender naked body – and her berating, angry voice. She stood upright in the hot sun, her hair blowing in the salty sea-breeze, screaming at him like an angry hawk now, as her impatience grew.

The fisherman looked anxiously down the sweep of the bay and shuddered. Her cries were attracting attention. A stooping figure far down the beach was straightening up. Another was cupping an ear with his hand under a conical straw hat, listening, squinting unbelievingly at the barbarian; and then he called to his neighbour and began to make his way towards them, slowly at first and then running.

The fisherman covered his eyes and groaned. The sound of the sea was loud in his ears, almost drowning the barbarian woman's imperious calls. There was no way to hide this now. The others would come; the headman would know; and the daimyo, Lord Nakano, would have to be sent for. He could not let the other men from the village see him helpless in the sand. Shutting his mind to the presence of the sea witch, he rose stiffly to his feet, swaying a little, still feeling adrenalin hum in his system as he fought for control.

More of the villagers came running, forming a curious circle in front of the naked barbarian. She vibrated with intensity, with life and sensual awareness as she paced in the sun. Tiny grains of sand clung to her naked flanks, falling as she moved. They drew the villagers' eyes and the fisherman saw betraying movements under the indigo garments his friends wore, and he knew that their penises were stiffening even as his had. Who could blame them? She was incredible. Look what she had done to him, and at forty-two he had thought he was long past sexual excitement. He slyly rubbed his toes in the gritty sand, hiding the evidence of his ejaculation. Then he looked back at the naked barbarian.

Her slender hands made a pantomime at her full pink lips. The fisherman realised that he now understood her. She wanted water, of course, and food. Despite her looks she was human, and had a human's needs. She would need succour after her ordeal in the waters of the storm. The fisherman gestured to her to follow him to the village, a little sad because his thrilling intimate adventure was over; it would be for the headman to feed her, and house her and to decide who to send with the news of her arrival to Lord Nakano.

Chapter One

'Oh, mistress,' groaned the young man, glinting beads of sweat trickling over the silk of his skin. 'I'll do anything for you; anything at all. Command me! Tease me! Please me! I'm yours.'

His head fell forward. His blond curls brushed against his wrists and gleamed against the dark wood of the curving walls of the tiny cabin. He tugged ecstatically against the hemp ropes that bound him to the rough beams. Annabel Smith took a step back. The long black whip she was holding trailed on the oak floor behind her, the lash rolling this way and that as the ship rose and fell with the swell of the waves. The light from the one, brass-rimmed porthole dimmed and brightened as green waves slid over it, throwing rippling shadows over her slim blonde figure in its stiff Elizabethan dress. She braced herself against the motion with the ease of long practice and regarded the young man critically.

He was lean, thin to the point of emaciation, as they all were, and his ribs were visible under his white skin; but he was strong and his fitness was evident in the healthy muscles that corded his tall body. His skin was pale but healthy. He was one who had hoarded his dried fruit and eaten sensibly, and so the scurvy had not got him. His billowing white shirt lay discarded on the wooden bunk, but canvas sailor's jeans still clung to his well-shaped legs. At the point where his legs met, a bulge strained at the fabric. Proof! He was enjoying the treatment that Annabel was handing out to him.

She lifted the whip and let the lash trail lovingly over the sweep of his broad, muscle-corded back. Red weals already marked the white surface, but he wanted more. Fine shivers ran over his pale skin as she caressed him with the black lash. 'Anything?' she enquired softly.

'Anything,' he whimpered. He twisted against the sisal ropes that held his hands above his head and lifted his buttocks high, thrusting them towards Annabel in mute supplication. She dropped to her knees in front of him, the long skirts of her dress rustling about her, and put her hands on his waist to hold his body steady. She tipped her head back and looked up into his tormented, pleasure-glazed eyes. Teasingly, she ran light fingers across the washboard ripples that outlined his belly. She smiled as she heard him suck in his breath. She watched his lips quiver as he ran his tongue along them, moistening them. His chest rose and fell as his breathing quickened. Annabel's teasing fingertips reached the point in the fabric behind which his penis lay, then they stopped, poised for action.

'Then why don't you show me your maps,' she cooed.

His head snapped forward and he stared at her in disbelief. 'My maps? To a woman? Whatever do you want to see them for?'

A drop of sweat ran down Annabel's forehead. Only a thin partition separated her bunk-bed from the black iron stove in the galley, so her cabin was always warm. It was comforting, but sometimes it was hard to think in the stuffy air. And she must go carefully. The pilot hadn't refused her outright. She may yet get her way. Annabel tried to make her face and voice soft as she said casually, 'Oh, I'm just curious. You know how I like things that are considered unusual for most women.'

'Unusual! Unheard of more like. They say you never forget what you read or hear. Though the good Lord alone knows what a woman wants with a book.'

He still hadn't refused outright. Annabel trailed feather-light fingers over his belly just above the waistband. Tiny beads of sweat formed under her fingers and her lips curved in secret satisfaction. It was sweet to have this power at least: the power to control men sexually. 'Show me your maps,' she cooed. 'It would be so interesting, and it would be something to pass the time on this endless, dreary voyage.'

He thrust his pelvis towards her. 'Is sex not a pleasant enough pastime?'

Her fingers slipped under the fabric of his trousers, teasing him, taking her time about reaching his cock. 'Pleasant enough,' she allowed, 'but sex only amuses the body. My mind needs pleasure too.'

He stared at her in honest bewilderment. 'What pleasure is there for a woman in man's affairs? And a pilot's maps and notes are secret. I have not even shown them to your father. I show them to no man – and certainly to no woman.'

Annabel's hands fell away from the area of his crotch in frustration. She sat back on her heels in despair. She hardly cared that the pilot's mood was changing, that he was escaping the sexual thrall she had woven around him. 'I'd like to see them,' she murmured.

His brows snapped together and he spoke with some of the force that made him the most powerful man on the ship: 'Why do you waste my time on such things? I didn't come to your cabin to talk to you.'

Annabel masked her anger, as she had so often had to do since she had boarded her father's ship. Her fingers trembled as she raised them back to the opening of his trousers. She undid another button before she pleaded,

'Sweetheart, don't refuse me.' He must not refuse. Search as she may, she could not discover the pilot's hiding place. He must show her his maps.

'Of course I refuse. And I grow bored with this conversation. Get back to attending to me, woman.'

Bored! What did he know of boredom! She was going out of her mind cooped up on this stinking sailing ship with its crew of stinking men. Every endless day the creaking wooden shell ploughed on over the endless waters towards the endless horizon. The men at least had jobs to keep them busy, but the ship-owner's daughter was practically a prisoner in her cabin. She had taken the opportunity to learn Dutch and perfect her German, but there was little more the sailors could teach her. And, apart from the old black Bible her father read the burial services from, there were no books on the ship.

Annabel wanted to see those maps. She wanted to learn how men recorded their passages around the stormy seas of Japan. If the pilot would just let her see the books once it would be enough for her eidetic memory. She needed to learn what he knew. All the hours of the long dreary voyage her restless mind worried at the problem of escape, and she had finally come up with a plan.

There were no available maps to the seas of the world, and so the pilots were powerful – they had handwritten records of the paths across the sea to fabulous China and further. Those books were the key to the rich pickings of the ports of Araby and India and the oceans beyond, and vessel owners would pay good money for them.

So much money that the sale of even one personal log, this pilot's personal record of the seas he knew, would fetch enough to keep a woman in independence for the rest of her life, in a little cottage with a maid. Annabel yearned for the comfort and security of that cottage. So much so that she dampened the little voice that argued that what she planned was theft and therefore a sin. She

14

knew that her fabulous memory would allow her to produce a perfect record of what she read. But she must at least glance through the books first, and this pilot balked her.

Annabel picked up the whip and stroked its black length slowly. She regarded the blond pilot steadily. She didn't think he was aware of the calculations running through her busy mind. His eyes were fixed on the way her breasts bulged above the narrow waist made by her tightly laced corset. He relaxed back into the ropes and muttered, 'Aye, that's it. Take my pleasure in your hands. Tell me what I am to do.'

'You are to repent and suffer,' said Annabel slowly. 'And I shall punish you until you do so.' His nipples stiffened as she spoke and she leaned forward and licked and nibbled sexily at first one pink tip and then the other before drawing her mouth away to say: 'What do you deserve?'

His groan was harsh in the sultry heat of the tiny cabin. 'To be punished,' he gasped. The words seemed to come with some reluctance through the moist pink lips that twitched inside his bushy golden beard, but Annabel could see that his penis was rock hard.

'What do you deserve?' she repeated wickedly, running the black leather thong of the whip over the bulge in his sailor's jeans. The smell of musk hung thick in the air. There was a short pause before he answered. Annabel listened to the creaks and groans of the old sailing ship while she watched his body reflect his internal struggle. His lips fell open and his breathing quickened.

'Punishment,' he groaned. 'I deserve to be punished.' His head fell back displaying his bare throat and his muscles went taut under his sweating skin.

Annabel ran pink fingertips over his shivering stomach and knew he was hers once more. She dropped the whip and bent before him, taking the opening of his trousers in both hands and allowing his cock to spring free. There was both pleasure and torment in his eyes. His fair pubic hair curled out. Drops of sweat winked like diamonds in the thickets of wiry hair. The smell of musk grew stronger. Despite her anger, lust rose within her as she uncovered his penis. It was so very hard, so very long and hard, and yet so velvety soft in her hands.

She stroked the length of his shaft gently before slipping her hands to the waistband of his rough trousers and rolling them over his bare legs and feet. Then she stepped back to look at him, making him wait, enjoying the anticipation he must be feeling. Finally, she reached up and unhooked his bound hands from the overhead beam and pulled him, unresisting, the few steps that led to her bunk.

He collapsed on to Annabel's bed in an eager rush, burying his face in the vivid silk counterpane that covered it, rubbing his distended manhood against the shiny, slinky surface, groaning softly in helpless delight.

'Bend over the bed and stretch your arms out,' ordered Annabel. He complied with eager swiftness. She slipped the ropes that bound his wrists over a hook that she had fixed into the oak planks of her cabin wall for this very purpose and ran a stern hand under his belly, forcing him to raise his quivering white buttocks into the air.

She cast the whip aside in favour of a thin whippy cane. It was as vicious as her mood. It made a mean whistling sound as it flashed through the air. She breathed deeply as she plied it. Each blow left a thin red line across the pale mounds of the pilot's bottom. It satisfied the anger in her heart each time it cut into his shivering flesh.

In between each blow she slipped her hand between the crack of his buttocks and tickled the hairy globes that swung there. She knew that if she touched his penis now, there would be no holding back the incredible orgasm that would take him, but if she touched his balls, lightly, teasingly, she could keep him hovering on the edge of ecstasy as she whipped him and tormented him further.

But what else could she do to him? He deserved something special for thwarting her today. Something that would take him to the very edge and force him to recognise the nature of his sexual desires.

She paused, stroking his hot wet balls absently, chewing her full bottom lip. And then she heard the softest of scratches at her door. A frisson of sexual excitement shook her lightly. Should she? Her skin glowed softly and arousal throbbed sharply between her legs. Tormenting the pilot was fun, but it did nothing to satisfy the lust that flowed through her. She slaked her sexual thirst with other men, and the one who scratched so discreetly at her door at this very minute was her favourite.

Should she invite Peter in? Shivers ran down her spine at the wicked barbarity of her thoughts: to make love with two men at once! Should she try it?

She slipped to the door and whispered softly, 'Peter?'

'Of course.'

'Can you wait? Just a few moments?'

A throaty laugh. 'For you I wait longer.'

'I'll only be a moment,' she promised, and slipped softly back across the shadowy cabin.

The figure stretched across her bed shuddered under his bonds. Ecstatic terror trembled in his voice. 'Who was that? Are you crazy? You must not let anyone see me like this?'

'Must not?' said Annabel gently, noting the iron-hard penis and melting arousal of the body that quivered before her. 'Is that any way to talk to your mistress?'

A pause. She ran the lightest of fingertips along the deep crack that separated his buttocks and then pressed at the crinkled-oyster of his anal opening with one cruel fingertip. His cry was a fervent sigh, 'Oh no, Mistress. I'm so sorry, Mistress.'

17

'That's better,' she said approvingly, absently parting the thick muscled opening and inserting her fingertip a little further into the hot dark crevice. He shuddered and groaned and she knew he was in heaven. 'Depraved little beast,' she hissed gently.

She twisted her finger against his melting, warm-muscled anal walls. She laughed softly at his helpless response. She knew how he loved her to violate him. She kept her finger inserted in his anus and bent over his naked white back to whisper tormenting words into the nape of his neck. 'I know what you want,' she hissed. 'You want to suck cock and that's what I've arranged for you. Standing at my cabin door is a nice, thick juicy penis and I'm going to make you suck it.'

He groaned again and she felt his body go lax, limp with the terrible rapture her words had caused. She pulled back and slipped her other hand under his belly once more. The penis that sprang into her hand was taut, aroused, only seconds away from orgasm – if she allowed it. 'Don't you want to suck cock?' she demanded.

The pilot was almost sobbing into the crimson eiderdown. Annabel withdrew her finger from his anus and picked up the cane. She reached in between his legs and pushed his buttocks high in the air. She felt his whole body tremble with conflict. She was aware of his dilemma. He was the pilot. On board ship he gave orders and all obeyed him. Yet here in her cabin he was the one who obeyed her orders. He loved obeying her orders. And the more depraved the orders, the more he loved to obey them.

Annabel waited patiently, wondering if this time he would refuse her. But no, as she took her hand away, he kept the white half-moons of his buttocks lifted in the air, allowing her to reach under him and grasp his sexual organs. His penis and balls were hot and silky in her hand. If she touched him gently, he would orgasm, but

18

she had no intention of allowing that. Instead, she brought down the thin line of the whippy cane across the base of his penis.

The pilot screamed in rapture. The soft scratching came at her door again. Annabel ran across the cabin and whispered urgently at the panel, 'Wait!' Then she returned to the pilot. He was lying shivering across her silk counterpane, but his face was contorted in ecstasy. 'You'll suck cock and you'll like it,' ordered Annabel. Her heart beat fast as she waited for his response. This was going to be fun!

'Make me,' came the soft and tortured whisper. 'I want you to make me do delicious shameful things. Acts I will repent of later, but I cannot resist now.'

Annabel licked her swollen moist lips. 'Are you sure?'

'Yes. But he must not know who I am. I could never control the men if they knew . . .'

'Knew what?' demanded Annabel mercilessly.

She heard his fast light breathing as his desire forced him to answer, 'That I am a depraved and sinful monster; that I have fallen for the temptation of tasting a man's organ in my mouth.'

'Trust me,' said Annabel softly. She knelt swiftly at her cabin trunk; it was brass-bound ebony and had belonged to her mother. From it she pulled out a length of fine Chinese silk. The bright gauzy cloth was cool and gossamer fine between her fingers. She buried her face in its perfumed folds briefly, inhaling the faint scent of exotic China, before draping the vivid orange fabric over the pilot's prone and naked body, hiding him completely.

Then she took the few steps to the door and lifted the oak latch. A big, thick-set sailor entered in a rush, pushing her up against the wall, silencing her squeal of protest with rough kisses, nibbling and biting at her neck, licking at the cleavage that her low silk dress exposed. Peter was so large that he seemed to suck up

19

all the space and air in the tiny womb-like cabin, but merry points of light twinkled in the slits of his laughing eyes and he was Annabel's favourite lover.

She leaned back on the wall and relaxed into his caresses, giggling, throwing her head back in delight. She made a face and laughed at him. His hot, wet, red lips were conjuring up delicious feelings. Heat and moisture gathered in her secret place and she felt a sexy smile curving her lips. She tipped her head back again and felt Peter's wild curls tickling her skin as he pressed his lips into her throat and all the way down her body.

He looked up at her and she enjoyed the admiration and desire she could see in his eyes before he dropped his head and knelt swiftly before her. He slid his big hands down to her ankles, caressing them before making to pull up the skirts of her dress. He was always wild to see her naked sex.

Annabel put out her hand to stop him. 'Wait,' she said softly, kneeling down so that they were both on the floor. He was watching her, his handsome bearded face close to hers. 'I've something special for you today,' said Annabel with a happy smile.

'You're always special,' he growled.

She smiled and twisted away from his grasp. He held her waist, pushing her skirts up, kissing what parts of her naked flesh he could reach, complaining at her movement. Shivering under his caress, Annabel leant over and reached into her still-open cabin trunk. She pulled out a black velvet mask, relic of a night in Venice. 'I want you to wear this,' she said, running it softly through her fingers. Her eyes met his with a little shock as she caressed the soft velvet.

Peter leant forward and grasped her hand, sucking one finger after another into his hot wet mouth, licking wetly at the mounds at the base of each finger. 'Why?' he enquired between sucking and licking, letting one finger fall and sucking on another. His eyes touched hers avidly. 'You know that I love to watch you. Nothing turns me on like the sight of your nude body.'

'Remember that luscious whorehouse you went to in Buenos Aires? The one you told me about, the one where a hot and delicious mouth sucked and licked your manhood into a shattering orgasm while another soft mouth bit and nibbled at the nape of your neck?'

'Aye! It is my favourite fantasy, as well you know.'

They still knelt on the swaying oak floor. Annabel grinned at him knowingly and they both laughed. She wrapped soft coaxing arms around his neck. He leant forward with the motion of the ship and kissed her. He smelt of brandy and fresh air. There was a fine layer of sea salt frosting the vigorous curls of his hair and beard. He must have come to her straight from his watch as helmsman. 'How would you like to experience those thrilling sensations again?' murmured Annabel against his eager lips.

'How do you mean to . . .' He broke off. A quiver from the body under the orange silk on the bed caught his eyes. He ran hot lustful eyes over the outline of the body beneath its fragile covering, while Annabel laughed softly at his surprise.

'But you must wear the blindfold,' she said, meeting his startled gaze. 'You are not to know who it is.'

She felt his skin grow hotter under the palms of her hands. His muscles flexed and he licked his lips lasciviously. His eyes narrowed with lust. 'Blindfold me then,' he said in a throaty growl.

Annabel bent forward and slipped the black velvet mask into place. She tested it with gentle fingers. Her lover looked sinister, menacing, in the dim green light of the cabin. She gave a little shiver and reminded herself that it was only Peter under the mask, not a stranger.

Then she turned to the silent shape stretched helpless across her bed. She whisked away the soft silk that draped his trembling form. The pilot groaned and his pale body undulated as he rubbed against her crimson counterpane. Annabel picked up the cane and slashed it across his bottom: once, twice, three times.

The blindfolded helmsman started in surprise when he heard the first stroke, then, as Peter realised what the noise was, what was happening only inches away from him, his lips pouted out in a full sensual smile under the black velvet, and he seemed to derive extra titilation from the sounds of the cane falling and a man groaning in rapture.

Judging that the pilot was too close to orgasm, Annabel gave him several sharp cuts across his sensitive penis tip with the cane. He shrieked in real agony, but she knew that pleasure would return, and it was the only way to keep him in a prolonged state of exquisite arousal.

Finally, she bent across the bed and unhooked his hands. Then she untied the ropes that bound his wrists. He rubbed his skin with fingers that trailed lovingly over the red weals. His eyes were half-closed as he stared at the marks dreamily. Then he looked down at his cock. Already, his penis was hard again, purple from the treatment it had received, engorged to its fullest extent. Knotty veins decorated the shaft. The huge purplish head dribbled juice from the slit.

The pilot lifted his gaze from his organ and slid a sneaking, terrified glance at the blindfolded male figure who dominated the dim warm cabin. A dollop of creamy fluid fell off the end of his penis and dropped to the oak floor of the cabin as he fell in a heap at Annabel's feet and kissed her bare toes in a frenzy of abasement. 'Mistress!' he groaned. 'Oh God! What vile acts are you going to make me perform?'

Thrills ran all over Annabel's bare feet as his beard and his lips tickled her. She struggled to control her voice over the outrageous stimulation of his wet mouth. Her whisper was husky as she hissed wickedly, 'You will commit hot, dirty and sinful acts that will haunt you for ever – though whether in pleasure or remorse I cannot say.' The pilot gripped her white feet in a sobbing ecstasy. Her skin could no longer stand his touch. She drew her feet away and said sharply, 'Stand up.'

The pilot rose at once and stood shivering before her. Now there were two men in the room, waiting for her commands, under her total control. But only one of them was naked. 'Strip that man,' she ordered.

Trembling, the pilot moved over to where Peter, the black blindfold making him look like an impassive statue, stood waiting. The big sailor shivered slightly as the pilot's fingers tugged lightly at his clothing.

He had no idea who was stripping him, of course, and Annabel wondered what kind of pictures he was making in his brain as the pilot's yearning hands removed his billowing shirt and rough sailor's jeans. They must have been good pictures. The penis that sprang free from his trousers was fully erect. A creamy drop of fluid winked on the tip of the glans.

'Kneel down behind this man and lick his naked bottom,' ordered Annabel. Moving with an eager speed that betrayed his pleasure, the pilot got into position and began work with his long probing tongue.

As the mystery tongue flicked across his hairy bottom into the crevice that led to his anus, Peter shivered slightly and began to sweat.

It was hot in her cabin. Annabel rustled her way out of her voluminous silk gown and then, clad only in her corset, moved to stand in front of Peter. She picked up his hands and ran them down the front of her soft body. 'Unlace me,' she ordered. She enjoyed the touch of Peter's hands as, even blindfold, he unlaced her skilfully. The restricting corsets fell away, and Annabel breathed a sigh of pure pleasure as the sultry air touched her naked skin. Peter buried his face into her freed breasts and began to nuzzle at them. Rapturous shivers tingled

23

in the tips of her nipples and Annabel felt ripples of hot desire forming at the base of her spine. She pressed her naked thighs together and abandoned herself to the urgings of her body and the immediacy of the moment.

Remembering the pilot, she made him move away from Peter. She placed her legs astride the pilot and pushed her pubis into his face. The ship was rising and falling in a more marked motion now, and she allowed her body to sway along with it, setting the rhythm. The pilot's hot lips and long tongue burrowed eagerly into the slit between her sex lips. She twisted to one side so that Peter could continue to suckle on her breasts. The pilot's soft lips caught the hot straining bud of her clitoris. She had taught him exactly what to do. His tongue flickered over the surface of her clitoris and his lips mumbled at the sensitive surroundings. He sucked hard, and then eased off, sucked hard and then eased off. His hands dug exquisitely into her buttocks, pulling her towards him. Peter's mouth closed imperatively on one nipple and he pinched the other responsive pink tip between his fingers. His spare hand circled her belly lightly.

Annabel went limp. She was hot. She was drowning. Her knees were weak and moving in circles. The ship swooped and flew below her, swinging her body through the air in delicious swaying movements. Her hips were twisting in urgent, melting movements. She threw back her head. Her hair brushed down her back. Her breath shrieked in her ears. She felt a flush stinging the sensitive skin above her breasts. Her open lips felt swollen, hot, sensual. And the pleasure, the pleasure she was trying to hold off and yet felt so desperate to welcome, grew imperative. It rushed up to take her over and she was dimly aware of Peter's strong arms reaching out to hold her up as the pilot's sucking lips and rhythmic tonguing generated the most delicious spasms all around her body as she came and then came again.

Smiling at the sharp rapture, even as she fell forward in a sweating, panting heap on to Peter's naked chest, Annabel cried out loudly with the final heavenly spasm.

Peter held her gently as she slowly drifted back to earth. Her skin felt soft and sensual and Annabel stretched lazily before rubbing herself against his corded sailor's body with a smile. She could feel his manhood rubbing against her. She would keep her promise to him. 'Now I'll make your dreams come true,' she murmured languidly. He should have the next ecstatic experience.

She made the pilot kneel in front of Peter. 'Take his penis into your mouth,' she ordered. The pilot sucked Peter's cock deep into the circle of his moist pink lips. His rampant and twitching penis betrayed his deep enjoyment of the forbidden situation. A soft groan broke through Peter's red lips. He bent his knees slightly, and Annabel moved behind him to nibble on his neck. She slid her hands around the front of his chest to play with his nipples. They were hard little nubs between her fingers. She felt him grow hot and a fine sweat broke out on the skin under her breasts.

She smiled languorously as she allowed the sway of the ship to push her breasts over the skin of Peter's back in a teasing massage. She could feel his heart thudding under her hands. She could hear eager sucking and slurping noises as the pilot took Peter's thick-set cock right down into his throat. She felt as near to content as she ever felt on the prison of her father's ship.

And then, a harsh noise beat at her ears. The sensual, erotic mood within the cabin was shattered as the wooden panels of Annabel's cabin door shuddered under the repeated blows of a fist.

'Open up in there!'

25

Chapter Two

'*O*pen up in there!'

The wood seemed to tremble under the angry onslaught.

'My father,' whispered Annabel.

Peter's hands flew to his black mask.

The pilot spat Peter's penis out of his mouth and stared at Annabel with terrified eyes.

Annabel put her hand on top of Peter's, stopping him from tugging at the velvet mask. 'Don't take off the blindfold. I'll tell my father to go.' She moved over to the door, lurching with the ship's movements, and cried, 'Go away, Papa. I'm sleeping.'

The wood trembled again. 'Open up, by God, or I'll take an axe to this door. Do you have the pilot in there?'

'The pilot?' said Peter. He bellowed with laughter at the thought. 'The pilot's been gobbling my cock?' His hands were still at the edges of the mask, just holding the black velvet, not pulling it off yet.

'Don't take off your mask! And wait!' hissed Annabel urgently to Peter. 'It wasn't the pilot and I'll get rid of my father.'

The pilot was limp, trembling at Annabel's feet. She

tugged at his shoulders, pulling him upright, pushing him on to her small bunk and covering him with the crimson counterpane. Once she had him hidden, she picked up Peter's clothes from the floor, thrusting them at him, tearing the mask off.

Urgent heavy blows still thudded at her door. 'I'm just getting dressed, Papa,' she called, trying to keep her voice light, clutching for her clothes with trembling fingers.

Her elbows kept bumping into Peter as he scrambled into his white shirt and canvas trousers as fast as he could. 'Just a few more seconds,' she called, cursing the smallness of her cabin and the complexity of her dress and corset.

The blows on her door did not slacken. The wooden latch was bulging under the pressure. And then it gave way and splintered open.

An extra lurch of the ship propelled her father right into her cabin. His bullet-shaped head cannoned into the half-dressed Peter, and he stood glaring up at him, his tiny piggy eyes molten with hot anger.

Peter stood tense, muscles rippling in indecision, as Annabel's father breathed sour rum fumes into his face. Walter Smith was his boss and the father of the woman he had been caught with, but if it came to it, he would fight him – to the death.

Annabel dropped her dress and corsets. There was no point in trying to pretend that she had not been naked. Her father had caught her. Shaking with fear, Annabel reached behind her and picked up the fragile Chinese silk that was lying on the floor. She wrapped the gossamer orange silk around her trembling body. The flimsy fabric felt like no protection at all from the angry feelings that blistered the air of her cabin.

Peter and her father glared at each other, their tension filling her tiny room. The vibrations between them pulsed and flowed as each male tried for dominance.

Walter Smith ruled his ship by the authority of his ownership and the cat-o'-nine-tails. He was no lover of personal combat. And Peter was his best helmsman.

The captain's eyes fell first. 'Where's the pilot?' he growled. 'Mother of God! Is this ship run by idiots? What the hell are you playing at with a storm blowing up?'

The ship lurched again, badly this time, and began a slow, sickening climb that told Annabel that the waves had suddenly become dangerously large. Now she was aware of confused shouting. A sound like sheets tearing in the wind told her that the sails were being dropped rapidly. Feet thumped on the deck over her head. Only a typhoon could blow up this fast. The most dangerous storm of them all.

Her father looked across her cabin. She saw him looking at the body-shaped bulge that shivered under the crimson silk of the bed cover. His lips curved in a cruel smile. Still trying to protect the pilot, Annabel laid a futile hand on her father's wrist. He brushed it aside and twisted the covering away. He uttered a sound of disgust as he uncovered the naked pilot.

The pilot's red-slashed buttocks shook, and he kept his face buried in Annabel's pillow for a moment longer before slowly, reluctantly, turning his head to meet Peter's eyes. Peter stared at the pilot triumphantly: now he could dominate the man who was technically his senior. The pilot's eyes fell, but not before everyone in the cabin had seen that they were miserable with his desire for Peter's cock.

'Disgusting perverts,' muttered Annabel's father, not fully understanding, but seeing enough to revolt him. The wind shrieked outside the cabin and the ship lurched violently. Footsteps hurtled pell-mell down the ladder in the passage outside and a filthy, terrified seaman burst in.

'The pilot,' he shouted. 'For Christ's sake! We need the

pilot!' There was a moment's tense silence as he took in the arrested, erotic nature of the scene in Annabel's cabin, then the urgency of the moment took over. 'Pilot, we need you,' he said urgently. 'And you too, Peter. The other helmsman is not strong enough to hold the wheel. This storm is a mother. And there are rocks. I don't know where. You must come.'

The physical force of the wind, which was increasing every second in the treacherous, fast way of tropical storms, jolted Peter and the pilot out of their erotic tension. They became seamen again. Peter picked up his boots and sprang for the cabin door, his untucked shirt billowing as he went. The pilot grabbed a few garments and rushed after him, leaving Walter Smith staring at Annabel across the lurching cabin. The sailors did not need him. He was useless in an emergency.

Annabel clutched the folds of orange silk that were trying to slither down her naked body and faced her furious father. Something ugly, both angry and wicked, jumped at her from his eyes. With the departure of the men she knew that he was secretly afraid of, it seemed that he felt brave enough now to vent his anger on his defenceless daughter. 'You're a bloody whore,' he spat. 'If your mother was alive to see you now —'

Tears made a fist in Annabel's throat. 'If my mother was alive I would be living safely with her instead of being dragged across the world with a drunkard.'

Her father was enraged by her defiance. His eyes were ugly dark pits as he took a step forward and slammed his open palm into Annabel's left cheek. 'I work hard to keep you,' he howled. She could barely hear him over the ringing in her ears. His eyes blazed with all the rotten insincerity of a drunk. He was working himself up into believing his own lies. 'There's many men who would have dumped you to get a living as you might! Indeed I should have left you to it. You'd have done well. You're a natural-born whore. I had to fight the men

29

to get a woman on board at all, but you're not a woman, you're a slut. Fornicating with sailors! By Christ! You're ruined for a decent man now.'

'What decent man would have me?' Annabel cried bitterly, spilling out the thoughts that she had tried to bury since her mother's death. 'After Mother died, you drank and gambled everything – even my dowry.' A sudden memory of the charm and serenity of her old life rose to torment her. 'Everything has gone,' she screamed at him, 'because you pissed it away!' She slammed one fist into the lurching wall. The pain of her lost life was so acute that it cut through her fury. Her anger drained away and she turned from her father. She rested her forehead on the wide oak planks and added softly, 'And, yes, I am ruined. I have known that since I was left with only you to care for me.'

'You ungrateful whore!' bellowed her father. His wet red lips worked in a furious outburst. 'You should fall on your knees in gratitude to me. Do I not provide for you? Did I not take you on me own ship?'

'You had to,' said Annabel dully. 'You gambled away the house, the garden – Mother's garden – all our furniture. Dear God, you even sold the servants' belongings, and turned them off without a penny.'

'I'll whip you, by God!' screamed her father. 'If you answer me back like an ignorant gutter-whore, then by God I'll treat you like one. I'll teach you some gratitude. Aye, and the proper way for a daughter of mine to behave.' His black eyes fell on the line of orange silk that was slipping over Annabel's breasts. The sight seemed to enrage him. 'Whore,' he shouted again. 'Whore, whore, whore.'

The ugly word echoed and bounced off the walls of the cabin. Annabel pulled the soft fabric closely to her, trying to cover her nudity. The smell of sour wine was strong in the air and nausea rose in her throat. She shook her head, she did not know why, and heard herself make

30

a little sound of protest. She had seen her father work himself up into these killing rages before. It was as if he could not flog a man without them – only this time it was his daughter he was proposing to string up to the mast and flay to the bone. She had seen men die from his whippings.

'Come up on deck!' He almost snarled the words out, then menacingly, he walked towards her. 'I'll show you some gratitude. I'll show you how a daughter should behave.'

Annabel tried to step back, but all she could do was press more closely against the swaying walls of her cabin. Her father stretched out a hand. Annabel's heart beat like a sounding drum as his black, hairy hand darted closer and closer to her like some monstrous spider. His hand brushed the skin of her breasts and she wanted to scream. Then his hand latched on to a handful of the flimsy orange fabric and twisted it, stretching the material out, using it as a rope to draw her closer to him.

A floating dreamlike horror descended over Annabel as she met his eyes. She had never seen much that was decent in them, but now they were opaque silver discs of horror. She knew it would be no good pleading with him, or appealing to his better nature. He was determined to flog her, and in the mood he was in she might die.

Her innocent scheme to pass the afternoon away pleasantly could not have gone more wrong. And not only for herself, for the pilot, too. She wished it had not. The pilot and the helmsman were already enemies, and now Peter had a weapon to use against the pilot. Not that she cared. She hated them all, she realised. She hated her life and her father and every human being on this cursed ship. Her life was a misery to her. How different it had been when her mother was alive.

Terrified feet raced down the ladder. 'Captain Smith!' shouted a toothless sailor. He brought in a gust of cold salt air with him. His clothes were drenched. Pools of water spread beneath him as he panted, 'Captain! The pilot's gone! Washed overboard.'

Walter Smith spun around. He let Annabel go, and she fell against the oak wall of her cabin. Her father's powerful hairy hands shot out and clutched the scrawny neck of the scurvy-ridden sailor cowering before him. 'His maps?' he howled. 'His charts? Who has them.'

'Gone with him, sir. He took them up on deck, to consult he said, and a big wave took him.'

'Wasn't he tied to the frigging deck?'

A terrible cold premonition gripped Annabel. Was this her doing? Had shame caused the pilot to seek death? The voice of the sailor seemed to come from very far away as he answered, 'No, sir. He said he didn't want no lifeline.'

Walter Smith let the scrawny sailor go and sagged against the oak wall of the cabin. The sailor pelted back up on to the deck. Annabel looked at her father. All the blood had drained from his face, leaving a network of spidery red drinker's veins bright against the livid pallor above his patchy beard. 'We are all dead,' he said, and there was terror in his rheumy drinker's eyes. 'Without the pilot there is no way of knowing where we are, which way to go. Even if we escape the storm, we're all dead.'

Annabel marvelled that she was not scared. A heavy burden seemed to fall from her shoulders, as if gentle hands had lifted a stone away. In fact a sweet relief lifted her heart. She was happy. She wanted to die. She no longer wished to continue living. Not the kind of dreadful life that had been hers since her beloved mother died.

If there was no escape from life but death, then how sweet the concept of death became.

She looked at her father with a calm clear gaze. 'Are you afraid to meet your Maker?' she taunted.

His frightened angry eyes fell before the courage in

hers. 'This storm is all your fault,' he screamed. 'Distracting the men when they should be working. I should never have brought you on board. The sailors said a woman would be bad luck, and they were right. The sea will have us all and be damned for it.'

He paused, his breath coming fast and scared. There was a half-mad gleam of fear in his eyes. 'Unless we can placate her, the sea that is. Sometimes she'll take a sacrifice and spare the rest. I should throw you overboard. It might break the bad luck.'

He stopped speaking and looked at his feet, muttering something Annabel could not hear. For a moment she thought her father had gone mad enough to revert to the old superstitions, but then he crossed himself, and she knew that reason had reasserted itself.

Walter Smith looked up at his daughter and anger rekindled in his eyes as he remembered his previous complaint. 'You see what a good father I am – some would sling you to the fishes.'

'You don't have to throw me,' said Annabel. 'If the ship is sinking and the pilot is lost, then we are all doomed. Why should I wait? And I think I would choose to die alone.'

The ship's bell began to toll: 'All hands on deck. All hands on deck.'

Annabel was suddenly aware of the fury of the wind. Between the fast, urgent clamour of the bell, she could hear the wind howling as if banshees were perched in the rigging of the doomed ship, wailing of death for them all.

'Why are they calling the men away from the pumps? By Christ! I'll sort them out.' Annabel's father lurched towards the door, but he turned his head back long enough to scream, 'Don't think I've forgotten you,' before he scrambled up the ladder that led to the deck.

Annabel looked around at her lurching, disordered cabin. It was like the home of a stranger, and she knew she would never rest there again. It was a strangely liberating feeling. Did she not mind dying? The lightness in her heart persisted, and Annabel nodded. She no longer wished to live. She murmured aloud, 'My life is nothing to me now that Mother is dead.'

Her words seemed to echo sadly in her ears. Her body moved as slowly as if she were already swimming under the sea as she gathered up the orange Chinese silk, twisted it about her, and moved slowly out of her cabin. The gauzy fabric fluttered around her, moulding itself to her naked body as she mounted the ladder to the deck.

In the full force of the storm, the ship pitched and heaved so savagely that Annabel was almost dancing as she shifted her weight to keep her balance. Black clouds obscured the daylight. A few rags of canvas, all that remained of the storm sails, flapped uselessly from the masts.

The cold wind shrieked around the ruined sails, and spray blasted across the deck. Spume wet the thin silk where it touched Annabel's nude body. The ends of the fabric whipped out behind her like orange banners. Salt water hit her face, soothing the sting where her father's blow had landed on her cheek. The air was fresh, clean, and it spoke to her of freedom.

Those sailors who saw Annabel's slow pace across the deck spat at her, or made the sign of the evil eye. They had never wanted a woman on board at all. At one time, Annabel had hoped to win them over. Now, she didn't care what they thought of her.

The ship and all its concerns seemed very far away as Annabel moved slowly to the prow, her hair whipping behind her, the orange silk flying bravely. She stood facing the wildness of the storm for a few moments, her robust young legs holding her balanced on the deck. Her toes curled into the oak planking. She felt strong, cleansed of the contamination of her old life. She was ready to meet the new – whatever it may bring.

The ship pitched wildly, seeming to fall for ever into a dark green hell of surging water and tumbling foam, before beginning a slow painful climb towards the monstrous wave that was thundering down towards them with all the weight and inevitability of God's grinding mills on Judgement Day. Annabel heard terrified cries and frantic prayers behind her as the men took in the wave's awesome size and power. Annabel laughed, stretched out her arms in a wide cross, and stepped willingly into the all-enveloping glassy-green embrace of the killing comber that was bearing down on them all.

Chapter Three

Without her mother's gentle admonitions on the subject of decorum, there was nothing to stop Annabel's daily walk along the beach becoming brisk. Today it had become so brisk that it had been close to a run. Her body glowed all over in the early morning warmth.

Her crisp, blue-printed cotton kimono had become dishevelled. Still panting from the exercise, she stopped behind a sand dune. She checked that no one was near enough to the pale expanse of sandhills to see her, before untying her deep-blue sash and exposing her nudity.

The kimono fell away from her body in a shapeless mass. She smiled as she shook out the soft fabric, smoothed it over her breasts and pleated it from the waist into beautifully hanging folds.

She tied the dark sash in a skilful bow, and smiled again at the result. She loved to wear kimonos now: cool, elegant, practical, they were so much more comfortable than corsets and her heavy gowns with their scratchy ruffs – but Lord, how she had struggled before she could master the art of arranging a kimono's intricate folds.

Grains of sand clung to her bare skin and silky, low-growing dune plants popped under her feet as she sedately walked the last few yards to her house. She could hear birds calling in the clear salty air. Seagulls in the distance, and what sounded like the whistling of some kind of hunting bird, a kite perhaps, very high in the vivid blue sky.

It was going to be warm again today. The spring air that touched her cheeks was warm and moist. The sun was already too hot for her pale skin, and Annabel eagerly mounted the step that ran around her little building, glad to be home.

The house that the villagers had built for her was right on the outskirts of the village: the very last building in fact. They did not want her too close to them, but Annabel preferred it so, realising that privacy was a precious commodity in a town made of wood and paper.

She pushed open one paper screen, so that the single room that made up the bamboo and rice-paper house was open to the beach. A slanting oriental roof overhung the veranda that ran around the house and shaded her from the hot spring sun. Annabel folded her kimono under her and sat on her knees, looking out dreamily at the endless moving silk of the ocean. She wondered how far away England was; then she sighed and, with an effort of will, wrenched her thoughts away from the distant horizon.

She half-closed her eyes and squinted at the delicate branches of the cherry tree that grew close to the house. The wind lifted and shook the graceful branches, throwing dappled shadows. The dainty double blossoms were a vivid pink against the blue sky. An errant breeze lifted a few strands of hair and kissed her cheek. Annabel sighed. Nothing but the breeze had kissed her in four long weary months. Or was it five? It was difficult to keep count.

'Are you sad, Annabel san?'

The soft voice pulled Annabel from her reverie and she turned towards it with a slow smile. 'Hiroko san.'

Silk whispered as the dainty Japanese girl mounted the step up to the house and knelt on the plaited rice straw mat next to Annabel. She was dressed formally. Her black hair was piled high in a glossy blue-tinted sweep, and a delicious fragrance rose from it. She bowed low and placed the lacquer tray she had been carrying on the mat in front of Annabel. Then she sat back on her heels and looked at Annabel with earnest, gentle eyes.

'Sometimes you look out to sea, to the west, and then your eyes are sad. I think perhaps you are dreaming of the home you will never see.'

'Maybe I am,' said Annabel. 'Maybe I'm dreaming of the lovers who will never hold me.' She turned her head away impatiently, and then back again with a little smile. It was not by Hiroko's orders that she was held prisoner here. 'My body yearns for the touch of a lover.'

The Japanese woman lifted her gold and crimson fan. It shimmered and danced in the sunlight as it fluttered with exquisite movements. She regarded Annabel with grave steady eyes. 'It does seem hard, Annabel san. But we were instructed that no one may touch you.'

'Not even in love?'

Hiroko bowed again, and the sash of her bright silk kimono stuck up stiffly behind her as if an orange brocade butterfly had landed on her back. Threads of gold embroidery glittered in the sun. 'Our orders were not clear on that point. The headman decided that it would be best to be prudent. Did the pillow toys not help?'

'A little,' Annabel admitted. She put out a hand and pulled a carved ivory penis from under one of the flat cushions that were scattered over the pale yellow tatami flooring. She stroked the tip of the false ivory manhood with a gentle finger. 'I do use it sometimes. Thank you, Hiroko san.'

'It is nothing. I try to make your stay here pleasant.'

Annabel laid the dildo aside on the warm sweet-smelling straw mats that covered the floor of the room. Each six-foot mat was bordered with green and gold ribbon. Her eyes absently traced the patterns the rectangular blocks made across the floor. She had learned to like tatami matting. She patted the soft surface and inhaled the scent of freshly cut hay that rose from it.

Hiroko was still regarding her with anxious eyes. 'Don't be sad, Annabel san,' she said now. Without thinking, Annabel put out a hand to touch her friend, wanting to place a gentle finger on her olive-skinned hand, but Hiroko drew back sharply.

Annabel let her hand fall and sighed. The rules again. Hiroko's body seemed to vibrate with some hidden tension. Her eyes followed Annabel's slender white hand. Annabel watched her for a moment before asking softly, 'Would you like me to touch you?'

Annabel had been in the alien country barely five months but her language skills were the talk of the community. Already she was able to converse fluently.

Hiroko clasped her delicate hands in front of her golden kimono and then let them fall open again. Her fine full lips trembled slightly and just the tip of a very pink tongue slipped out between them. Her short bristly lashes fluttered on her cheeks for a moment before her eyes opened, and as the slanting almond gaze met Annabel's, a slight frisson passed between the two women.

'Yes, and I would like to touch you,' whispered the beautiful Japanese girl softly. The spring breeze stole her words away as she spoke and Annabel leant closer to hear her. 'More and more often, now we can speak more easily, I feel that our hearts grow closer together.' She paused, and Annabel noticed a tiny duck's tail of hair curling under her shell-like ear. 'I have wondered very much about how it would be, if we were free to allow our bodies to grow closer together.'

'Then we should do it,' urged Annabel. 'Don't take any notice of those silly orders. No one would know if you came to my room. Come to me – tonight.' Her whole body ached and trembled with a deep-seated desire to just touch and hold another human being close to her. She longed to feel the silky caress of the gentle Japanese girl's skin against hers. She dreamed of pressing her lips just lightly against the bee-stung fullness of Hiroko's pretty mouth.

But Hiroko sat like a silk statue under the frame of the pink cherry tree and said sadly, 'Honour would not permit me to disobey the orders of my lord. Not even in order to share the delights of the pillow with you.'

'He's your lord, not mine,' said Annabel sulkily. 'Why should I have to suffer because of his bloody rules.'

Hiroko's lips pursed disapprovingly. She suddenly looked very much like the teacher she was. 'The Lord Nakano makes very good rules,' she said primly, 'and it is in all our best interests to obey them. And, please excuse me, but you should not say "bloody", Annabel. It is not a nice word for a woman to use. I think you have been talking to the fishermen again.'

Annabel tossed her head. 'And why should I not? They teach me things too.'

'Of course they do. But, I beg you please to be patient with our customs. You must not use the same words that men do. I have tried to explain to you that we Japanese women have our own language, our own way of speaking –'

'Oh! Don't try to explain anything so stupid to me today!' snapped Annabel. 'My head hurts and I can't understand you. Words are just words and I'll say what I please. Go away!'

A cloud passed over Hiroko's face, turning it into the same unfriendly, unreadable blank that Annabel had first seen when she met the headman's daughter. Hiroko swayed gracefully to her feet, bowed coolly, and stepped down off the raised floor of Annabel's wooden house, pausing to slip on her wooden overshoes before she pattered elegantly away.

As Annabel watched the vulnerable nape of Hiroko's neck rising out of the folds of her bronze kimono with its bobbing butterfly of a sash, she wondered how she could ever have mistaken one Japanese for another. After the long winter she had just spent in the village, she could easily read the moods of those she was close to, like Hiroko. And the departing set of Hiroko's back said that she was deeply offended.

Annabel heaved an angry sigh, and stood up, her knees cracking. She stretched in the sun, arching her poor aching body. Perhaps she should run down the beach again? Spring fever was running mad in her veins. But it was a lover she craved for, not more exercise, and besides, it was already too hot to go out.

She looked into the achingly blue sky above, then at the graceful tree that shaded her house. Fat cheeky blue tits swung in the branches, pecking at the heart of the cherry blossoms, spoiling them, like her mood was spoilt. Why had she been so cruel to Hiroko when she owed her so much?

Annabel picked a delicately illustrated rice-paper scroll and tried to read, but she needed Hiroko's help with the more intricate symbols.

She turned to her meal. She fished out a pink shrimp and wrapped it in green seaweed. As she popped the salty morsel into her mouth, she remembered how Hiroko had taught her to use chopsticks. The shrimp tasted rubbery. She wasn't hungry. She rested the lacquer chopsticks on the blue ceramic fish that was used as a chopstick holder and jumped up. She would eat later. Her bedding was still airing outside.

The distant sea glittered in the sun behind her as she

lifted the warm, heavy sleeping mats off the green-scented furze bushes. She rested her face on their crisp white cotton cases and sighed. She had not had a good night's sleep until Hiroko had shown her how to arrange the Japanese bedding she called futons. And who but Hiroko had told her what everything was called?

Annabel stowed the armful of soft bedding into the one large cupboard that held everything in her house. It was a concealed cupboard that melted neatly into the rest of the paper-lined room. As she slid shut the paper door with its painted patterns of pale pink peonies and bamboo fronds, she suddenly said aloud: 'Oh! I should not have spoken so to her.'

She pattered across the sunlit room, stepped down out of her house, picked up her wooden shoes, and fitted them on carefully. She would hunt out Hiroko and do whatever it took to make things right with her.

Annabel had only taken one step along the sandy track that led to the cluster of slanting-roofed buildings that made up the village when she saw Hiroko running towards her. Patches of agitated red bloomed in Hiroko's smooth cheeks, and wisps of hair were escaping from under the wisteria blossom that was fixed in her glossy dark chignon. The bright light of unshed tears glittered in her eyes.

Apologising was suddenly easy. 'Hiroko san! Dearest friend,' cried Annabel as she started towards the Japanese girl. 'What can be wrong? Surely I didn't upset you so. You must know that I did not mean it. I would never want to distress you. I was coming to find you, to tell you how sorry I was –'

Her friend came to a stumbling halt in front of her, cutting short the apology. 'Do not worry yourself, Annabel san. I know your heart too well to take offence.' She paused to take in a snatched breath. Her breastbone rose and fell quickly, as if it were trying to escape the gorgeous folds of her yellow, bronze and orange kimono.

42

Waves of her own particular heady almond scent rose from her warm skin. Annabel breathed it in. She longed to press her lips to the point where the last layer of silk clung to the faint shadow of cleavage that tormented her imagination. But she knew that Hiroko would never allow it.

'I thought a lady should always appear tranquil?' she said teasingly.

Hiroko ignored her taunt and took in a deep breath. The urgency in her eyes was close to panic. Words tumbled from her panting, parted lips. 'It's the Lord – Nakano – the daimyo. He is here. He is come. He is to stay the night with his servants and his hawks. And he wishes you brought before him.'

A cold knot began spreading around Annabel's belly and insecurity rose all around her. She wanted to be left alone. Her quiet routine of studying Japanese and exercising on the beach had never seemed so appealing. Her house no longer seemed a prison to her, but became a haven in her mind. One she never wished to leave. 'I don't want to go,' she whispered.

Hiroko's eyes were wide and sympathetic. 'He is very terrifying,' she agreed. 'But there really is no choice. You must come now to the bathing area, and I will choose the most gorgeous kimono in the village for you.'

'A plague on him!' muttered Annabel in her own language, but she began to follow Hiroko along the sand-coloured grit path to the village.

Hiroko looked over her shoulder at Annabel, not understanding the English, but worried by the unmistakable tone. 'You must try, Annabel san. Try to please him and use all the polite words that I taught you. You must be very careful. I am afraid that his mood will not be good. His hunting was spoiled – his favourite bird has been hurt. We are very much concerned that his stay here should please him.'

'His stay here is nothing to me.'

'Would it be nothing to you if I were punished for not teaching you properly? If we displease him, even a very little, he can order us all killed – the whole village – it is his right.'

'He has no rights over me,' muttered Annabel defiantly. But her heart was beating very fast as she followed Hiroko to the bathing pool.

Chapter Four

The creamy opal-green pools of the bathing area were deserted. Annabel turned to her friend Hiroko. 'Where is everyone? The pools have always been full of naked bodies before.'

It had taken the English girl a long time to get used to the concept of immersing her naked body in water. She had always been told that washing was injurious to the health, particularly in winter, but she had gradually learnt to enjoy the touch of hot water on her skin; and she found that the sensation of being naked in the open air put her deliciously in tune with nature.

But however much she might have come to enjoy nude bathing itself, she had never learnt to feel comfortable with the whole village present while she washed her naked body. How often she had longed for privacy as she bathed! But now that the shimmering hot springs were silent and empty, the empty pools were worrying and unnatural. 'Where is everyone?' she asked again, staring at her friend. 'Is there something wrong with the water today?'

There was a worried pucker in Hiroko's olive brow as she answered, 'This is no time for bathing! Of course, we have known since we found you that the Lord Nakano would be coming – we have been preparing for this day ever since – but still, there is so much to do. All must be perfect for him.'

Annabel unwound the indigo blue sash that held her crisp cotton kimono in place and let the folds of printed fabric slip over her shoulders. She pushed her arms out behind her back, squeezing her naked white shoulders together, trying to ease the tension that bunched there.

Unable to choose which of the sinisterly empty pools to enter, she hesitated, looking around her, feeling the soft, moist air touching her bare body; she lifted her naked feet slightly, away from the rough surface of the volcanic rock that she stood on.

Beside her, Hiroko froze in the act of unwinding the length of orange silk that bound her waist and lifted her head sharply. 'What's that?' she hissed.

Wisps of steam rose from the hot springs that bubbled all around them. Mist saturated the air. Diamond drops of moisture beaded the needles of the dark pine trees that hung over the rocks of the hill. Mist drifted eerily over the smoky green surfaces of the water. The water vapour formed a gossamer cloud that protected them from the sun and enclosed the bathing area in a membrane of mist. Sounds echoed oddly within it.

'I hear nothing,' said Annabel, looking at her briefly, and then back at the cataract that fed the pools. 'Except the waterfall. It sounds loud today. Because all the pools are empty, I expect.'

Hiroko relaxed slightly and let the embroidered sash of her silk kimono slip to the floor. Annabel continued to listen to the waterfall that poured merrily over the rocky brim of the steepest of the walls that bounded the bathing area. Now she clearly heard another sound above its tumbling roar: the jingle of metal. Then the heavy regular tread of masculine feet. Annabel was unperturbed: every man in the village had seen her

46

naked by now, and besides, nobody stared at her nudity, not openly anyway.

But Hiroko was aghast. There was terror in her eyes. 'Pick up your clothes,' she whispered, turning away, bending to pick up her own discarded sash with trembling hands. The many layers of her kimono flowed open around her like the petals of a chrysanthemum, just disclosing the swell of one breast.

'Why?' asked Annabel, her eyes lingering on the sweet, exposed femininity. Then she caught something of Hiroko's fear. 'Is it . . . him?'

'No,' answered the Japanese girl. Her voice trembled. 'The Lord Nakano bathed first, of course, and after him, his samurai warriors. I thought they had all finished. But here are more of them. We must hide!' Clutching the folds of her disordered kimono around her as if she needed a silken shield, Hiroko took a few agitated steps and then paused to look around her.

All about them, hot water gushed endlessly to the surface in clouds of faintly sulphur-scented steam. The jade-green pools that lay in the hollow were completely natural, but over the years, generations of villagers had altered the flow of the water, deepening some of the green pools. They had also fashioned cedar walkways and arched crimson bridges over the gushing streamlets. And they had taken volcanic rocks and boulders from above the hillside where the waterfall began, and placed them in artful piles and zen arrangements, landscaping the area beautifully.

'Behind these rocks,' Hiroko whispered. She looked like a multi-coloured dragonfly as she darted for the safety of a huddled grey rock mass. Annabel followed her, marvelling that even in her agitation, Hiroko had chosen a hiding place large enough to protect them both without the necessity for their bodies to touch. Even now, Hiroko was mindful of her lord's edicts.

As Annabel settled herself behind the boulders, folding her kimono into a cushion to protect her from the roughness of the volcanic rock, her naked white body seemed to sway towards Hiroko, driven by her yearning for human touch.

But she knew that Hiroko would never permit contact. And, as Annabel peered cautiously through a chink in the cool grey rocks that sheltered her, her blood cooled: the men who were striding towards the soaping area had two large sword handles protruding from the left-hand side of their girdles. The hilts gleamed viciously through the mist.

It was obvious at once the men were soldiers: disciplined, muscled, dangerous. They laid their swords aside carefully, almost reverently, and one man stayed fully dressed, guarding the glinting pile of weapons while his comrades shucked off their kimonos and began washing themselves vigorously. They gave vent to such brutal expressions of satisfaction as they washed, especially as they touched their quickly forming erections, that Annabel felt that it was dangerous even to watch them. She let her lashes drift shut, closing out the world.

'They are the second guard,' breathed Hiroko, her almond-scented breath tickling Annabel's ear. Her voice was quiet, but her face was tense. 'How stupid of me. His samurai would never leave the Lord Nakano completely unprotected while they all bathed at the same time. We must wait until this watch are gone.'

Annabel nodded. It made sense. The men were obviously part of a group – a team. Each of them had the same haircut. Each of them wore an identical chestnut-brown kimono with identical insignia on the back, chest and sleeves. Each of them wore their killing-swords lightly, as if it would be a pleasure to use them. Effective guards, but not men to meet in the wrong place.

Feeling unprotected and vulnerable, Annabel shrank back behind the comforting bulk of the rough-surfaced boulders that hid her. The volcanic rock felt cool and scratchy against her tender bare skin. She considered trying to unfold her kimono and put it on – but it would be impossible to do so without a dangerous amount of movement, so she held still. But, oh, she felt so naked.

She sensed Hiroko stir beside her. Annabel couldn't resist a swift peek through the chink in the boulders. Three men were striding towards them, magnificent in their nakedness. It looked as if the soldiers were heading this way deliberately. Annabel's breath caught. Could they have been seen?

Her whole body subsided in relief as the sounds of splashing and wallowing made it clear that the men had simply been attracted by the pool that lay in front of the stones where she cowered. But then, as they began to talk, Annabel began to realise that the three guards must have left their fellows because they were seeking privacy.

Her anxiety surfaced anew as she began to understand that they were plotting against Lord Nakano, the very man they were supposed to be protecting. She closed her eyes again, but she could not shut out the voices.

'That was well done,' said one softly. 'No one could suspect our treachery. The accident looked completely natural. Wild birds will fight. Who could have stopped your peregrine from breaking the wing of the lord's favourite hawk?'

There was an amused inflexion in the tone of the next speaker that even Annabel, with all her inexperience of the Japanese tongue, could not misinterpret. 'So sad that Nakano's hunting was interrupted – and so lucky that this terrible event should take place near the village that houses the barbarian woman.'

That's me! thought Annabel as her heart crashed in her breast. Why should they be talking about me?

'She is an unknown factor and therefore dangerous,' said one of the men.

Another agreed with quiet satisfaction: 'Nakano will

find it difficult and dangerous to decide what to do with her. I think he was delaying any confrontation with the woman. His situation is ... delicate. An unknown factor at this stage could ruin him.'

'Why is our master, our true master, so sure that the barbarian will cause Nakano problems? I would hate Nakano to gain any advantage through her. He could use her as a bargaining counter with the Portuguese, or the Jesuits.'

'Stinking barbarians.'

'Quite so. But they have treasures that Nakano needs, muskets, gunpowder, information even. What if she turns out to be of value?'

'It is possible. She could be gifted to the Emperor, or even to one of the daimyo who are allied with Nakano –'

'Allied with Nakano today you mean!'

'Ha! Just so. But the point is, he does not know what to do with this sea witch. And by forcing him into this confrontation, our master felt that Nakano would be forced to take the time to consider her, and so have less time to spare for his resistance to our master's wish to control this area.'

'Nakano may choose to destroy the barbarian, and so have done with the problem.'

'He may. But his mind is subtle. He would not have kept her alive all winter if he had not been considering how he could make best use of her.'

The water splashed agitatedly, and one of the conspirators whispered urgently, 'Ho! One looks this way. We must not appear to be plotting. Take your peerless member in your hand. Make it seem as if we have merely slipped away to indulge in a little mutual relief.'

Annabel's eyes flicked open as if of themselves, and her gaze was drawn through the hole in the rocks to the three naked men who lolled in the pool before her. Their skins gleamed through the steam and the hot water had brought a glow to their faces. The bubbling water came up to their waists, covering their male parts, but from the movements of their arms, Annabel could see that the men were masturbating.

She watched the play of muscles in the wet arms as the men stroked and pulled in oddly familiar, rhythmical movements. One of the men moved a little closer to the largest of the three soldiers. He spoke deferentially, 'Sir, it would be an honour if I were to be allowed to masturbate you.'

'Ah, if you wish it. I like to be gripped so, firmly at the base, and then a long stroking motion along the shaft. Ah! That's good. Ah! Your touch is as sweet as a woman's.'

'Will you not take a woman later, sir?'

'By all means – although judging by this collection of stinking hovels that calls itself a village, I might have trouble finding a woman fit for even a quick coupling.'

Annabel felt Hiroko stir beside her and knew that the Japanese girl was listening.

The senior guard allowed his head to loll back, and there was a catch in his breath as he continued, 'But if I do find a slut to pillow with, I will last all the longer for a sweet orgasm now – Oh! That feels so good.'

Annabel felt her own breath quicken as she watched his pleasure. His head rolled back and forth as his physical delight in the moment grew. His eyes screwed tight shut as his orgasm took him over. He began breathing in tiny animal grunts: 'I'm going! I'm going!' he cried.

Annabel could hear the other soldier's fist hitting the surface of the water with increasingly urgent splashes as his whole body bent over in concentration, seeming to become one giant hand that existed only to masturbate the penis of his superior up to a point of true ecstasy.

The senior guard's entire body stiffened as his orgasm took him. His hips rose so violently that most of his body left the water. Annabel could see his cock jutting up stiffly from the water. She heard the man groan. His back arched, and white cream began to spurt from the slit at the top of his penis. The jets of sperm arched up into the air before splattering back into the water. His ejaculate floated briefly, in thick white clumps on the surface of the water, before sinking.

As his orgasm finished, the man sank back into the hot water with another groan, a gentle satisfied 'Ah,' and let his head lie back against the side of the pool.

Beside him the second man spasmed, then his comrade came too, and Annabel listened in amazement as each man called out that he was 'going' rather than 'coming'.

As soon as their orgasms were over, they seemed to find the water too hot. They scrambled out and lay on the ledge of smooth slate that had been set around the edge of the pool for this very purpose.

'It is sweet indeed to relax in hot water,' said one.

'And to take a friend with you into mutual release,' said another.

'And lay great plans,' continued the leader, with the contented air of a cat who has caught a very large mouse. His naked body lay limp and boneless on the cool slate. He was playing idly with his now-soft penis. Wisps of steam rose from the hot skin of his body as it cooled in the open air. 'Successful plans at that. Nakano's hand is forced. Just as our master wished.'

'Is there more that we must do?'

'No. All that was necessary was to bring them together, the great daimyo Nakano and the gaijin, the barbarian from the south. This we have done. Now we are to behave as if we were plain samurai, loyal only to Nakano – until the next order from our true master.'

'I understand. We shall act as the most ordinary of Nakano's men until then.'

A shout echoing across the steamy air sent the three men scrambling to their feet. Annabel was silent, watching as they strutted over to their fellows, waiting patiently until each soldier had dressed and carefully slung his sword around him. She was silent until she was sure that every single member of the watch must have had time to get well away from the bathing area.

It was not just caution. She did not know what to say. Her feelings were confused. Her first instinct was to expose such treachery, but she had no duty to Nakano, and besides, it seemed as if she were somehow involved in this plot. 'What did you think of that?' she asked Hiroko, glancing at her sideways.

'I heard nothing,' replied the Japanese girl. Beneath untroubled eyelids, a glint of hard obsidian warned Annabel not to persist with her questions. 'The Lord Nakano is sure to have the measure of his samurai. No need for women to interfere.'

Annabel could not resist one more exclamation: 'But it seems so wrong!'

'And if we interfere in the wrong way, perhaps spring a trap the Lord Nakano has carefully baited, then my whole village could die like animals. Leave it, Annabel san. You do not understand the politics of we Japanese.'

Hiroko stood up and slid her already dishevelled kimono over her wheat-coloured shoulders. The layers of silk fell to the ground like the crumpled wings of a butterfly. She lifted smooth arms above her head and unpinned the wisteria blossom that nestled into her glossy blue-black hair.

Annabel sighed. Behind the slim, naked body, mist hung in cobwebs over the fragrant dark pines and swirled around a tiny gold and crimson bridge. As the Japanese girl unpinned her hair and bent forward, allowing the glossy mane to fall free, Annabel felt that she was indeed a stranger in this oriental land. Better to accept Hiroko's advice and say nothing. Better to get on with the task before her – to prepare for her meeting with the Lord Nakano.

* * *

53

It was mid-afternoon by the time the last nervous preparation had been made and they were ready to leave Hiroko's house. Annabel was surprised when she realised that they were walking out of the plum-scented village. 'Where are we going?' she enquired.

Hiroko turned her head over her shoulder to look at Annabel. She pointed with her pleated paper sunshade as she spoke. 'To the main temple, of course. There is no building in our poor village good enough for the Lord Nakano. He is staying in the lecture hall.'

'Oh,' said Annabel. She retreated under her own turquoise and pink shade as if it would protect her while she considered this information.

From the seashore, it was possible to look up at the hillside and see glints of scarlet and gold through the green trees, so she had known the temple was there. Over the winter months, the leisurely bronze clang of the temple bells had become as much a part of her life as the sounds of the sea, but as a good Catholic, she had never dreamt of visiting a heathen shrine.

But am I a good Catholic? she asked herself. She remembered the nightly ritual of her childhood: comfortable in a white lace nightgown, kneeling in front of her mother's burnished wood prie-dieu, clutching her rosary. Her mother's softly spoken prayers had always made her feel safe. In her mind, she could still smell honey and beeswax, and see her mother's serene face as she bent over a melting candle to trim it.

But when had she last said a prayer? Uneasy now, Annabel remembered her despair as she had prayed by the bedside of her dying mother. Her prayers had gone unanswered then, and she had been too devastated by her great loss to even think of praying for relief from the horrors that had followed.

God had not seemed to care that it took her father only a few months to gamble away the family wealth. It had not occurred to Him to prevent the bailiffs from taking every stick of furniture out of the house or to stop them from digging up the vegetable garden before selling the buildings. Nor had it seemed to occur to Him that a stinking lice-ridden sailing ship was no fit place for a young girl. And, in return, she had ceased to think of Him.

It's too late now, anyway, thought Annabel as she recalled how long it was since she had even said a simple prayer, let alone been to confession. It was very wicked, of course, and perhaps one day she would try to put things right. But for now, they were pattering along an avenue shaded by cherry trees and the lovely pinkness of their smell returned Annabel's attention to the here and now.

She looked curiously at the neat patchwork of cultivated fields they were passing through. There was only a tiny strip of flat land between the hillside and the seashore. Rocks had been used to build terraces into the sides of the hill in an effort to extend the cultivatable land. Most of the fields were freshly ploughed. Their furrows lay open, ready for the green spears of the spring planting. Annabel inhaled the smell of country earth and felt happy.

It was delightful to be somewhere new. Apart from the shore, she had not been more than a few steps away from her house all winter. And because of that, her feet were beginning to trouble her. For months, she had run around on bare feet, rarely needing to slip on wooden overshoes except on the very few wet days of winter.

Now, for the first time, she was wearing the formal white socks that all women wore with their best kimono. The socks had split toes, and so she had been able to slip her feet into the elegant, heavily lacquered shoes that Hiroko had presented her with, but the shoes were a little heavy and awkward. 'Hiroko,' she called. 'These shoes . . . can we slow down?'

The paper shade bobbed and Hiroko turned to Annabel at once, concern in her eyes. 'Of course. So sorry, Annabel san. You are not used to our Japanese wear. Is the kimono comfortable for you?'

Annabel shook her head. She was uncomfortably aware of the fact that she was naked under her splendid outfit. They had dressed her in blazing pink layers of silk, silk almost as bright as the double cherry blossoms that now danced against the vivid blue sky. The soft brush of the kimono underlayers was a constant reminder of her naked skin.

Annabel had become used to the sensation of her bare breasts moving freely inside the Japanese costume, but today, conscious of the fact that she was to meet the man who had the power of life and death over her, she wished for the protection of a tightly laced corset. And undergarments! There was a throb of vulnerability from the heart of her woman's place as her bare thighs brushed lightly together and her pubic hair curled into the silk of her kimono.

The only part of the outfit that gave her any protection was the tightly wound sash that bound her body ramrod straight. Annabel brushed her hands lightly over the immense sash of chestnut-brown that swathed the centre of her body and tied behind her in an intricate fabric knot. She tugged at it fretfully. 'This sash, obi, did you call it? This obi holds me so tightly that I can hardly breathe.'

Bees zoomed around the dappled pink canopy over their heads as they stood resting. A cock crowed in the village behind them, and Annabel realised that the sound of the sea was receding as they climbed the hill, although there was still a salt tang in the air. Hiroko's hair gleamed in the sunlight. The sun made her dark eyes gleam like the pips from a passion fruit. 'Good posture is very important for Japanese women,' she said primly. There was reproach in her voice, but not in her eyes. 'Are you rested now, Annabel san?'

'I think so,' said Annabel, and she realised that she was reluctant to continue.

At the foot of the hill, where the cherry avenue finished and the tall pine trees began, two extremely imposing guards stood before a crimson arch. Two huge trunks of wood formed the sides of the arch. An even bigger trunk had been carved and gilded and placed as the top to the arch.

Sunlight bounced off the guards' gold-coloured helmets and glinted on their double swords. One of them put up his hand, making the girls wait. The guards' eyes were inhuman black slits. They avoided Annabel's gaze. They looked at the air above her, as if they had no interest in her face, or her mind.

Annabel looked at their brown kimonos and the identical insignia stamped on each side of their chests. The insignia looked familiar. It looked like the cream patterns inside the circles stamped on the sash of her kimono. She looked at the designs on the uniform of the guards more closely. Now she could see that each pattern represented a bird. And she knew that each great house had its emblem. This must be Nakano's.

She looked down at her sash. Cream-coloured cranes flew within the circles printed on the silk. She was wearing his mark! Her face burned. It was as if she were labelled with his ownership. If only she had realised earlier what the implications of the length of silk that bound her waist might be. She could have refused to wear it, but she had not even noticed that the colour was the same chestnut hue as that worn by the guards. And now it was much too late.

Four more guards marched into sight. A nervous villager scurried along beside them, and Annabel recognised Hiroko's father. The guards ignored the headman, who joined his daughter awkwardly. Two of the new arrivals fell in before Annabel and Hiroko, and two fell in behind.

The party set off at a great pace up the stone-paved avenue that led steeply up the hill, but Annabel slowed down and shook her head. One of the soldiers tapped his sword in a bullying fashion. Annabel pointed to her shoes and said, 'I can't walk fast in these!'

The man paused, eyeing her with anger and suspicion, not quite sure what to do. His eyes narrowed, but he must have understood for he slowed his pace until it matched Annabel's. She gave a faint sigh of relief.

The air was cooler as they proceeded through the green-scented pines. Now the shrill of clear-toned cicadas replaced the sound of the sea, and, as the path curved, Annabel caught a distant glimpse of blue. It made her realise how high they had climbed.

The path turned another bend, and they came to another major crimson arch. Once more the guards made them wait until another set of soldiers joined them. Six more in front and six more behind. 'They must think we are very dangerous,' joked Annabel. But Hiroko was silent and nervous.

The stone path had turned into stone steps. Annabel climbed them gingerly, placing the lacquered shoes carefully, pulling up the folds of her kimono so that the silk didn't brush along the dusty pine-needled ground. Some message passed between the soldiers, and they didn't try to hurry her. Annabel was grateful. The exertion was bringing her out in a fine mist of sweat. The exertion, and the apprehension that was growing in her belly.

At the top of the steps was another immense red arch. They passed through it into the sunlight of the temple grounds. The guards motioned them to halt and Annabel stood squinting in the bright light, looking around her curiously at the mountain-top shrine.

It felt like a holy place, despite the numbers of danger-ously armed soldiers who marched busily hither and thither. The sweep of the gravel court was so vast that it neutralised their warlike effect. Graceful scarlet roofs soared upwards over gold pagodas. A deep-toned bell clanged briefly and was silent.

'Where is this Nakano, then?' asked Annabel. She tried to sound insouciant, but her voice sounded reedy and thin. As they marked the irreverence in her tone, as one man, the guards shifted slightly and froze her with their malevolent eyes.

Hiroko seemed close to tears. Her voice shook. 'Please, Annabel san. You do not understand. You cannot understand. But, for my sake, will you not remember all I have taught you about polite behaviour?'

Annabel burned. What had polite behaviour to do with their foreign taboos? There and then she determined that she would not grovel. She would be polite as her mother had taught her, but she would not cower before the great Lord Nakano, despite the dominion he had over her.

Another detachment of guards stamped over and waved Annabel's party to follow them towards what seemed to be one of the main buildings. A broad flight of stone steps led up to its scarlet and gold bulk. A bronze cauldron swung over a charcoal fire in the centre of the path. Smoke from the incense sticks burning within the hot sand of the cauldron poured over its metal rim and scented the air.

At the entrance to the great crimson-painted building, to Annabel's great relief, the whole party paused to take off their shoes. Then they stepped into the building between the two fearsomely carved and gilded guardian deities whose statues flanked the entrance. Annabel stood very still inside the cool dim, tatami-smelling interior and waited for her eyes to adjust.

Spring sunlight filtered through the rice-paper panels of the outer walls, illuminating the gold of the straw matting and the brown of the ranks of kneeling samurai. All the men wore brown, the silk of their kimonos dyed the rich nutty hue of chestnuts in autumn. All wore the crane insignia.

Now Annabel realised that the samurai warriors were squatting in tidy rows, at their ease, sipping the green tea that the village women had already served them. As Annabel watched, the silk of women's kimonos flashed like hummingbirds as they knelt, allowing the men to choose from the bowls of rice and fish and pickled vegetables that adorned the lacquer trays they carried.

The guards urged Annabel forward, through the kneeling ranks of men, to an empty space where there was a dais at the end of the temple.

The dais was covered with rich, thick tatami matting. The gilded screens behind it were decorated with exquisite scenes of China. In a niche in the wall, an earthenware vase held spears of blue iris. Annabel could smell the yellow pollen that fell from the heart of the flower, fresh in the dim hall.

Her eyes slid away from the two men on the dais and went to the only woman present. She was kneeling, eyes modestly cast down, waiting for the men to notice her. She wore green silk embroidered with silver cranes over a brilliant scarlet kimono, and a wide peach sash bound up her narrow waist.

She was bowing low over a black lacquer tray full of food. Scraps of blossom and elegant leaves decorated the bowls of white rice. The food was untouched. A pair of black chopsticks banded with dull gold lay unused on an elegant ceramic rest.

Annabel noticed that the tray held a dish of spiny sea urchins. She shuddered as she spotted sticky, slimy bobbles of fermented bean paste. And then her gaze fell on the crumpled black puff balls that tasted of bile.

The tray looked beautiful, but Annabel knew that the more a food was considered to be a delicacy, the more likely it was that she would find it repulsive. She hoped that the Lord Nakano would not ask her to eat with him.

The Lord Nakano! Annabel could delay looking up at him no longer. Slowly, she took her eyes away from the silently kneeling serving-woman and lifted her gaze to the dais.

Beside her, she was aware of Hiroko, kneeling low on the tatami matting, her head resting on the floor in front of her, her hands placed on the straw matting, one on each side of her dark chignon.

The headman, Hiroko's father, had prostrated himself near by, although with far less grace than his daughter. The samurai who had brought them into the temple were also bowing low before the great daimyo. But Annabel had sworn that she would not grovel.

'Down!'

She ignored the curt whisper from the guard behind her.

'Please, Annabel san!'

She ignored the low whisper that came from the parted lips of her friend.

And finally, the majestic figure on the dais turned slowly to look at her. The huge, winglike shoulders of his starched overmantle gave him a formidable presence. His eyes were too cold to express any kind of feeling. They simply stared silently across the abyss of two cultures.

Annabel felt his impact like a blow. A cold, malevolent, alien intelligence burned in the eyes that met hers. She had expected him to be powerful, an authority figure, but she had not expected him to be so hostile, so unreachable and other-worldly.

She was shaking all over and she wished that she had obeyed orders and was safely prostrate on the matting. But she was committed now. It was too late to take a servile approach to the great daimyo.

Hiroko had told her enough about Japanese protocol for Annabel to know that her behaviour could be read as a deadly insult towards any samurai, let alone the

61

daimyo. But she was not Japanese, she was from the West, and she would show him only the deference that was suitable from an English citizen.

She blessed the stiff bindings that held her spine so straight. The restriction seemed to make it difficult to breathe, but at least it held her wildly fluttering heart in place. Annabel willed her blue eyes to stay calm. She could not speak because her tongue was stuck to the roof of her mouth, but she forced a polite smile to her lips. Then she bent her knees in a graceful court curtsy.

And all the while he watched her. The lamps of male power burned in his eyes and he measured her with the cool, steady intelligence of a king.

The tight narrow silk of the kimono skirts prevented Annabel from curtsying as deeply as she would have liked to, but she was deliberate in her movements as she made her obeisance. She kept herself under control as she straightened, and then settled herself on to her knees next to the motionless, prone figure of Hiroko.

Nakano still watched her with expressionless malevolence. Annabel did not want him to think that she was uncouth, so she bowed low as Hiroko had taught her. But then, although her heart was pounding and her palms were sweating, she raised herself up again and sat calmly on her knees. And, although it was terrifying to do so, she lifted up her blue eyes to meet the powerful dark gaze of the man before her.

He held her eyes with a steady, measuring look. Annabel felt as if he had caught her up in the nets of his eyes. As if she were being dragged unmeasurable fathoms into the depths of his intelligence. All the sights, sounds and scents of the world around her seemed to grow pale and fade away. Only the gaze of the dark lord remained.

And even when he seemed to come to some decision and broke the gaze, turning away to the man who knelt before him, Annabel didn't feel as if she had regained her freedom. All her thoughts seemed bound to him. Her gaze seemed chained to his figure.

His body had grown massive as it moulded itself to fit the power of the mind that inhabited it. He was larger by far than any of the warriors in the hall. Rich silk gleamed in folded wings across the breadth of his shoulders. A short sword glinted from its scabbard. A long sword lay on the tatami beside him. He did not look as if he ever went unarmed. His dark hair was cut in the same way as the soldiers', but his topknot was higher and his regal face was more impassive. Although he was turned away from her, Annabel could feel the heat of his male testosterone.

The tight band around her waist seemed to become tighter as she struggled to calm her breathing, to regain some measure of control. She was aware of her chest, lifting and falling rapidly beneath the silk of her kimono.

She was aware, too, of the naked vulnerability of her woman's place. Heat spiralled there, and a pulse beat fast and hard. She tried to ignore the signals her body was sending her, and turned her attention outward, towards the two men on the dais. She forced herself to concentrate on what they were doing.

The man kneeling before the daimyo was old. He still wore the uniform of a samurai warrior, and the swords, but the hand and arm that he held stiffly up towards Nakano were gnarled. A large bird with fierce talons gripped the leather band that protected the old arm. It was a hawk, a hunting hawk, and as Nakano reached for the bird with a gloved hand, Annabel saw that the bird was hooded.

Disturbed by the motion of being passed from one man to the other, the hawk protested, and flapped her wings vigorously. Tiny bells jingled on her feet. The soft leather hood held her blind, preventing her from flying away.

'Be easy now, my beauty.' Even in a low croon, the

voice resonated with power. Annabel watched, fascinated, as Nakano held his hand steady and gentled the hawk with light but commanding hands. Beneath his touch, she quietened, dropping her wings and letting the feathers settle into place.

Within moments, the hawk was allowing Nakano to examine her, to spread her magnificent wings and check her for damage. There was an injury to one wing. Towards the end of its spread, the wing bent in a sickeningly unnatural dip. Annabel thought a bone must have been broken.

A cloth full of mysterious paraphernalia lay spread open before the daimyo. From the jumble of contents, Nakano selected what looked like a piece of washed bone trimmed into a quill. Then he took a needle already threaded with black thread and stitched the white cylinder to the wing of the hawk.

His hands moved in a way that was almost rough, yet they were precise and competent, and the hawk lay silent and unprotesting in his grip, seeming to understand that he was healing her. The needle flashed swiftly as he pierced her flesh, then bound the wounds together. Annabel watched intently, until the job was complete.

'There,' said Nakano, gentling the hawk so that she allowed herself to be passed back to the old man without protest. 'I think she'll heal now. Keep her under your protection for a few weeks. You can bring her back to me when she is ready.'

The old falconer bowed low and backed a few paces before turning away with the hawk. Annabel's heart began to speed again as Nakano wiped his hands on some clean white cloths. First a damp one and then a dry one. The damp cloth was perfumed, and the gentle odour of flowers dissipated the dusty reek of the hawk.

The daimyo took his time over the cleansing, rubbing the cloths over his fingers so slowly, so thoroughly, so much as if he were delaying, that Annabel thought that what the conspirators had said by the bathing pools was true: he did not wish to confront her.

And as he turned slowly to face her, gazing steadily at her across the vast distance that seemed to separate their two lives, the chink of sword metal reminded her that if she posed him too great a problem, there was no force or rule in Japan to protect her.

Chapter Five

The Lord Nakano kept his dangerous dark eyes fixed firmly on Annabel, but he inclined his head slightly in Hiroko's direction to tell the Japanese girl that she could address him.

'So sorry, lord. Please excuse me for disturbing you, but here, as you requested, is the barbarian,' whispered Hiroko. She raised her body a little, but she punctuated her words with deep, low motions towards the floor.

Nakano's voice was as sharp as one of his swords. 'Have you managed to teach the barbarian nothing?'

Annabel's heart crashed painfully into her throat and lodged there like a boulder. She tried to work up enough saliva to unglue her tongue, to speak up in her friend's defence, but her mouth would not obey her. The strange taste of fear silenced her. Her hands lay trembling in her lap, and her belly crawled, as she saw that her knees were jerking uncontrollably in fine, nervous spasms under the pink silk that covered them.

'So sorry, sire,' Hiroko was saying. 'I did my poor best. So sorry. So unworthy.'

Beside Hiroko, her father lay prostrate on the matting.

He, too, was trembling too much to come to the aid of his daughter.

Nakano was silent for a long, dangerous moment. But then he shrugged. His eyes never left Annabel's face as he said, 'No matter. They are unteachable. I have never met one that could do more than grunt a few words. And at least this one does not smell. You have cleaned it up well.'

'You are most kind. You deal with me so graciously. I thank you, Lord Nakano. But this barbarian can speak many words.'

'Very good. Show me what it can do.'

'Yes, sire. If you please, Annabel san, be upstanding. Say a few words for the honourable daimyo.'

Annabel got slowly to her feet. She felt very tall as she stood above the kneeling serving-woman, the prostrate headman and Hiroko, as they all lay flat on the tatami matting.

She could hear a faint murmur of conversation from the great hall behind them, but she had a feeling that much of it was fake, and that the attention of both the samurai and the women who served them was trained upon the dais where the Lord Nakano sat.

He did not look small although he was seated. He knelt on some wide, flat cushions, and the stiff wings of his magnificent robe gave him height; yet Annabel felt that even if he had been naked, he would have kept his imposing stature.

She made a curtsy, the English way once more. She thought of the hours she had spent practising her curtsy in case her papa's ship should come home with a fortune and she and Mamma should be taken to meet Good Queen Elizabeth. It felt strange to be sweeping low before a royal personage so very different from the one of her childish dreams.

She lowered her blue eyes for a moment, then looking up at Nakano, she inclined her head gracefully. Her mouth had freed itself, and the words came easily now. 'It is a very great honour to meet you, Lord Nakano. Please do not chastise dear Hiroko. She has told me much that is interesting of Japanese protocol, but I chose to greet you in the manner of the English court.'

Her voice rang a little high and shaky in her ears, but Annabel was filled with triumph. Her curtsy had been graceful despite her shaky knees. Her smile had been judged to perfection. And, at last, she had found the courage to speak up on behalf of the woman who had, indeed, taught her all that she knew of this strange and exotic oriental country.

Nakano had started violently as she began to speak, but his control was perfectly in place by the time Annabel had finished her little speech. His eyes bored into hers with renewed intensity. Although they were black, they burned with a dark, intense passion. He seemed to be judging Annabel, examining her every pore; weighing her up.

'Very pretty,' he said approvingly, still addressing Hiroko. 'You have done well. Even if the barbarian has memorised only that one speech, it is still more than I've ever known one achieve before.'

It was infuriating to stand silent before Nakano while he discussed her with Hiroko as if she were a side of beef. Annabel felt anger flare up in her. Nakano was weighing her up as if she were a commodity for sale. For the sake of her friend, she dropped her eyes to hide the hate she knew must be sparking there. But she didn't drop them quickly enough to hide their expression from the Lord Nakano.

'Ha! It has eyes like a wild thing! Such anger as burns there. It's almost as if it knows that we are talking about it.'

'If you please, Lord Nakano, I think you will find that this barbarian comprehends a very great deal.'

'Nonsense!'

'If it would please you, sire, why not try a little test: ask her to do something, to perform an action for you.'

'You really think it could understand?'

Hiroko's forehead touched the mat. 'Sir, Annabel san, this barbarian, she is most intelligent.'

'Very well. We shall try it.' He turned his full attention to Annabel. 'You! Barbarian! Look at me!'

Annabel raised her head slowly, obeying him because she had no choice. She was so angry that now she hoped that all the hatred she felt for him was clearly visible in her eyes. His gaze met hers like a blow. His eyes were dark, unreadable.

'Ha! Those eyes still spit hatred, like a hawk before taming. Hiroko san, it cannot be possible that such a barbaric creature could understand all the graceful complexities of the Japanese language. It is well known that the barbarians are too stupid, or too primitive, to understand culture.'

'Sir, I beg you to direct your questions directly to her.'

Nakano stared down his nose at Annabel and spoke directly to her for the first time. He spoke lightly, as if he would not be surprised to be ignored, or misunderstood. 'Why so angry, Barbarian?'

'Because of the way you are treating me.'

When Annabel answered his question in good Japanese, Nakano leaned forward intently. He looked at her sternly and his eyes never left her face. 'How so? Were you starved? Ill-treated in the village?'

'No, not in the village, now! You are treating me like an object. Calling me "it". Speaking about me as if I had no intelligence, had no feelings.'

Nakano still seemed to be testing her. 'How would you have me treat you?'

Annabel's tangled feelings about her complete dependence on Nakano's goodwill expressed themselves simply. Her voice was soft and sad as she answered him: 'As a woman.'

69

'Ha! It shall be as you wish.' He paused for a second and added, 'Show me your breasts.'

He said it with such force that Annabel was startled and looked directly into his eyes. She felt blood pump into her cheeks and sting them red. 'What?'

Nakano's hand just lightly touched the hilt of his sword. 'If you want to be treated as a woman, you must first prove to me that you are indeed a woman. I have never seen a human being with blue eyes and yellow hair. No, not even a barbarian, for the Portuguese are strange and stinking devils, but they are coloured as we are. I have never seen your like before, and I wish to examine you thoroughly.'

For the first time, he smiled at her. The expression was pleasant, but there was a hint of something chilling in his eyes as he repeated: 'Show me your breasts.'

Annabel's eyes were drawn to his sword hilt. Another large sword lay on the matting next to him. Visible symbols of his power. She realised that she was completely and totally helpless; powerless to stop him from doing anything he wanted. Her only hope lay in winning him over. 'Yes, lord,' she whispered.

Nakano looked at her gravely, searching her face, and then relaxed, settling himself back on his cushions, relieved perhaps by her submission.

'If you please,' faltered Annabel. Her voice was a barely audible whisper, muffled by the thought that, in only a few moments, she would be baring her breasts before him.

Nakano looked at her with black danger in his eyes. Annabel gestured helplessly with her hands. Then he realised that she was so tightly bound up in the giant silken obi that it was impossible for her to undo the intricate bow that fastened behind her.

'Help the barbarian!' Nakano growled to the two prostrate females on the matting. Hiroko and the serving-woman rose instantly and went to Annabel.

She felt the soft hands of the women tugging at the silk that bound her, and then a feeling of release as the sash fell free.

The skirts of the kimono brushed against her legs as they loosened, but they did not fall open. Annabel stood trembling. She sensed rather than heard the two women settle back on to the tatami matting behind her, waiting patiently in case their lord had any further orders for them. It made her nervous to know that they would witness whatever might happen next.

Slowly, holding her gaze as he rose fluidly from the cushions, Nakano got to his feet. He retrieved his large sword from the tatami and slid it into place at his side. He acted as if from long habit rather than as if he thought he would need his sword. As he walked a few paces towards Annabel, she was uncomfortably aware of the agitated movement of her heart.

He was only a few inches taller than her. She was surprised. His aura was so powerful that she had been expecting him to tower above her. But his physical body was not so much bigger than hers. It was by the force of his will that he dominated.

She began trembling again as his scent reached her nostrils. He smelt of the outdoors, and horses and oiled steel, and, under that again, lay the tang of musk, the scent of a sexually active male.

He stood looking down at her for an endless moment. Annabel's heart pounded in her chest as she made one last effort to stop him from humiliating her, using the formal Japanese phrase, 'Please, I beg you most honourable one, treat thy humble servant kindly.'

'Come now –' Nakano hesitated for a moment over her name before deciding how to address her '– Annabel ... san. We are agreed, are we not? You wish to be treated as a woman?'

Annabel paused while her mind reviewed her situation. Then her head dropped slowly as she nodded her acceptance. 'How else can I prove to you, Lord Nakano, that I should be treated kindly?'

She felt his soft breath on her cheek. 'This is the best way.' His voice was a soothing whisper. 'And I will deal with you kindly. Let me just part these folds of silk a little way. I wish to expose your charms.'

Annabel's hands reached up as if to stop him. Then her hands fell apart in surrender as she felt his gentle fingers brushing at the fabric that hung loosely over her breasts. Now her body was reacting to the closeness of a male, to the first gentle touch to brush her skin in so many lonely months.

As his fingers pressed into the softness of the kimono fabric, parting it, then gently brushing over the thrusting softness of her breasts, Annabel's breath caught in what was almost a sob and she struggled to force back what could easily become tears.

Her eyes remained downcast as she felt his hands roam at will over her breasts. He touched her gently. Her breasts felt as if they were growing, swelling and hardening as he cupped and fondled them. She wanted him to squeeze her breasts harder, his feather-light touch arousing and tantalising her, making her nipples ache. But instead of pressing harder, he took his hands away. 'Breasts like white doves,' he said softly.

A pain as sharp as the feelings clutching at her throat burned at the base of her spine, one sharp locus of pain on each side of her bone, just above the buttocks. Annabel knew what that pain was – desire. The need for a man was pushing her, shaping her reactions, rushing over her with such force that she trembled, knowing that she could not control her body, hungry as though after the winter famine.

Nakano was standing before her, looking at her very openly. The folds of her kimono were spread open now, allowing her breasts to poke out softly. Annabel looked down at the creamy pale curves, and she knew that she wanted Nakano to touch her breasts again.

His eyes lingered over her pale skin and the pink tips that hardened there. 'Beautiful, Annabel san! You have such fine pale skin.' He stepped back.

Annabel kept her head down submissively, unwilling to meet his dangerous gaze, or to let him know how much he had unsettled her.

Nakano said harshly, 'Now, show me everything.'

Her head jerked up as if he had slapped her. He had not used that blatantly sexual tone of voice to her before. She looked into his eyes, trembling. 'I don't understand. What, what do you want me to do?'

'I want you to show me your *momo*.' His voice was forbidding in the shadowy room.

Annabel felt the deepening throb of arousal between her legs. Way down inside, her womb clenched and unclenched, readying itself for this man. The long dark tunnel of her vagina was black velvet closing on nothing. Her flesh longed to cling on to male flesh. The flower of her woman's place yearned to curl and wrap itself around the satin hardness of Nakano's manhood.

Her body had no doubts. Her body understood nothing of the social restrictions that confused her need. It understood only simple desires.

When Annabel heard the slight rasp of Nakano's quickened breathing and knew that she was exciting him, her body responded by producing the first silvery secretions of desire. A delicious wet trickle of love dew began to gather between her thighs.

But her mind still objected, and Annabel felt the useless desire to cup her hands protectively over the pulse that beat so warmingly between her legs. Perhaps if she pretended not to know what he meant? Annabel stared at him in confusion. 'What must I show you?'

A thin smile lifted Lord Nakano's lips. 'Your *momo*,

73

Barbarian san. Your lovely, delicious, peach of a woman's cunt, that's what I want you to show me.'

Annabel stared into the smooth buddha's mask of his face. If only that stonelike expression would soften into warm creases – just for her, how easy it would be to obey him.

When she still made no move, Nakano walked behind her. Annabel shivered all over as his dangerous tones pierced the silence of the room. 'You're slow to respond, Barbarian san. But it doesn't matter. I'll help you undress.'

Annabel felt the smooth brush of fingers as he trailed his hand across the nape of her neck. 'Don't hurt me,' she whispered.

A soft chuckle buzzed in her ear. 'Oh, I'm not going to hurt you. On the contrary, I want you to feel pleasure.'

She felt his breath on her back, and soft, warm, human lips momentarily touched the warm flesh at the base of her hair line. Frissons of pure ecstasy shivered down Annabel's spine at his fleeting touch. She felt as if the imprint of his lips were branded in crimson ink upon her neck for all time.

Her lips parted as the breath hissed through them in an involuntary moan. Waves of lust swept upwards towards her throat. It was the most meltingly delicious sensation she had ever known.

Nakano stood before her again now. He looked enraptured as he faced her, but he was still very much in charge. 'Pull aside your kimono,' he insisted. 'I want to see you naked.'

Annabel cringed at his order, but she reached down and took each side of the unloosened kimono in trembling hands. Then she slowly parted the fabric, drawing it across the front of her body, feeling it brush gently over her skin as she drew the concealing folds aside, exposing her nakedness.

As more and more of her pale white flesh was exposed,

Nakano's eyes never left her body. His lips parted slightly, but Annabel could see no other reaction.

Annabel stood like a statue, holding the kimono wide-open, feeling like a whore for exposing her nakedness to him in this way. Her head drooped softly as his eyes fell to her pubic curls.

'Yellow!' His voice held wonder and reverence. His eyes stared at her so intently. 'Take off your clothes – completely.'

Annabel shivered, but she obeyed, dropping the sides of the kimono. They brushed softly down to hang across her body as she reached down to her feet. She peeled off her white, Japanese, split-toed socks. She lingered for a moment, bending, feeling the warm yielding tatami beneath her bare feet. But she could not delay for ever. She must face him once more.

Her breath caught in her throat as she straightened. Nakano was watching her dreamily, his face soft, but she knew something of the steel that lay below, and she knew she must strip for him.

She slid her hands under the clothing that obscured her naked body from his view. She pushed the layers of pink fabric backward over her shoulders. The silk smelt of sandalwood as it whispered down her body to lie in a crumpled mass around her bare feet.

A glimmer of admiration floated into Nakano's eyes as their gaze drifted down the slender curves of Annabel's naked body. His voice was just a whisper, but there was a command in it she dare not disobey. 'Slide your fingers down into that soft, golden peach-fur.'

Annabel's hands brushed so lightly over her perfumed skin as she obeyed. Her belly felt taut and shivery. Nakano's voice was just a whisper as he looked at her naked sex. 'Like the first ripe peach of summer, and as fragrant.'

Annabel crossed her hands protectively over her mons.

Again the soft, compelling whisper, 'Bend your knees.'

Eyes downcast, she did so.

'Now, spread those petal lips with your fingers. Show me, frankly and clearly, what lies between the legs of a barbarian.'

The coral-pink folds of flesh felt heavy as Annabel spread them open.

Nakano inhaled deeply. 'Perfumed,' he murmured. 'And beautiful. Like a fragile pink flower.'

Then he added, in a deeper, rich, amused tone, 'The petals are glistening with the evidence of your excitement, Annabel san.'

As Nakano bent low, looking closer, Annabel knew that it excited her to be looked at; a heady, intoxicating excitement, but it made her feel vulnerable too.

The daimyo stretched out one wondering hand and touched her softly between her legs. His fingers explored the lips, the folds of the labia. They circled the clitoris and just lightly tapped at the entrance to her vagina.

Nakano's voice was a barely audible whisper. 'Ah, it feels like a *momo*. The soft touch is the same, and the wet heat of it on my palm is the same.'

Annabel flinched away from the shocking intimacy of his touch, yet she felt herself floating on waves of dreamy, sensual delight. And she knew that his touch was the cause of all her pleasure.

Nakano stood watching her with a slow smile. Then he said softly, 'You are a woman, Annabel san, and I shall treat you so.'

She was afraid to discover how that might be. To experience what he would do next. Her heart fluttered strangely at his gentle words, and her delicate lips trembled as she lowered her head. Her lashes slid shut, as if they would shield her from his presence.

For an eternal moment, nothing happened, then Annabel shivered as she heard Nakano come up softly behind her. Her clitoris tingled all over as she felt his hands cupping her buttocks. She could hear his rasping breath plainly now, as he hefted the soft weight of her bottom, rolling the taut flesh, squeezing one globe against the other.

A deep and heavy ache began within her as his hands explored the length of her slender back, running briefly over her shoulders to clasp her neck – a dark play that turned her bones to water – before sweeping down again, over the curve of her hips, down the lush curves of her thighs.

She felt his breath on her back and she realised that he must be kneeling or squatting behind her. His hands travelled lower and lower. Her skin almost sizzled as she felt the soft blow of his warm breath touch her buttocks, and then the gentle press of his hands demanding entrance to the crack that ran between the lush slopes of her cheeks. She clenched her buttocks together, and then tensed even harder as she waited for his reaction to her denial.

His hands slipped back down a little, pausing to caress the flesh of her legs before pressing on the inside of each knee, pulling her legs apart. Shivering, her face burning with shame and embarrassment, Annabel slowly parted her legs. She kept her eyes tight closed, but the buzz of conversation seemed to have faded, and she couldn't help feeling that all the people in the hall were watching.

And she wondered what Nakano was seeing as her legs parted. Her sex lips felt stiff and engorged as they swung free. The blood in her labia pounded in time with her heart, thrilled by the knowledge that Nakano was looking at her sex, was so close to her intimate secrets. Her clitoris swelled softly inside the gentle creases that held it, and she knew that soft moist liquid was dropping like gentle rain from her gently clenching womb.

'Bend forward.' The order was barely a whisper.

Keeping her legs straddled, she bent forward. She knew that the purse of her sex was now open, displaying all her treasures. Her heart beat in an odd rhythm as she waited.

Then Annabel felt a soft tongue touch her anus. A long sigh escaped her lips. Her eyes remained closed. Her body remained motionless. She felt the tongue again, this time sliding along the slit between her legs. Nakano's face pressed under her buttocks, pushing up between her legs, as his tongue slipped into the pool of moisture that dewed the entrance to her vagina.

Annabel murmured, a long shiver passing through her body. The tongue slipped away from her entrance, pausing briefly to lap up her love dew, and slid up towards the button of her clitoris. Annabel's knees weakened. They shivered below her, letting her sex drop further towards the exploring tongue. She wanted that velvet touch so badly. Her whole being yearned for his touch.

It was so strange that he chose to explore her this way, from behind, pressing his face into the curves of her buttocks as he strained to reach forward, but it was so arousing, so delicious in its intensity. She had never wanted the relief of a touch on her clitoris so badly. It moaned as it waited for him.

But she felt his tongue drop away. The pressure of his face on her buttocks stopped. The comforting warmth of his body left her.

Annabel swayed slightly as she stood, naked and abandoned in the centre of the temple hall. There was movement around her, footsteps and bustle.

She opened her eyes to see a thick-set man staring at her in total disbelief. He wore a splendid blue kimono with a different insignia to that of Nakano's. The samurai crowded about him wore the same uniform. They too stared at Annabel. Their eyes burned into her nakedness. She turned away from them to look at their leader, the man who had distracted Nakano.

The new daimyo's accent was thick and difficult to

follow. '*Nan-da*, Nakano Sama?' He grunted. 'What in the name of hell is this?'

'Yoritomo san. A surprise visit, indeed,' said Nakano. He would have moved away, but Yoritomo remained transfixed in front of Annabel.

'What is it?' he asked again.

'It's a barbarian woman.' Nakano moved to join the man in front of Annabel. 'Did you never see one before?' he said casually.

'Never! The men are stinking pig devils! I assumed the women would be as degraded – but this one! What colouring! She is incomparable!'

'I admit to being quite enchanted with her,' said Nakano.

A haze of sensual delight drifted over Annabel at his words. She floated dreamily on a cloud of pleasure, content now to wait for the resumption of his sweet attentions to her body.

'Annabel is a wild and savage creature,' said Lord Nakano to the newcomer, 'and quite untaught in the pillow arts, but I desire her. We shall see what Mamma san can make of her.'

'A barbarian geisha? Is that possible?'

'Oh yes,' said Nakano, smiling down at Annabel with all the sweet intimacy of their sensual encounter in his eyes. 'As soon as I touched her perfumed valley, I knew she must be trained as my geisha.'

As Nakano spoke of Annabel's womanhood, she saw the blue-clad daimyo's eyes slide to the secrets between her legs. He looked lustfully at the tell-tale glisten of love dew.

'Ha! She likes your touch, then,' said the older man coarsely. He exchanged a knowing glance with Nakano and continued, 'She's juicy, all right! And those nipples might be pink – but they are stiff and erect. Just as perky as any Japanese woman's might be.' Lust clouded his eyes. 'I've never touched a barbarian before.'

'In that case, Yoritomo san, please, be my guest,' said Nakano in a polite silky voice.

Annabel stared at him in shock and outrage. She had not expected this! Still trembling from the intensely personal nature of her encounter with Nakano, her senses rebelled at the thought of another man's touch.

She shrank back as the stranger reached out a rough hand and rubbed it over her breast. The skin flinched under his touch.

But because Nakano's dark eyes followed the motion of his colleague's hand, watching intently as Yoritomo pinched her nipple roughly, Annabel was aware of a wild and sneaking excitement. Her nipples grew harder yet as the strange hand stimulated them, and, in the glance she threw to Nakano, there was as much embarrassment for her arousal under this stranger's lewd caress, as there was pleading to be rescued from it.

'She likes it all right,' observed the strange man once more. 'I'm touching a barbarian! I'm overwhelmed! She has the whitest skin I've ever seen.'

He began to pinch the skin around the tips of Annabel's nipples. The red blood that flowed into her ivory skin seemed to fascinate him. He pinched her again, and again. Hard. Too hard. Red welts formed in her delicate white skin and her lips trembled as she lifted her eyes to Nakano, begging him for relief.

'I see she intrigues you. Perhaps you would accept the barbarian as a gift?' said Nakano. 'Then you could treat her as you wished.'

The rough fingers fell away. 'Your pardon, Nakano. Your very pardon, indeed. No insult was intended. She is so beautiful, so peerless, and so very unusual in her beauty – I was tempted into rude behaviour. I do beg your pardon.'

Annabel struggled to contain the feelings that swept over her. The depth and strength of the instinctive outrage and denial she felt at Nakano's words were a revelation to her.

She now realised that Nakano's offer to present her to the newcomer had acted as a rebuke. Yoritomo was bowing low before Nakano in apology.

'Your pardon,' he said once more. 'Perhaps I could beg a few moments of your time. I am come to request a favour of you.'

Annabel stood to one side, momentarily forgotten, examining the strange feelings in her heart. In theory, she should not care which daimyo dealt with her. One Japanese lord should be much like another to an English girl. But this was not true.

She had not known Nakano long, and he was certainly intent on demonstrating his dominion over her. He had forced her to strip and display her naked body for his pleasure. He was talking about 'training' her, which did not sound comfortable. She had no reason to like or trust him.

Yet, almost before he had touched her, she had been aware of a mysterious link between them. And once that first kiss had sent shivers down her spine, she had known beyond doubt that there was a bond. Fleeting, ineffable, impossible to explain the transcendental nature of her feelings towards him, but they were connected. Their relationship might not be happy, but she was destined to work out their mysterious connection, whatever it may bring.

'Annabel san,' said Nakano, and there was fleeting regret in his eyes as he spoke to her. 'There is much I must see to now that my friend has unexpectedly joined us. You must say goodbye to these villagers. I must leave at once, and you are to accompany me to my fortress.'

Annabel bent to pick up the crumpled silk petals of her kimono, but he put out a hand and stopped her. She glanced at him, an open question in her eyes.

'You don't need that. You must wear more suitable garments,' said Nakano. A tenderly sensual smile played about his lips. 'Garments that will not only make you look beautiful, but will also make you aware of the nature of our relationship.'

A servant hurried over and, bowing low, handed Nakano a confused black bundle. Annabel stared with horrified eyes as Nakano separated the black mass into two long black strips of fabric.

He took a step towards her and she felt his breath just touch her face. He stroked the black fabric over one cheek. It was soft, delicate, with a slight nap to it. Annabel smelt leather and realised that the fabric must be the softest kid. She moaned slightly and pressed her face into the leather.

Her response pleased Nakano. His eyes were tender and warm. 'Ah, Annabel san. You make me wish for more time with you. But that is impossible, so let me bind you to me in such a way that you will yearn for my return.'

He shook out the black garments, and Annabel now saw that they were gloves. Two long black gloves that would come up over her elbows.

Nakano picked up her left arm and began easing her fingers into one glove. His touch was sensual, heavy with the promise of delights to come. Annabel's breath came faster and faster between her parted lips as she felt the warmth of his body pressing close to hers as he bent over his task, intent on getting each finger smoothed into a black case.

She shivered because she longed to put her arms around him, but because he seemed to wish it, she stood passively and let him dress her.

When he was finished, Nakano stood back and looked at her with possessive pride. 'Good,' he nodded. 'It is good.' *

Annabel languorously stretched out her black-clad

arms before her. Now she saw that the gloves had loops stitched into the leather, all the way up the seams, but more at the bottom of the glove, around the wrists, than at the top of the gloves by the elbows.

She looked up at Nakano. He was watching her intently. 'Put your arms behind you,' he said.

Annabel saw that he was a holding a long black cord that looped and dangled between his fingers. A faint premonition stirred in her belly, but she obediently put her arms behind her. As she did so her breasts lifted up and out, and Nakano flicked one pink nipple approvingly. 'Now turn around.'

She turned. She was facing the great hall now, and many faces watched the dais. While she had been standing with her back to them, she had managed to just about forget how many, many people were in the temple. But now she was facing them, and they were all looking at her, watching avidly.

Annabel slid her eyelids shut, blocking them out. In the darkness, she felt her wrists grasped, and gentle tugging sensations as Lord Nakano began lacing the wrists of the black gloves together behind her back.

The movements were gentle but firm. She felt her hands drawn together at the wrists. Then a pull as her arms were drawn together and then let go. When she felt her arms pulled together once more and then let go again, Annabel realised that Nakano was experimenting with the mobility of her arms, seeing how high he could lace the black gloves without hurting her.

She shuddered as she stood there and her head drooped. She wished she could let down her hair so that it covered her face. With her arms tied behind her, her breasts stood proud. The red marks where Yoritomo had pinched her were clearly visible around her nipples. They tingled and ached. The stimulation had aroused them. She longed for Nakano to take the yearning tips into his soft, wet mouth and suckle and ease them. Fresh moisture slid between her legs, and a soft chuckle behind her told her that it had not gone unnoticed.

With a final tug on her wrists, Nakano came back to stand in front of Annabel. His eyes rested on the breasts that poked out so invitingly towards him, but he made no move to touch them.

'Beautiful contrast, Annabel san. Black bonds on white skin. I will have no time for dalliance until we reach home. But tied as you are now, I know that you will not forget me.'

Nakano lifted his eyes from her breasts and met Annabel's gaze. She knew that her arousal must be plain to him; hot desire sprang into his expression, but his voice was perfectly controlled as he continued. 'You will travel in a palanquin and will need no clothes. I have no maids to give you, so sorry, but two of my men will attend to your every need on the journey.'

'Every need?' said Annabel faintly. 'How long is this journey?'

There was wicked, knowing glee in the dark eyes. 'Only a few days.'

Annabel's eyes slid shut. 'A few days? How am I to . . . My natural . . .'

The voice that answered her was smooth, knowing and utterly implacable. 'It is only natural for a woman to be uncomfortable without her man. I want you to be aware of my absence, Annabel san. I want you to yearn for us to reach home, and yearn for the relief I will give you there.'

Annabel was curled sleepily on the silk cushions inside the palanquin. She had been half-dozing, but some faint premonition shuddered through the air towards her, or some quality about the hoofbeats that thudded towards her sent a message, and she knew that Nakano was approaching.

She yawned and sat up. The palanquin lurched to a

halt and she felt it tip and then drop as it was placed on the ground. It was not a comfortable way to travel, and she had asked if she might be allowed to walk, but the only response to her request was a blank stare and a slight shake of the head.

Annabel lifted her gloved hands to her head and smoothed out her hair. It had fallen loose during the journey. Its length and mass were a comfort to her. She was still naked. Whenever the party had stopped for food, she was given a padded robe to wear, but once the palanquin was ready to leave, she was not allowed to keep it, nor was she allowed to take off her gloves, although, despite Nakano's threats, they had been unlaced as soon as she was put in the palanquin.

Through the curtains that enclosed her in the stuffy darkness, she could hear the jingling of horse harness and hear low-toned male voices. She was expecting the hand that slipped between the curtains and pulled them open. Cold mountain air flowed in and touched her body. It smelt thin and fresh. Its caress hardened her nipples. Annabel began to shiver.

'Out!' grunted one of the guards.

Annabel unfolded her long naked legs and bent her head so that she could pass through the palanquin door. Sandals stood waiting for her on the ground outside. They felt cold as her feet slid into them. She looked up.

Nakano was there, waiting for her. He wore golden armour, the light overlapping metal squares held together with red lacings. His eyes were unreadable, as if he had become a stranger again on the journey.

'Come with me, Annabel san,' he said. She could not read his mood from his voice, either.

One of the guards brought the padded robe. Nakano took it from him and tenderly slipped it over Annabel's shoulders. The robe was the same shape as a kimono, but stuffed with cotton wadding and then quilted. Anna-

85

bel drew the warm folds around her, grateful for its warmth and the evidence that he cared for her.

Nakano gestured Annabel to follow him. He left the narrow mountain path and began striding towards a rocky ridge that looked dark against the sky. It was just after sunset. The sky still glowed with faint colour, but night was approaching fast.

Annabel looked back at the horses and porters and samurai in the party behind them. They were all strolling about aimlessly, waiting for Nakano to be ready to resume the journey. Two or three hundred people, all wearing brown. No sign of the other daimyo or his men, the uncouth speakers who wore blue. 'Has your friend left us?' she asked.

Nakano gave her a slanting look, but he answered her readily enough. 'He left us at Okitsu, when we stopped at the staging post on the Tokaido.'

'That little path was the Eastern sea road?'

'It's big enough to connect Edo and Kyoto.'

'I thought we would turn on to the Tokaido, towards the city of Edo.' Annabel felt a stab of disappointment. After a long winter in a fishing village, she wanted to go to a city. Hiroko had told her that Nakano had a place in Edo, where political power was concentrated, she had hoped that they would go there. But he seemed to be taking her into the mountains.

Nakano did not answer her. He picked up his pace as they breasted the rocky ridge, and Annabel had to hurry to keep up with him. Then he stopped and caught her by her black-gloved wrists, holding her so that she had to face him. His eyes turned down towards her as he bestowed on her a tiny smile. 'We are going to Shimoyama,' he said. 'Castle Mountain. My father established us in Edo, but this is my fortress – I built it.'

Then he put gentle hands on Annabel's shoulders and turned her to face out over the view that lay below the rocky promontory they stood on. Annabel looked down.

Far below her feet, the bumpy top of a dark-leaved forest lay in a cloud of green cedars below them. The forest ran like the sea and broke in a bubbling green wave against the soaring white bulk of an enormous Japanese building. Annabel's eyes were drawn up over its many layers of steeply hipped roofs to a central tower that seemed to float up into the still, sunset sky.

The building seemed to gleam in the soft light, reflecting the hazy pinks, blues and greys of the sky as a pearl might. Behind it stretched range after range of dark grey mountains, their sharp peaks etched against the soft sky. Annabel could pick out the unmistakable outline of a volcano, Mount Fuji, and her lips parted with the wonder of the scene below her.

She looked at the round, full moon that floated over the blue-black hills to the left of Shimoyama's slanting roofs. The moon glowed like a pink lantern in the sky, at exactly the same level as the highest point of the castle building. The central keep, the donjon of the fortress, seemed to hang glimmering over the great bulk of its foundations.

Annabel smiled up at Nakano with a look of wonder on her face. 'I'm glad that you brought me to this vantage point to show me your home.'

She turned back to look at the incredible tinted white bulk of the fortress as it reflected the pink moonlight. Time passed. The sunset cast faded from the moon, and the sky and the colour of the night became dark blue as she stood quietly next to Nakano, feeling the cold mountain wind blow softly by her ears.

The moon was silver and the sky a very dark indigo before Nakano stirred. He was looking beyond the magnificent outline of his fortress, out to where the simple line of the far mountains pierced the sky. 'The full moon makes me feel that the world is mine indeed,' he said softly.

But as Annabel followed his gaze, a grey cloud drifted

up from the horizon and draped itself over the cone of the distant volcano. 'Ha!' said Nakano. 'The spring rains are coming.'

The metal of his armour stirred as he turned. There was a look of peace on his face that Annabel had never seen there before as he said, 'Come! Shimoyama – your new home – awaits you.'

Chapter Six

Despite the lateness of the hour, Mamma san was waiting for them just inside the entrance to the main tower of the fortress. Her tiny upright figure glowed in the light of a lamp that stood on the floor behind her. The light glimmered on the green and silver rushes embroidered on her black kimono. Her underskirts and obi were a strongly contrasting red, printed with leaves and berries. More berries graced her hairstyle.

Her face was a well-bred, powdered white mask until Nakano acknowledged her, then it broke into a slightly toothy smile, and she turned and pattered along beside him. 'Such a long time since we saw you, Lord Nakano,' she crooned. 'I thought you might be hungry so I've arranged for food to be waiting for you, totally delicious, and we can change it at once if my poor selection does not appeal to you.'

Annabel followed behind, feeling grubby after the long journey, and frumpy in the padded kimono-coat which she was still wearing. The black gloves clung to her hands. They tired her now, and she longed to be rid of them.

Mamma san continued to ignore Annabel as they pattered along polished wooden corridors and up flights of steps but she carried on with her soft flow of comments to Nakano: 'So unfortunate about your hawk, but mended most skilfully, I hear, so clever as you are, Lord Nakano. And the spring clouds arriving, so people tell me. Sad, don't you agree? Because there will be no more moon and cherry blossom parties this spring; but we should be so thankful for the rain because there would be no rice harvest without it.'

They had climbed a great many floors by this time. Annabel thought they must be nearing the top of the central tower. Nakano's personal guard strode before and after them, but the rest of the people who had been travelling with them had melted away, peeling off into stables and kitchens and corridors and dormitories as Nakano's party walked through the keep. In fact, Annabel realised, she was the only person left, besides the guard and Mamma san, who was saying, 'I thought you might care to dine in your quarters this evening, Lord Nakano. You'll pardon my presumption, sire, but I asked the lady Kiku to join us. And, oh, there is little Kiku chan, just waiting for her lord.'

The right-hand side of the corridor seemed to be the outer wall. Fresh air flowed in through the embrasures that were cut into the white plaster. The left-hand side of the corridor was walled with paper screens. Annabel saw that two of these bamboo-coloured screens were slightly open. A graceful figure knelt behind the opening, peering out into the corridor. When she saw Nakano, Kiku bowed until her head touched the floor.

Like Mamma san, her kimono was black, embroidered with rushes and pools and golden fireflies hovering over water lilies. The big red bow of her sash stuck out stiffly behind her. When Kiku raised her head, Annabel saw that her face was a porcelain white mask, with doll-like features and painted, arching eyebrows. Her mouth was a crimson slash as she trilled: 'Welcome home, Lord Nakano.'

Like Mamma san, she appeared to take no notice at all of Annabel, but Annabel had a feeling that Kiku was looking at her from the corners of those dark narrow eyes. Annabel did not need a direct look to inform her that the Japanese girl was her enemy. Hostility flowed through her pores and hovered in the air. Hostility that intensified when Nakano said: 'You are most kind, but please, don't wait up. I shall dine in my room this evening, with the barbarian, with Annabel san.'

Mamma san bowed low, hiding her eyes, and there was nothing but tender concern in her voice as she answered, 'Of course, Lord Nakano. I shall have the maids take food there at once, and hot sake, the honourable daimyo will need hot wine after his journey, and green tea, the very best naturally. Kiku! Hurry, child. Rouse the maids, lazy good-for-nothings. Have them see to it at once.'

Kiku swayed to her feet and vanished gracefully into the dimness of the room behind her. 'We shall bathe first,' said Nakano. 'Have a clean kimono brought for Annabel.'

'Certainly, lord,' said Mamma san, bowing low. When she lifted her head, she looked directly at Annabel for the first time. There was a hostile, wary superiority in her eyes that was at great variance with the honey-soaked tones that she spoke to Nakano with: 'If you would care to use the copper room, the bath is ready prepared and so full. Probably not hot enough for you, sir, the servants are so useless, but, please, come this way, the attendants are waiting to bathe you.'

The room they were led into was obviously a private bathroom, meant only for use by the daimyo. The floor was lined with cedar wood the colour of sweet potatoes, and it smelt powerfully of resin. A single large copper tub steamed in the middle of the room. Only two

91

samurai actually came into the room with them, the others took up position behind the paper screens. They made dark, warlike shadows behind the rice-paper walls.

Nakano removed his swords and laid them aside carefully, then he lowered himself on to one of the low-legged washing-stools with a grunt. Uncertain as to what she should do, Annabel stood waiting by the door, breathing in the pine-scented steam and looking around the room. Several lamps burnt with the smell of sweet oil. The wick of one lamp spluttered and trembled, throwing golden shadows across the steam.

Attendants came forward, bowing low, to undress the warlord. As they began unlacing his armour, Annabel saw that the bath attendants wore only white loincloths, but they were tattooed so fabulously that she stared at them until Nakano looked up at her with a quizzical gleam in his eye. 'Well, Barbarian san? Do you not know how to sit down and wash yourself?'

Annabel's skin felt hot in the thick robe. It was far too heavy for the steamy room. She let it drop over her shoulders and stood proudly naked in the soft lamplight. She lifted her hands before her in mute explanation. The long, black gloves trembled slightly as she held them out.

'Ha! Your pardon, Annabel san, I had forgotten.' Nakano then barked at one of the tattooed attendants, and the man rushed forward. He took Annabel's arm, but instead of removing the gloves as she expected, he led her over to stand in front of Lord Nakano. 'Kneel, Annabel san.'

Slowly she knelt before him, aware of her nakedness. Hot air touched her skin. Her nipples stood proud, dark pink in the lamplight, and while Nakano was gently easing her fingers out of the gloves, she wished that he would touch her breasts. Wished he would ease the ache that made her nipples heavy, made her breasts droop softly downward with the longing to fall into his hands.

But when the gloves were thrown aside, it was her face that Nakano framed with his hands, and his lips brushed across her forehead. Then she felt his hands bury themselves in her hair. He lifted the hair and let it fall. It sparkled in the lamplight. Annabel saw that the slight curl that any damp always brought out had appeared at the tip of each lock.

Nakano's face was reverent, wondering, as he stroked the fine pale yellow mass of her hair, and there was awe in his voice as he said: 'It is so fine! So soft and silky! Never did I see such hair. It is more beautiful than gold, more beautiful than sunlight.' His large hands were soft and warm, running over her head, brushing past her ears, exploring her hairline.

The attendants waited, kneeling, while Lord Nakano admired Annabel's hair. When he finally shook his head, as if he still could not believe in such magical hair, and let his hands fall away, the attendants ran forward, and Annabel moved back, so that they could continue unwrapping the stiff layers of silk that encased Nakano.

Annabel stood waiting, absorbed in watching the daimyo's costume being removed. As more and more of the silk was stripped off, sections of Nakano's naked body were revealed. He was compact, well-muscled. She could see a hollow in his thigh where several big muscles crossed. His belly was a hard-ridged marvel.

Nakano lifted his powerful arms so that his silk over-robe could be stripped off, and, as the chestnut silk peeled away, leaving him naked, Annabel saw that he had very little body hair, just a few smooth dark curls that were oddly attractive.

His skin was a delicious, smooth colour. An even honey-tinted hue that shaded down to dark olive. He was good-looking! So much more attractive than a sailor, thought Annabel. No pallid, flabby belly, no lumpy red feet, no grubby beard, or chest hair crawling with lice. He was clean, healthy and muscled, an enticing figure naked in the flickering amber glow of the lamps.

Her breath came a little faster because she knew that his manhood would be uncovered next. She longed to see it, but an attendant urged her away. A frisson of disappointment ran through her. She wanted to see his male organ. She wanted to know what he looked like. The delay was tantalising, but she had to sit on one of the low wooden stools and be washed.

It was strange to be attended to by a man, especially a naked, tattooed man. But his blue-patterned hands were impersonal as he massaged her skin with a rough towelling mitten, making her arch her back like a little kitten and go limp and boneless in his grasp. It was so very nice to be washed; to feel competent hands shampooing the dirt of the journey out of her hair.

Once clean, she was urged to lie on a warm white towel. She lay on her belly, and the firm, tattooed hands began a massage that melted her body. The attendant's hands dug into her, and sometimes even hurt her, until she discovered that when she relaxed the pain stopped. The magic fingers massaged out all the kinks and stiffness in her spine.

When the attendant gestured to her to roll over, she did so willingly, not caring that his strange hands ran over her naked body. There was nothing sexual in his ministrations. He just smoothed out her aches and pains and tension with an almost maternal touch.

On the other side of the room she could see another attendant bending low over Nakano, massaging the daimyo. The whole of the attendant's back was tattooed with a gigantic blue carp. The stylised, plump bare figure of a samurai clung to the fish's dorsal fin as its tattooed form swam up the back of the bath attendant. When the attendant rose to his feet, in the dim light, the fish seemed to swim across his skin as he escorted the naked figure of Lord Nakano to the bathing tub. Bowing low, the attendant retreated to the corner of the room, where he squatted on his heels, waiting.

Now Annabel's attendant was bowing low, too. Her massage was over. She was led over to the big copper tub where Nakano floated, his eyes closed in bliss. The bristly dark fans of his eyelids flew open as she approached. A merry light gleamed in them. 'Ha! Annabel san, I suppose you want me to move over?'

She looked up at him, catching his mood, dimpling. 'There seems to be plenty of room for two.'

'Bold miss!' grumbled Nakano, but his voice was as indulgent as the smile in his eyes. The water splashed as he moved over, patting the water to indicate where she might sit.

Annabel put one cautious leg over the edge of the tub. Then she stopped, balanced in mid-air. 'Oh! That is so hot!' she cried.

Nakano's smile was lazily sensual as he tipped his head back and let his eyes fall into the space between her legs. 'Very nice position,' he murmured. 'As I wish to further my studies into the mysteries of a barbarian's peach, you have my permission to stay there.'

Embarrassment as hot as the water flamed in Annabel's cheeks and she hurriedly lifted her legs over the edge of the tub. Her breath hissed between her teeth as the hot water crawled up her legs and lapped at her belly. 'I can't sit in it!' she gasped.

'Did you not bathe in the village?'

Sweat beaded her face and dewed her breasts. 'Yes, but outside. The pools, they were all different temperatures. I chose a cool one.'

'I see,' said Nakano, his eyes very dark. 'But you must bathe, Barbarian san, if you are to pillow with me.'

She hesitated, savouring the import of his words. Well, she had known what was coming, hadn't she? Ever since he had brushed off Mamma san and Kiku, a floating, fluttering sensation between her legs had told her what was going to happen, that she would be sleeping with the daimyo. An intimacy she both feared and longed for.

Nakano broke her train of thought by snapping: 'Sit down!'

She lowered her body a little and then cried, 'It's too hot!' The hot water was a torment, biting and stinging at her skin. Every instinct urged her to get out of the tub.

But a fierce light glinted in Nakano's eyes. 'Get down!'

She dared not disobey him. Annabel sank into the blisteringly hot water until only her head and neck and the round curves of her shoulders were showing above the water line. She was unable to stop her reflex reaction to the heat of the water: her body lifted slightly out of the water before she forced it back down again. Her skin had turned scarlet already, from only that brief contact with the water.

Nakano chuckled, not unkindly, watching her face. 'The secret, Annabel san, is to keep very still. Then your body will cool the water as it touches your skin.'

Obediently, she floated as still as she could be, feeling her heart speed as it tried to cope with the strain; feeling sweat beading her forehead, trickling down to sting her eyes.

Another long, hot moment went by, and she tasted salt in her mouth as the drops of sweat on her upper lips formed into beads big enough to break and run over her lips.

'That's good,' said Nakano san. He rose to his feet, steam rising from his hot body. He had been in the water for more time than Annabel, and she looked at him, wondering if he would make her stay in it longer, but he smiled at her and said, 'You can get out now.'

She went dizzy as soon as she got out, clinging on to the sides of the tub, hearing a black roar in her ears. Nobody fussed; they just left her until the giddiness cleared, and she was able to lift her head once more.

Then she felt soft brushes and pats against her fizzing skin as the attendants dried her with cotton towelling. Then she sat on a low stool once more to have her hair combed out. Opposite her, an attendant was doing the same to Lord Nakano's hair. She stared at it frankly.

'What is so strange, Annabel san?'

'Your hair! I have never seen men who arrange their hair as you samurai do. Do you shave the sides?'

Long black hair streamed down Nakano's back, but on each side of his head, some way above the ear, was a bare patch. The haircut was designed to give him a marked, and very attractive, widow's peak in the centre of his forehead.

'I shave it every day, as does any well-regulated samurai,' answered Nakano, a hint of mischief in his eyes.

'What?' enquired Annabel, daring to tease him, 'even when you are ill?'

'Of course, not when I am sick.' His smile crossed the space between them, creating a warm link of fun.

'Then you must go all bristly,' said Annabel, eyeing him cheekily. 'What do you do about that?'

Looking across at her he laughed again. 'Then I stay at home and I do not show my face in the world until I am a respectable samurai once more.'

Nakano held her gaze, not turning away or continuing their teasing, and a certain tension developed between them. His eyes were frighteningly intense.

Annabel looked down, twining a strand of her hair around her long, delicate fingers. The lock of hair was drying rapidly. It glinted in the lamplight, and Nakano's eyes fell to watch her fingers as they slipped around the lock of hair. Then he stood up.

She still had not seen his penis, and Annabel kept her head bowed, feeling strangely shy, knowing what she would see if she looked up. She could hear her own

97

blood drumming in her ears. She could feel the weight of his gaze upon her, willing her to look.

It was an article of faith among the sailors that Orientals had no penises worth the mention. More than one grinning sailor had assured her that the Japanese and Chinese had such tiny organs – smaller than my little finger if you'll believe it – that they had to resort to artificial penises made of wood or ivory in order to satisfy their women. 'And that's why the women love us Britishers so much,' the pilot had assured her. 'They never knew what satisfaction was until they met us.'

Now, curious to know if the old tales were true, she slowly lifted her head to examine Nakano. He stood proud and naked above her, enjoying her inspection, and Annabel knew as she looked at him that he had nothing to fear.

His manhood was like the rest of him: a smooth delicious tan colour. Not overlarge, no, but as Annabel looked at the neat, arrogant erection that jutted away from Nakano's taut belly, she suddenly had the impulse to take his cock into her mouth. It looked as if it would fit between her lips. As if it would be a pleasure to swallow that warm, friendly length of penis and nuzzle into the dark hair that grew around the base of it.

She was glad that the foreskin of his penis had not been cut, the way she had heard some foreign men's were. She liked its wholeness. It seemed to fit in with his natural healthy body. Desire blossomed softly between her legs as she examined his balls, the tender skin between his thighs. His hard, dark, muscled body was so very different from her own soft white one, but the contrast only increased her desire. She wanted him.

'Wrap yourself in this kimono, Annabel san,' he said softly, holding a robe open for her. She approached him a little shyly, her eyes cast down. The robe was pink, made of heavy woven cotton like damask. It brushed lightly over her skin as Nakano slipped it over her unprotesting shoulders. She wrapped the clean-smelling fabric around her. It tied with a crimson sash that slipped softly between her fingers as she tried to knot it becomingly.

Lord Nakano was tying the indigo sash of his own blue-printed robe, calling for his samurai. The screens of the wall slid open and he stepped out, gesturing Annabel to follow him into the cooler air of the corridor. She stepped into the wooden sandals that had been laid for her and followed his striding figure. Some way along the corridor the paper walls were the colour of burnished gold, and two of these were open.

Annabel kicked off her sandals and entered the room behind Lord Nakano. It was plain, the plainest room she had been in yet. The ubiquitous tatami matting was soft beneath her feet and she inhaled its familiar summer-hay scent gratefully. It smelt like home. Like the security of her room by the sea.

There was nothing else in the room, nothing at all, and Annabel saw that the effect of space was emphasised by the black ribbons that bordered the tatami matting and the black paint that coloured the bamboo squares of the shoji screens. It was a dim, shadowed room. Vastly peaceful.

All the wall-screens were closed, but Nakano strode across the room and slid two of them open. At once, the scent of fresh air and cool moonlight poured into the room. He stood looking out for a moment. Clouds dimmed the moonlight just as servants entered with lamps. 'It will rain tomorrow,' said Nakano, turning back to face Annabel.

There were footsteps in the corridor and a shoji slid open. 'As it rains every year at this time. As it must, if the wells are to fill and the peasants are to produce the rice we rely on,' said Mamma san as she entered the room from a screen behind Annabel's shoulder. She held a black and gold lacquer tray that was exquisitely decorated with pickled seaweed and slivers of ginger. Annabel didn't want the older woman there. She had the uncomfortable feeling that behind Mamma san's smoothly correct façade, she, Annabel, had been judged and found wanting.

More servants fetched in a low table and flat blue cushions. Then they brought steaming lacquer bowls full of sticky white rice, delicious miso soup and tiny flasks full of hot wine.

Nakano, Annabel and Mamma san knelt around the table. Mamma san chatted pleasantly, serving both Nakano and Annabel as if she were happy to do so; but as Nakano bent low towards Annabel, gallantly filling her tiny cup with the hot sake, Annabel was aware of a feeling of hostility flowing from the older woman. It was almost too faint to be measured, but like the squeak of a bat, Annabel knew it was there, so it was with deep alarm that she heard Nakano say, 'From tomorrow you will study with Mamma san. She will teach you the pillow arts, Annabel san, but also music, poetry and singing. It is most important for a geisha to be civilised. Indeed, strictly speaking, a girl is nothing but a common prostitute if she knows nothing of culture.'

'That is so true, Lord Nakano,' said Mamma san, bowing low. 'You understand the matter very well. Common whores are to be met with anywhere, but a beautiful, refined, truly elegant girl like your devoted Kiku san is a star who shines high above the multitude.'

And Annabel knew that those comments were directed at her; and she knew, too, just what category Mamma san put her into. Her heart pained her, but she took some satisfaction from the fact that Nakano immediately waved the older woman away.

He leant over the table and refilled Annabel's thimble of a sake cup. As Mamma san was no longer there to do it for him, greatly daring, she bent across the low table to refill the cup he was drinking from. She had to tuck up her kimono sleeve to prevent it from trailing over the table. The little sake flask was scalding between her fingers, but she managed not to spill any as she poured the hot wine.

Still concentrating, she carefully put the sake container back on to the low lacquer table. There were flying cranes etched faintly in the pearly-grey glaze of the flask. 'Prettily done, Annabel san,' said Nakano. She dared to lift her eyes. He was smiling at her approvingly. 'You learn quickly. Your movements are exquisite. You will make a good geisha.'

A tiny kimono-clad maid came in and knelt by Annabel and leant gracefully over the table to remove the food bowls. Other dainty servants were removing everything but the wine. In a moment they would be alone. Annabel's quim was heavy with that knowledge as she sat waiting, waiting for the inevitable.

Her body felt good now. Better than good. It felt as if a whole layer of dirty skin had been stripped off in the hot tub, leaving her light, clean and refreshed. The red glow had subsided from her skin, leaving her feeling pink, clean and a little sleepy, but although she saw the servants were now bringing in futons, the heavy bedding encased in gleaming white sheets, she did not think that she was going to sleep peacefully, not yet at any rate.

The servants drew closed the paper screens as they left the room. The gentle sound of lamps burning was loud in her ears. A faint chink of metal rang harshly as one of the samurai stationed in the corridor outside shifted his position slightly. Those men will be able to hear everything we do! she thought. This sent a tingling through her body. There were at least six of the massive shadows stationed in the corridor.

Annabel took a sip of rice wine. The hot, rich liquid flowed over her tongue and slipped down her throat, settling sweetly in her belly. She kept her gaze fixed on her cup. Waiting. Waiting. Waiting.

Nakano's voice was a caress in the warm room. 'Annabel san. Stand up for me.'

Her knees were quaking beneath her as she got to her feet. She let her head fall forward, and her hair fell about her face in a soft curtain.

A small sigh, hardly above a breath. 'Turn your back to me.'

Hesitant, slow ... How significant her movements felt, because he watched them.

His command was a gentle, distant sound. 'Untie your sash.'

Her fingers were unsteady as they untied the knot.

'Let your robe slip from your shoulders.'

Annabel felt the damask slide over her skin. She caught the deep pink folds to her breasts. The fabric dipped sweetly behind her, held up across her elbows.

'Let it drop a little further.'

The skin on her back felt so sensitive. She could feel the stiffer neckline of the robe as it lay on the curve above her buttocks.

His voice grew softer. 'Now let it drop.'

The robe whispered to the ground and pooled around her feet. Annabel stood waiting, wondering, glad that Nakano was enjoying her body.

Behind her she heard fabric rustle. He must be undressing.

'Turn around.'

He was lying on his back in the centre of a mound of futons, watching her intently. His head rested on a pillow that lifted it slightly. His dark hair streamed over his shoulders. The amber-gold glow of the lamps transformed the plain tatami room into a place of warmth and magic, and her lover into a mythical being. His chest and arms were so heavily sculpted that Annabel realised that Nakano must practise with his weapons every day.

His waist was slim, but she could see lines of muscle ridging his stomach. Each muscle on his spread-open thighs stood out clearly, although he was resting. And his manhood – her eyes dropped to examine his private parts – his manhood was the sweetest sight of all. His testicles dropped on to the futons between his thighs. His penis was erect, noble, rampant, waiting for her.

'Come here.'

Softly, Annabel crossed the room to stand by him.

'Sit on me.'

'On you?'

'On my face. Sit on my face.'

A shiver of delight passed through Annabel as she met his intently lustful expression. Her hands slid to the plump mound of her mons, her fingers prying the labia apart so that he could look up at the pink lips of her sex as she stood above him. Then she stepped over him, turning so that her back was to his face, because she knew very well what he wanted.

Her knees bent slowly, carefully, as she lowered herself so that she could keep her balance. She used her hands to support herself until she was down, and then she balanced herself on her knees. She felt them sink into the exquisitely clean bedding as she gently eased her buttocks down on to Nakano's face.

Her breath caught in her throat as she tipped her head back. Her loose hair brushed her neck and shoulders. Her breasts felt heavy and aroused. Blood was racing to the heart of her woman's place as her excitement grew. She could smell sex in the room, her own secretions and Nakano's, musky with heady delight.

She felt hard hands grasp her buttocks. It felt so good as Nakano pushed her yielding flesh into position. She heard him make a muffled sound. She could feel his face pressing against her buttocks, his nose in the crack, his chin pushing against her wet sex.

A faint sound came to her own lips as she reached back, pulling her buttocks apart to make it easier for him. 'Oh, yes, that,' she heard herself gasp, and gasp again, as his hot seeking tongue slipped into the crinkled opening of her anus.

The sucking, licking sensation was divine. Annabel leant forward, so that her breasts were resting on her knees, lifting her sensitive, private, but now open anus so that Nakano could continue his careful licking, and the wet noisy slurping that was so intense, so blissful, so very close to making her faint.

Scarcely breathing, Annabel felt her whole being submerged in an ecstasy of delight. A quivering happiness engulfed her as firmly as Nakano's lips. She lifted her head slightly. Her half-open eyes travelled over Nakano's naked form, over his slim waist and belly, to the softly rounded promontory covered with dark hair.

She wanted to move down, to take the stiff and gorgeous penis that jutted out between the soft skin of his thighs into her mouth. Her mouth felt empty. She opened it and the tip of her tongue slid out between her lips, as if to softly tongue the spear that dazzled her.

But Nakano's lips were sucking at her anal opening and it was good, much too good to leave. She straightened her body slightly, increasing the pressure on his face, wriggling her buttocks, mounting him completely, knowing from the hardness of his organ and the bead of pearl-like liquid that just seeped from the tip of it, that she was giving him pleasure. And he was giving her pleasure. His tongue felt marvellous, like a soft wet petal nuzzling into her private spaces, as he began licking the entrance to her vagina.

Annabel groaned again, and her hands came up to slide over her breasts. Her nipples were pink and pointed. As she touched them, they responded sweetly. Pleasure was all she knew as the hot point of his tongue slipped and wriggled inside her.

Hands gripped her buttocks, lifting her. Nakano rushed forward and tipped her on to the bedding. Annabel rolled over quickly, then lay back in the crisp soft cotton and looked up at her lover. His chin glistened with saliva and her secretions. He wiped them off as she watched. 'Delicious,' he said, inhaling deeply and then licking his fingers. He fell forward and kissed her and Annabel tasted her own female sweetness on his male lips and smelt it on his breath as their mouths met. His kiss was deep, slow, passionate and ethereal.

Why this man? wondered Annabel. Why is it this Japanese warlord who makes my body sing to heavenly music? I am his prisoner, yet he is treating me gently, acting as if he values me.

She returned his slow, open-mouthed kiss with fervour. But still her feelings were mixed. She knew so little of him, of his world.

Could there ever be love between us? Love? Is it love that makes me feel so sensual? Or simply divine lust? The agony of my body, the sweet pleasure of my soul . . .

Her thoughts broke up and dissolved as his hard lips slid down her throat. His teeth grazed the curve of her ear. His tongue nuzzled into the warm, pulsing spot below her earlobe before slipping over her breastbone and down to find her bare breasts.

His mouth sucked at one nipple. His tongue came out to follow the faint blue line of a tiny vein that radiated out from the areola. One hand slid over her other breast, taking the nipple firmly between his fingers, applying exactly the right amount of pressure.

Annabel fell back into the pillows with a cry of sheer helpless pleasure. She heard Nakano's rough breathing as he looked up from her breasts. He held one nipple in each hand as he looked at her. Despite the lust that burned hot in his expression, there was something very tender for her in his eyes, and she felt safe as she drifted, melted, allowed all conscious thought to leave her as she sank deeply into the blissful experience of love.

The intoxication of his nearness, the subtle musk that rose from his body, all conspired to lift her to the heights of sexual pleasure. Nakano's eyes slid down to examine her perfumed valley as she lay swooning in the soft bedding, seemingly helpless, her legs opened wide, spreading themselves open of their own volition for his inspection; for his touch.

Nakano bent his head and covered her entire labia with his mouth. The lips of her sex were slick with moisture as they slid open to welcome him. The broad surface of his tongue was smooth and hot as it slid over her clitoris and back towards her vagina. Annabel gave a deep sigh and her fingers slid into Nakano's hair. Her hands pressed down on the top of his head.

It was all the encouragement he needed. He grabbed the soft white globes of her buttocks and lifted her up so that her sex met his mouth easily. She felt his tongue licking, slipping around as he gathered up the wetness that seeped out of her vagina. The swollen bud of her clitoris rubbed against his nose. She cried out, and he instantly took the little pip into his mouth and began sucking vigorously.

At once Annabel felt a deep and vibrant tremor beginning inside her. She cried out in warning and pressed the flesh of her thighs into Nakano's cheeks as she began to yield to the insistent, pulling, sucking summons of his mouth. He would not stop. He sucked her harder. He was making her orgasm.

The spasm was unstoppable. As the flow of sweet release took her, Annabel was aware of Nakano's face pressed hard against her sex, experiencing the violent spasmodic shivering that rippled the whole area between her legs as she came. A hand came up to the entrance to her vagina and she felt cool fingers collecting up the sudden flow of moisture that gushed there. His touch was delicious, and then it was too much.

Her hands came up to push at him. 'Wait,' she gasped. 'It's too much . . . I can't . . .'

His dark eyes were bloomed with lust, but even now

he understood her. 'Sensitive after your orgasm? It will pass.'

He reached out for a pillow in a white case. 'Put this under your buttocks,' he said, passing it to Annabel. Annabel reached for the pillow. Little hard peas shifted and rustled inside it and she felt them give under her buttocks as she slipped the cool hardness of the pillow below her. Her vaginal muscles began to clench softly and relax, readying themselves to take a man. To take his organ deep inside her.

She lay back, feeling her balance shift as her back arched and her knees splayed open across the pillow, lifting her pelvic area towards Nakano, opening her sex for him, wide as could be.

Nakano knelt above her, holding his cock in one hand. It glistened in the lamplight as he circled it with his fingers, rubbing along the whole length of it, from the swollen head that now poked out of the wrinkles of his pushed-back foreskin, to the thick stem of it that vanished into his dark pubic hair.

Annabel watched him, feeling her breath come fast between her softly parted lips, feeling her sex open itself for something it wanted very, very much. Nakano looked up from his fully aroused penis. A sweet knowing smile curled her lips as she met his intent gaze. He wanted her. He might be in control at this moment, but he wanted her. The woman in her could tell.

She let her eyes slide half-shut and heard him shift closer to her, pushing a fold of one futon out of the way. His figure was a dark shadow against her lashes, bending, stooping over the entrance to her dark velvet tunnel. Her breath came softer and faster as she felt the first soft brush of his penis against her vagina.

He didn't enter at once. Instead, Annabel felt the soft, insistent touch of his manhood nudging her sweetly. The tip of his penis felt slicker as it moved. The secretions that pooled at the entrance to her vagina were wetting it, coating it with a layer of glistening love dew.

Annabel reached out to Nakano as if she would gather up his hot pounding heart and hold it in her small hands. She wanted him. She wanted him inside her. And the soft, maddening caress as his penis brushed by her hole was too much. Her hips lifted towards him, inviting, twisting, urgent.

Her mouth fell open and she bit softly on her lower lip. The soft pink of her tongue brushed over the sensitive surface of her lips before she spoke, her cry soft in the shadows, 'Let me feel it!'

Nakano pulled back so that his cock was clearly visible. 'This?' he enquired.

Her eyes could not leave it. The head had gone purple. It looked fat, and polished with her juices. A slow pearl-like tear oozed from the slit.

Mesmerised, Annabel lifted herself off the white bedding and reached for the organ before her. The flesh throbbed with hot vitality as she touched it. She could feel a pulse as she ran her fingers lightly up and down the shaft, tracing the veins.

Then, with one gentle fingertip, she collected the juice that leaked out of the slit. She coated the length of his penis with it, until the whole, long, delicious length of his shaft glistened wetly. The musky smell of him made her shiver.

Annabel looked up at Nakano's face. His cheeks were flushed and he was breathing heavily. Responding to the hunger in his dark eyes, she fell back on to the soft pads of the futons and lifted her hips once more, spreading her legs in a blatant invitation. And this time he responded.

Annabel felt the knob of the head of his penis slip up the groove of her labia, then push at the tight ring of muscle that closed her vagina. The entrance opened at once, and she felt the purest, most exquisite delight as the entire length of his shaft plunged into her scented valley. The soft walls of her woman's place wrapped themselves lovingly around his male hardness as he began to move, pumping hard, slamming into her sweetly for one, two, three, four, five driving strokes.

And then he stopped, holding the weight of his body on his arms, totally in control as Annabel lifted her hips and ground up against him, crying out in the black frenzy of her need.

He looked down at her, smiling, for a long moment. 'A girl with spring desire,' he whispered. And then he began moving again. Softly, exquisitely.

The slow, marvellous sensation as the full length of his cock pulled gently out of her vagina and pushed leisurely back in again, sent ripples and shudders of sensual delight around Annabel's body, and she melted into his sensitive movements. 'Desire for you,' she admitted softly.

And then he went hard again. His balls slapped against her thighs. The fast, urgent compelling thrusts as his penis slammed into her wetness and rammed home into her cunt were just about to force her into the most violent orgasm imaginable – when he stopped.

Annabel clung to him gasping. His body was hot and sweaty. His heart boomed in his chest. Her head tipped back and hot lips touched her throat as he moved, so slowly, so sweetly as he fucked her gently once more. Waves of languorous pleasure rolled over her with every controlled, gentle movement.

And yet her need was urgent too. And when his movements became hot once more, she lifted herself up to meet him. His body was her master now. His urgent movements controlled her experience. His hardness was sinking into her softness. Exquisite. His shaft was impaling her. Ravishing. She was breathing in harsh, passionate, unstoppable gasps. Ecstasy.

Nakano's body tensed. His orgasm was near. He felt

heavy as he plunged into her. Responding to his climax, Annabel cried out. Her own orgasm seemed to rush at her out of the darkness. Tears came to her eyes with the violence of it. She could feel Nakano's manhood striving against her dark female muscles as they gripped his shaft in passion and held him tight while the great good release swept over her.

Panting, she fell back, and her internal muscles let him go. There was a flooding sweetness as he orgasmed. Or she came again. Annabel no longer knew which sensations were hers and which belonged to the dark lord who lay on her, gasping, crushing her with his masculine bulk.

Nakano recovered in seconds, and took his weight on his arms. Annabel drew in a deep breath, relieved to have the weight of him gone, and yet she felt the loss of him too and turned her head to him. Dark eyes met her own. Serious, tender, a little sad. Annabel wanted to ask those eyes if the gulf between them had been bridged, but the words would not come.

Nakano sighed deeply as he watched her. He sat back on his heels, rearranging the piles of spotless futons. Then he gathered up Annabel to his broad, strong chest and fell back in the warm, fresh-smelling bedding with a happy sigh.

Sated, she sank against his warm skin, floating on a cloud of nothingness. His strength made her feel safe, protected. Oh, her body felt so good after that long, long, lonely winter. She'd forgotten the sweetness of the afterglow. The delicious feeling of curling up with a man.

But she still had the urge to know if their minds had grown closer as well as their bodies. Under the pretext of pulling one of the heavy wadded covers over them, she moved so that she could look up at him with the fullness of their loving in her eyes.

He met her gaze for a second, then his eyes flickered

closed. Her heart melted at the beautiful curve of his eyelids, the gently slanting eyelashes. She spoke using the soft English words, 'I love you.'

His eyes did not open, but a tender hand groped for her hot face, swept the wet hair from her forehead. 'Annabel san? Was that your language? What did you say?'

She did not quite know how to phrase her feelings in Japanese, or even if it was wise to share them. 'Nothing,' she answered him.

His eyes slid open, and he smiled down at her. He clasped her tenderly as he spoke. 'Then sleep now, little savage.' And their bodies grew limp and boneless and drifted into sleep together.

Chapter Seven

Mamma san's lips pursed into a disapproving frown. 'Even a barbarian should be able to play the shamisen better than that, Annabel san.'

Annabel put the instrument to one side with a despairing sigh. The room seemed very quiet without the discordant sounds she had been plucking from the strings. She could hear the spring rains beating on the roof and swirling out of the gutters. The light filtering into the room through the rice-paper screens was grey, matching her mood, and the air was moist and chill.

Mamma san was resplendent in a gold and orange kimono embroidered with stiffly formal blooms, but her eyes were icy. Annabel met her disdainful expression and tried to explain: 'It just doesn't sound like music to me,' she moaned. 'I was never any good at English music, but, Japanese music...' Her voice trailed off dolefully.

'You should play the music like this, Annabel san,' said Kiku san smugly. She picked up the long-necked instrument and began plucking at the strings. Discordant, oddly spaced sounds floated out from the square body of the shamisen.

Mamma san nodded her head approvingly. 'Beautifully played, Kiku san,' she crooned. 'Such talent, such artistic feeling as you display.' She closed her eyes and sat back on her heels. Her pose suggested nothing but delight in the bizarre sounds she was hearing.

Annabel schooled her features into a mask of polite interest. All she could hear was a senseless twanging. She couldn't hear any difference between the horrible noise Mamma san and Kiku made when they played the shamisen, and the horrible noise she produced when she attempted to play the instrument. She was honestly bewildered when they winced and protested.

She sighed again as she watched Kiku performing. The Japanese girl might sound appalling, but she looked beautiful in her bright orange kimono. So dainty, so groomed, so elegant. She possessed a fragile doll-like charm that Annabel knew she could never emulate, no, not if she trained for a million years.

She felt as if Mamma san was trying to crush her into a mould that she could never fit. High-class courtesans were supposed to not just hold their own, but entertain and astonish with the intelligent breadth of their knowledge. Annabel enjoyed learning about literature and poetry, and her fabulous memory enabled her to soak up the history and politics of Japan with ease; but the ritual and protocol Mamma san tried to teach her she found pointless and boring, and also worrying. What exactly was her role at Shimoyama going to be?

Annabel did not want to be a courtesan. She did not want to spend her life in a scented parlour waiting for her lord to have a few minutes to spare. She wanted . . . What do I want? Annabel asked.

I want it all! she answered herself passionately. I want love and adventure and romance. I want to feel alive. I want to be by his side in the morning and I want to ride out to battle when he does. I want to eat and drink and live with him. I want to hold him in my arms when he's tired and sleeping. I want to be there when desire stirs and he reaches out for love in the dark night.

Annabel's head drooped and she sighed softly. She had not seen Nakano since the night they had spent together, which now seemed like a dream. She had tried several times to get information about his whereabouts from Kiku and Mamma san. They turned all her questions adroitly, putting her off with soft platitudes, turning every conversation into an opportunity to lecture her about her shortcomings.

'Please excuse me for intruding, ladies.'

Annabel turned towards the soft voice. Kiku put down her instrument and Mamma san opened her eyes. 'Ah! good boy. So good of you to come. Please, step inside and be seated in our poor room.'

Annabel looked curiously at the young man who was stepping through the shoji screens. She felt a delicious shiver run down her spine. All the young men they sent for her to practise on were young, clean and healthy, but this boy was particularly good-looking as well. A lithe young man, perfumed and pretty, his hair well oiled and very neat. He was about twenty years old, as near as she could judge – she often thought that the Japanese looked younger than they were – and he glowed with an attractive sensual vigour.

Annabel joined Kiku and Mamma san in the rituals of greeting, bowing so low that she became aware of the sweet haylike smell of the tatami as her nose touched the floor. The youth might be a paid hireling, sent from a brothel in town run by Mamma san's sister, but he was greeted with all the pretty deference that the two women bestowed on all the males who came their way.

He turned down all their offers of food, green tea, a shoulder massage. His attention was obviously fixed on Annabel. He stared at her with frank wonder and admiration as she straightened from her bow and sat back on her heels, returning his look.

'Well, if you are ready to begin,' said Mamma san crisply. 'Take off your kimono, there's a good boy.'

The young man responded eagerly. His kimono dropped to the tatami with a soft rustle. Out of the corners of her eyes, Annabel could see that he was already semi-erect. It looked as if he was eager to be touched by the barbarian.

Kiku was shaking out a futon, laying it carefully on top of the tatami matting. 'For your comfort, young man,' she trilled sweetly as she settled herself on her heels in a position where she could watch everything that was going to happen.

'Thank you, sweet lady,' said the youth politely. He lay back on the crisp white bed in a lordly manner. He threw his naked arms over his head, posing, flirting with his eyes, trying to catch Annabel's gaze with all the confidence of the good-looking. She couldn't help smiling. He was so young and cocky, so very appealing in his masculine vanity.

She bent her head swiftly, before Mamma san could catch her expression and read her a lecture on impropriety, but she could still feel the smile tugging at the corners of her mouth. She didn't know yet what she was going to have to practise today, but she had a feeling she was going to enjoy this session more than usual.

'Mamma san,' asked the youth hopefully. 'Will you require me to unclothe the barbarian?'

Mamma san's carmine lips pursed thoughtfully, then she shook her head. 'No. The barbarian lacks decorum. I want her to learn to remain unruffled while she ministers to a man. You shall be naked; she shall remain dressed.'

'What pillow art will you teach her today?' asked Kiku brightly.

'I think today she should work on using her hands to stimulate a man's penis to glorious orgasm,' said Mamma san. 'There are so many strokes to master.' She turned to the naked youth. 'You won't believe it, but she knew nothing of skilful penis manipulation when she came here, and she has barely mastered the rudiments even now.'

'It's true,' said Kiku smugly. 'We practised the hand orgasm yesterday, and the day before, and she never can stroke a beautiful barb with the grace and delicacy befitting a high-class female.' She gave the tinkling laugh which Annabel was learning to loathe. 'She enjoys it too much for true artistry. She gets carried away.'

Annabel shot the Japanese girl a vicious glare. The smile vanished. Kiku's face crumpled slightly before going blank. She would be quiet now, for an hour or two, but then the tinkling laugh and the barbed comments would begin anew. Annabel sighed. She had no friends in this place.

'Come now, Annabel san,' said Mamma san.

Annabel moved over to the youth. She smoothed down the skirts of her gold kimono with a gesture that was becoming automatic and settled herself on her knees next to his naked body. Close enough to smell his clean spicy perfume. She had not placed herself at the right angle to suit Mamma san and she felt tiny, but steel-like hands tugging at her waist, pushing her closer to the naked man.

'You must not be too far away,' scolded Mamma san. 'Your posture must remain upright and graceful at all times. Now, take his peerless barb into your hands. Oh! Truly you are a barbarian! Don't crush it! Remember that you are dealing with a delicate instrument.'

'Yesterday,' said Annabel through gritted teeth, 'you told me that the rule for the clitoris may be the gentler the better, but that the rule for the penis was the firmer the better.'

But she did loosen her grip, holding the shaft more gently. The penis between her hands did not seem to object to her handling. The satiny soft skin was warm against her palms, and she could feel it stirring slightly, growing as she touched it. His testicles looked dark and swollen as they lay in their hairy nest. Moving her hand away from his penis, she jiggled each egg carefully, just using her fingertips.

'Rest your index finger on the little thread going from the head of his manhood to the shaft,' ordered Mamma san.

Annabel changed her position. The feel of the warm thick cock in her hand was delightful. She lined up the rest of her fingers along the underside ridge. From the corner of her eye, she saw Mamma san open her mouth. She was going to remind her about the position of the thumb again. Annabel quickly placed her thumb so that it could lie against the rim of the shaft, on the topside of his penis. The trailing silk sleeves of her kimono just brushed the skin of his belly as she began to gently stimulate his penis.

'That is so poor a grip,' said Mamma san. 'Take your hand away. I think you must have forgotten where the most sensitive areas of the male organ are.'

Annabel felt the penis in her hand shudder protestingly as she let it go. She began to recite her lesson, just brushing the satiny hardness of the youth's cock with her fingertips as she spoke, sympathetically touching each area as she mentioned it. 'First there is the head,' she said. 'That's very sensitive.' She teased the sheath of skin that covered the swollen tip up and down the hard cylinder of his cock.

A slight groan escaped the lips of the youth she was ministering to. Annabel sneaked a quick look at his rapturous face. She was glad that he was finding his experience more pleasurable than Mamma san's ceaseless criticism seemed to imply.

Moved by a sudden sense of mischief, she bent her head and licked the salty tear that oozed from the slit in a swollen head that was getting pinker and more bulbous by the second. Then she quickly lapped her tongue

117

around the whole area of the head, pausing to run her tongue over the raised area where the head joined the shaft. She raised her head. 'The rim at the bottom of the head is very sensitive too,' she continued wickedly.

'Hands only,' snapped Mamma san, looking at her with displeasure. 'You have no discipline, Annabel san. You should have mentioned next the long ridge that runs along the underside of the sword of a samurai.'

Annabel's fingers obediently danced up the pulsating length of the ridged area. The youth shuddered and swooned beneath her fingers. Whatever Mamma san might say, the penis in Annabel's hands seemed to be a happy one.

'Now touch the slender string of skin that connects the head to the shaft on the underside,' said Mamma san, seeming not to notice that Annabel's fingers were there already. 'That was terrible, Annabel san. I do not see how a man could ever gain enjoyment from the mauling of your untrained paws.'

Annabel looked at the youth who lay sprawled beneath her. His eyes were shut in ecstasy. His chest rose and fell with the quick shallowness of his aroused breathing. A faint dew of sweat had risen to the surface of his skin, intensifying the spicy scent he was wearing.

His penis looked huge, a long thick cock jutting out from the patch of springy black pubic hair. The shaft had darkened, with the veins now standing out prominently. The fat knob at the end of his cock was swollen. The tight skin had a purplish hue. His testicles looked bloated, ready to explode.

'Yes, Mamma san,' said Annabel. She could afford to ignore the older woman's carping. She knew what effect her hands were having as they fondled the penis of the naked youth who lay so blissfully on the futon before her. She smiled as she placed her hands on his shaft in the perfect position for his pleasure.

'A lady's stroke is always consummate in its artistry,'

said Mamma san, hovering over Annabel. 'Your movements must be flawless.' Annabel moved her soft white hands along the pulsating dark cylinder of Japanese manhood as the old woman nagged, 'Do it firmly! Do it smoothly! Oh! Annabel san, you're so clumsy!'

Annabel felt Mamma san's strong tiny hands cover her own. She shuddered at the alien touch. The skin was chill, and slid across her hands with a dry, cool rasp, not unlike the touch of a snake.

'A nice gentle rhythm,' said the older woman, using her hands to regulate the movement of Annabel's, as their twined fingers slid up and down the length of the pulsating cock below them.

Mamma san, finally satisfied that the correct rhythm had been achieved, took her little claws away. 'The twig is now a mighty branch,' she crooned approvingly, looking down at the youth's engorged cock. Then she sat back on her heels to watch every movement.

Annabel hoped that the older woman wouldn't intervene again. It made her feel creepy, and spoilt her enjoyment of the occasion. And, now, she was beginning to enjoy herself.

The sight of the youth's pleasure – he writhed and squirmed between her hands as they moved on his penis – was making Annabel's heart race. She felt guilty for her enjoyment of such a bizarre sexual situation: bringing a complete stranger to sexual climax while Mamma san and Kiku watched! But at the same time a knot of excitement was building in her chest.

She bit her lips in arousal. She was aware of her breasts as they swung free inside the silk of her gorgeous gold kimono. She would have liked to slip her hand beneath her kimono and cup her sex with her hands, but she knew that Mamma san wouldn't allow her to touch herself while she was bringing the youth to orgasm. Her own satisfaction would have to wait until later.

'Stop!' cried Mamma san. 'You don't want him to

climax too quickly. He's getting too excited. Take your hand off him. Gently and smoothly, you fool. Now, wait a few moments and move again. That's right. Now, this time, bring him to the cloudburst.'

Annabel made a ring of the thumb and index finger of each hand. Then she placed one hand above the other in the middle of his erect and eagerly waiting shaft. She could smell the musk of his sexual secretions and she knew that he was ready to climax. Moving gently at first, she pulled the warm, straining skin of his penis in both directions at once.

She saw his hands clench by his sides and his face contorted. She did it again, with a nice, gentle rhythm that even Mamma san would have approved of. The breath hissed between his teeth and the skin between her hands grew slippery as another great dollop of liquid oozed from the tip of his penis. Annabel massaged it into his skin as her hands stroked his shaft. His breathing rasped loudly. She increased her grip, and her speed.

As his orgasm took him, the youth relinquished his passive role. His back arched. His body tensed. His pelvis lifted. He began pumping his hips, ramming his swollen organ through Annabel's caressing hands. 'I'm going,' he cried, and with that he drove forward one last time.

Boiling seed spurted from the tip of his penis. Annabel lifted her hands to try to stop the jets of milky liquid hitting her silk-clad chest. Sperm flooded over her hands and ran between the gaps in her fingers. The smell was sharp in the room, and she heard a light pattering as drops of the viscous liquid fell on to the youth's naked chest.

The youth fell back limply on to the white futon, breathing heavily. Annabel smiled down at his sweating figure as she wiped her hands on the clean white towel that lay waiting. She took another towel and cleaned up the pearls that jewelled his dark curls and clung to his now-soft penis.

Then she sat back on her heels and looked at the youth's happy, sated expression. It was nice to think that she had given him so much pleasure. A wet patch bloomed between her legs. If only she could guide his hands there. She shivered as she imagined light, cool fingers gently touching her woman's place.

Mamma san's voice was a harsh intrusion into her pleasantly sensual dream. 'That was pathetic, Annabel san. Even a peasant could give a man a better experience than that.'

Annabel bit her lip in vexation. How she longed to be free of restrictions and criticism. She opened her mouth to answer angrily, but she was interrupted by a light, pleasant masculine voice. 'Oh, I don't know, Mamma san.' Behind Annabel, a rice-paper screen slid fully open. 'I arrived just in time to see the climax, and I thought it one that any man would enjoy.'

Annabel twisted around so that she could see the newcomer. Even the many starched layers of his splendid kimono did not disguise his slight build, but he had a handsome smiling face, and he carried himself with regal confidence. Mamma san gave a faint squeak and prostrated herself on the tatami matting. Kiku flung herself to the ground next to the older woman. The naked youth joined in the orgy of prostration, his bare buttocks bobbing comically as he bowed, and bowed again.

The newcomer ignored them all. His eyes were fixed on Annabel. She bowed once, as slowly and as gracefully as she could, but then she sat up, as much as she could on her knees, and returned his gaze levelly. She would not, could not bring herself to grovel.

'So this is the incredible barbarian,' said the newcomer slowly. His eyes examined Annabel ceaselessly. His outer kimono was chestnut brown, but Annabel noticed that the crane insignia was smaller, and placed in a different position from those the guard wore. She wondered who he was as the light voice continued, 'I thought it might be a trick, a matter of dye and clever make-up; but the reports did not lie! She is the most astonishing creature. Eyes like the sky and round like the sun! Who would have thought it possible?'

'You are so right, Mr Hiroshi. She is very strange, all must be agreed on that,' twittered Mamma san, raising her head from the floor. 'Something quite out of the usual, don't you think, Mr Hiroshi?'

Mr Hiroshi! Then this is Nakano's younger brother, returned from the family castle at Edo. Annabel hunted for a family resemblance in his face as he smiled at Mamma san and said, 'Oh, I agree. But really, I'm quite lost for words. Speaking frankly, I had thought the others were lying. Of course, they came back to Edo and said that the barbarian looked a certain way and acted a certain way – but I thought they were lying, as young men do. I did not think that she could be a real foreign woman. Where is she from, Mamma san?'

'Of course, you already know that she is from a country called England, Mr Hiroshi, so clever as you are. Like Japan, it is a small island, but governed by a queen, a woman, which sounds most unnatural to me.'

'Not the same place as the smelly priests, then? But I can see that she is quite different from those debased creatures. What does she think of Japan?'

'If it would please you, Mr Hiroshi, you could ask her yourself. She speaks Japanese.'

'No! This is too wonderful! A talking barbarian!' The small shiny eyes turned full on Annabel. There was a light, sparkling glee in them that made her uneasy.

She was uncomfortably aware that, like all samurai, Nakano's brother wore two swords at his side, one short and one long. Since moving to the fortress, she had learnt that those swords meant that the wearer was perfectly entitled to lop off her head if he chose to. For any reason, or no reason at all, except that he was samurai, and it was his prerogative to do so.

As she waited for Hiroshi to speak to her, she could hear the rain beating down ceaselessly outside. It must be the chill damp of the atmosphere that was making her thoughts gloomy. Nothing could have been more pleasant than the light, smiling countenance now turned her way.

Hiroshi spoke slowly, clearly, enunciating each word as if he were speaking to a child, 'So, Barbarian san, how do you like Japan?'

Annabel inclined her head gracefully. 'I find it most charming,' she said sweetly, 'and although I preferred the dry, crisp winter weather of the first months I spent here, I have to admit that these spring rains remind me of England; for in my own country it rains a great deal.'

Hiroshi's eyes opened wide. 'Your pardon, Annabel san,' he said, laughing a little. 'All my previous encounters with barbarians ... I have only met merchants and sailors, and they truly are barbaric. I had not realised that the women were so very different. Is it because you are a woman? Or is it a matter of education?'

She smiled at him. 'A little of both, sir. Just as in Japan, different lifestyles exist in Europe. One could not expect a poor sailor to have the leisure to study.'

'I quite see your point.' He looked thoughtful. 'Is it possible then, that there are barbarians who do not stink like dead dogs?' His nostrils flared as he inhaled deeply. 'For you smell only as a woman should, a subtle fragrance to inflame a man's senses.'

'None of my friends and family smell,' said Annabel, somewhat stiffly. 'I fear that you have met only the lowest type of sea-merchant.' People were always telling her that Europeans stank, and although they invariably added that Annabel was different, their comments irritated her.

'Delightful!' cried Hiroshi, his eyes sparkling. 'I have always been curious about lands across the sea, and when I was a boy I had a private fantasy about having a barbarian friend. Now it seems as if the fantasy may become real.' He broke off and laughed aloud. 'Although I was such an innocent boy then. It never occurred to me to dream of a female barbarian!' He straightened a fold in his already impeccable kimono and adjusted his swords. His voice became husky and dropped slightly. 'Nor to dream of certain delightful things that we could do together.'

Tension crept into the pause that followed. Behind her, Annabel was aware of furtive rustling sounds as the boy from the brothel gathered up his clothing and tiptoed out through the rice-paper screens. Mamma san had raised herself from the tatami. She was kneeling forward, poised, ready to spring into any action that the daimyo's brother might demand. The screens slid open, noiselessly, and Kiku appeared in the entrance. She carried a tray of green tea.

'Thank you,' said Hiroshi, absently accepting a thin, handleless cup half-full of tea. He sipped it delicately while he continued to watch Annabel. A wisp of bitter steam rose from his cup. Her feeling of unease returned, but he was still smiling at her, his face friendly. Then he turned to Mamma san. 'I hear my brother is having her trained in the pillow arts. How does she go on, Mamma san?'

The older woman bowed low, her orange and gold kimono glittering as she moved. 'Slowly, my lord. I do my poor best, but would you believe that she knew nothing, nothing at all when she came to me?'

'Is that so?' Hiroshi looked curiously at Annabel. 'Did your mother not teach you how to please a man?'

Annabel wondered how to explain the absurdity of such a question. She settled for a simple, 'It is not the custom, sir.'

'Really? That seems most strange! How then does one keep a husband from sampling the erotic delights that an expert practitioner of the pillow arts can promise? Why, even the simplest of peasant girls knows that the cheapest way to keep a man at home is to make sure that he lacks for nothing in bed.'

'I do not think that English husbands stray,' said Annabel, tossing her head.

Hiroshi's little black eyes sparkled. 'Then they are nothing at all like any other man in the world! For all men love to stray. All men like to experience something a little different.' His voice became slower, thoughtful. 'A little out of the ordinary,' he mused. 'A little ... exotic, shall we say?'

A sharp thrill ran over Annabel as their eyes met. His expression was intent, dreamy, and sensual. Desire for her was plain in his face. His hand drifted to the area of his kimono that shielded his manhood. 'You are not too tired after your earlier exertions?' he enquired.

Annabel's heart slammed into her throat. What was he suggesting? This was Nakano's brother! She cast a startled glance at Mamma san, wanting the older woman's help. She could not have understood his meaning properly! She could not be expected to become intimate with the warlord's brother.

But the older woman was smiling. 'Oh, Mr Hiroshi, of course she is not too tired! She will be most happy to participate in any sexual act you would care to experience.'

'Her mouth is delicious,' said Hiroshi, staring intently at Annabel's lips.

Annabel bent her head. This country! This crazy country! How could she be expected to understand a place where she was encouraged to make love with Nakano's brother?

The sensual area between her legs softened as she looked at Hiroshi's thoughtful face. He was still watching her mouth. She licked her parted lips, feeling the soft pink weight of her tongue with a sensitivity that told her she was becoming sexually excited. Yet apprehension mingled with her arousal. Would Nakano get to find out if she had sex with his brother? Would he be angry?

'Your mouth, Annabel san,' said Hiroshi dreamily. 'I yearn for the delicious feel of your wet lips.'

Paralysed by the turmoil in her head, Annabel continued to kneel where she was, too confused to move. Mamma san cast an anguished eye at the waiting male figure of Hiroshi and hissed across the matting, 'Move, you stupid barbarian!'

Dreamlike, Annabel moved across the sweet-smelling tatami matting until she was close to Hiroshi. His head was tipped back slightly and he regarded her from half-closed eyes. His hair was very thick and so dark it was blue-black. 'I would not wish to force you.' The words fell from between his sensually parted lips.

Annabel bent her head in acknowledgement. 'You do me great honour,' she said, falling back upon the ritual phrase, not sure how true the words were, but conscious of desire, curiosity, and a sensual mix of emotions running around her body. Emotions too tangled to analyse.

Hiroshi bent his head and slowly pressed his lips to her mouth. His tongue slid between her lips. It tasted of bitter green tea. His soft wet tongue licked and teased at her own tongue. Then it seemed to stiffen and he pushed it hard into the warm depths of her mouth. Annabel sucked at the soft muscular bulk of his tongue with tight lips, as if she were sucking his manhood, and she felt his face grow hot.

He pulled his lips away with a wet smacking sound. He sat back and ran incredulous fingers over his lips, as if he could still feel her touch there. 'That lovely face! Those soft pink lips! What excitement. My cock grows stiff. My family jewels are quivering as I speak. Mamma san!'

'Yes, sir!'

'Take her hair down. I wish to see that fabulous veil of gold as she sucks me.'

Annabel felt Mamma san's cold fingers scrambling with the pins that held her blonde hair. Then a soft tickling as the heavy mass fell loose over her shoulders.

Hiroshi reached into the folds of his kimono and extracted his penis. Annabel felt her breath quicken as she saw how the reddish-purple head pulsed in an almost hypnotic rhythm. The base of his penis was still hidden in the folds of kimono fabric, but what she could see of the shaft was fleshy, engorged and taut. A shiver ran over her as she contemplated the approaching intimacy.

'Would you like me to undress you, Mr Hiroshi? The barbarian could be naked in one moment if it would please you.'

Hiroshi's eyes never left Annabel's mouth, but he answered the older woman politely, as if he was cherishing the delay; as if it pleased him to prolong the moment before he thrust his rampant cock between Annabel's tender lips. 'Most kind of you. But I have not the time for a lengthy dalliance. Indeed, I had only the intention of popping over for a moment to meet the fabulous barbarian, but now I have met her, I find I cannot bear to continue on my way without the pleasure, the very great pleasure, of relieving myself inside that tender, but terrifyingly sensual, pink mouth.'

'Just as you wish, sir,' said Mamma san, bowing and crawling backward out of the way. 'Do please carry on. You do us all honour by entrusting your pleasure to our hands.'

'The pleasure is entirely on my side,' answered Hiroshi. His eyes became blacker and, despite his apparent calm, there was a faint tremor in his voice as he said, 'If you would care to begin, Annabel san . . .'

A shiver of apprehension ran around Annabel's belly as she leaned forward. Her face brushed against the disordered folds of Hiroshi's kimono as she pushed into the warm mass of soft silk and crisp cotton and slid her lips over his manhood.

The smooth flesh of his cock filled her mouth. The erotic taste and smell of it assailed her senses. His organ surged with life as her lips enveloped it, and she felt her lips stretching to accommodate its warm, satiny bulk.

She felt her own blood begin to stir. Warmth spiralled in her belly as, deep within her, her woman's place responded with a gentle quivering to the erotic stimulation of a penis in her mouth.

Her tongue curled over the satin bulb of his knob. She ran her tongue over it, washing it with firm, warm strokes. She heard his sharp breath. His hands moved over her head. They were gentle, encouraging her to please him. Feeling her cheeks hollowing with the suction, she drew the hardness of his erection deep into her throat. Her eyes flickered open briefly as she felt the head of his cock touching the back of her throat. His face was intent, his eyes wandering over her blonde hair, her foreign face. He seemed fully aware that it was she, Annabel, the barbarian woman who was sucking him into ecstasy.

Annabel resolved that he should enjoy the experience. She moved her head back, the gleaming wet length of his cock shining as it slid wetly out from between her parted lips. Her lips made a faint slurping noise as she sucked his shaft back into the cavern of her mouth. The sound embarrassed her. She felt blood rising to her cheeks and knew she was blushing. But Hiroshi's penis jumped in her mouth like a live thing and he cried ecstatically, 'The sounds of heaven!'

More confidently now, careless of the wet sounds and

the saliva that poured from her mouth, Annabel sucked at his straining flesh with growing relish. She heard herself mewling with pleasure as he writhed in delight. She was surprised at how excited she was becoming. Her sex was heavy within her as she worked upon the slim brown length of Hiroshi's cock, her head bobbing faster as she slid her lips up and down his shaft.

The sensuous feeling of his naked organ moving around in her mouth was so seductive, so enjoyable, that she wished she knew how to delay the exploding finish that she could sense building within his tense body. But even as she briefly considered if she should attempt to pull back and so delay his orgasm, the first thin stream of liquid flowed into the back of her throat, almost gagging her before she could swallow it.

She gulped hard as his organ paused for its next eruption. Then she whirled her tongue over the fleshy head of his penis, waiting for the next swelling throb. When it came, she swallowed another heady mouthful as the thick cream flowed warmly over her tongue and down the back of her throat. She sucked gently, and was rewarded by another gush of sperm. Her own body shivered exquisitely in sympathy with Hiroshi's climax. His soft hands patted her head helplessly as he spasmed.

She held his penis gently in her mouth as it went limp. When it began to shrink, she opened her mouth wide and just let the soft organ roll out. She nuzzled briefly into the darkness of Hiroshi's kimono, inhaling the warm scent of him and the musky tang of his sex, then she pulled away and sat back on her knees.

Annabel folded the gorgeous silk skirts of her kimono beneath her, patting them smooth. Her embroidered obi still held her waist stiffly, it had not loosened, despite the sensual way she had been writhing inside it. Her hair, however, now flowed freely around her shoulders. Annabel tilted her head to one side and used her hands to gather up the golden cascade into a long tail, which she then twisted into a casual knot.

Hiroshi's breathing was slowing now. He looked at Annabel with a dazed expression. He shook his head. He appeared to be hunting for words. His eyes were stunned. Kiku and Mamma san bobbed up, holding out hot wet towels. He took one absently, dabbing at his genitals in such a random fashion that Mamma san tut-tutted audibly and took the cloth away from him. She rubbed the cloth over his privates as if he were a helpless child. 'There we are, Mr Hiroshi, sir,' she crooned. 'All nice and clean.'

Hiroshi said vaguely, 'Yes, I thank you. I must ... the fact is ... I am expected at the war council meeting ... I am already late ...'

He took a deep breath and seemed to catch hold of himself. His opaque eyes, which had been bloomed with unreadable fantasies and veiled with a mysterious sensuality, cleared and returned to the untroubled, shiny black buttons Annabel had first seen. 'Ha! Most remarkable experience,' he said crisply. He bowed deeply. 'Annabel san. I do thank you for your most exquisite attentions.'

He released the bow and stood up, arranging his kimono with capable movements. 'As ever, I am in your debt, Mamma san,' he said smoothly, moving towards the rice-paper shoji that Kiku held open for him. He strode past her kneeling figure without appearing to see her. Annabel heard metal armour clinking in the corridor as his escort stirred, and then footsteps departing with an even, military tread. The taste of his sperm was still in her mouth. She felt overwhelmed, exhausted by the erotic intensity of the experience of fellation.

'Please, Mamma san,' she said urgently. 'May I be excused? I need to retire to my room. I need to be alone.'

Chapter Eight

*A*nnabel lay on her stomach on the warm, sweet-smelling tatami matting and gazed through the open rice-paper screens to the wet green garden beyond. Because she had already been told she would not be needed for training that day, she was wearing a simple blue and white kimono tied up with a plain red sash. It was nice to feel free. Even the heavy rain could not completely dampen her holiday feeling. She had slept late, and had been lying on her belly for about an hour now, dreamily watching the rain fall over the garden.

The heavy drops formed silver rings the size of an English shilling as they fell on the surface of the water where the koi carp lived. The dark orange fish swam lazily under the water lily leaves that bloomed in one corner. The pond lay in a curve under the moss-covered boulders that bounded Annabel's tiny garden. She thought it a very strange garden, consisting mainly of boulders and gravel and moss-covered stones. Yet the ferns that bloomed in the corners had a tranquil air about them, and no one came there but herself.

She was daily thankful that she had begged and argued and pleaded and insisted until she had been

131

given a room – tucked away in a forgotten corner of the fortress – for herself. She didn't think she could cope with Shimoyama without a private space to escape to. She was much happier now that she slept on the same futon every night. Bedding taken at random from a communal cupboard might be warm, but it lacked the secure feeling of home.

She hated the way the Japanese lived without privacy. Rooms were communal and multi-functional: furniture, cushions and bedding were brought in and out as necessary. It was practical, but it wasn't cosy, or restful, or private.

One of the rice-paper screens of her room now opened with a scraping noise. Annabel tensed as Mamma san entered, scolding as she came, 'The distance I have to travel if I want you, Annabel san. Why you have to lurk in this dark corner is beyond me, unless it's so that you can laze in that ungainly position! A well-bred young lady does not lie on her belly! Get up at once.'

Sighing as she did so, Annabel sat up and bowed politely. The warm moist air of spring seemed to clutch at her throat. She wondered if a thunderstorm was building. Over the last few days she had been aware of a feeling of oppression, as if the air pressure were dropping. It made her feel claustrophobic.

In the weeks she had been at Shimoyama, she had not been allowed to go anywhere, except her room and the corridors that led to Mamma san's domain, so she was surprised when she realised that the older woman was saying, 'Quickly now! We are to go to the sumo wrestling tonight. Lord Nakano himself has invited us to be present.'

Nakano! She was to see him at last. And Hiroshi? Would he be there? Annabel trembled. Would they be there together? How would she face them? Her mind worked busily as she followed Mamma san's back through the damp, echoing corridors. She wanted to see

132

Nakano so badly, yet she feared the encounter too. Her clitoris throbbed sharply between her legs, and dark velvet muscles moved softly inside her womb, as her body responded to Nakano's name, his dark and potent image.

The emerald-green kimono that lay waiting for her in Mamma san's apartments was the most splendid Annabel had seen yet. She cried out in sheer feminine pleasure at the sight of the embroidery. The brightly coloured silk was thick with gold couching. Red and gold autumn leaves sprawled across the body of the garment, all mixed up with exuberant sprays of pink and purple plum blossom, and it was bordered by great bronzy sheaves of chrysanthemum blooms. Fantastic swirls of silver and ribbons of gold looped behind the design, holding the pattern together. To go with the kimono, Mamma san had chosen a stiff obi of deep-green silk embroidered with bright yellow dragons. The outfit was a riot of colour. It broke every cannon of good taste and fashion sense that Annabel had ever heard of. It was a glorious triumph.

As she often did, Mamma san had chosen outfits from the same colour palette for all three women: dark green silk embroidered with a twisted pine tree pattern for herself, and a pellucid jade for Kiku. Their minds might not be in harmony, but Annabel thought that the toning colour of their kimonos probably made them look like a family group as the three women pattered down from the central tower.

At the threshold of the keep, outdoor shoes of green and gold lacquer were waiting. Annabel pushed hers on without looking because she was so keen to examine the courtyard of the keep. It had been too dark to see much when she arrived.

The rain had slowed to a fine mist, but the sky was still grey, and the fresh outside air felt damp on her cheeks. The grey sky reflected the grey stones that gravelled the courtyard. Annabel shivered as she stepped out into the still and sombre scene.

The only movement came from four figures wearing dark, indigo-dyed garments and the conical straw hats worn by peasants, who were stooping over the ground. Annabel examined them curiously as she walked past, her shoes crunching on the gravel, and saw that they were sifting through the stones with curved metal tools, cleaning the grey pebbles. A woven basket lay next to each peasant, containing minuscule scraps of dirt and a few frail-looking weeds.

She looked back at the building she had just stepped out of, and saw that the whole massive, bulky, sombre fortress had a sparkling air of immaculate cleanliness. The sheer elegance of the structure belied its massive strength. From the way the dark tiles gleamed in the rain, it looked as if the curved and hipped roofs were polished daily. It was probably only rain soaking all the timber, but the wooden steps and latticed screens and all the windows, porches and balconies shone shiny polished black against the white plaster walls.

A gust of wind met them as Mamma san ushered them around a corner and towards the massive arch of the entrance and the road that led into town. A faint tinkling made Annabel look up. A shiny metal owl swung beneath the eaves of the roof she was walking under. 'What are those birds for?' Annabel asked, pointing with her bamboo and oiled paper umbrella, not knowing the Japanese word for owl.

'The owls? They are to scare the mice away, of course. We Japanese are vigilant against vermin. We maintain good hygiene.'

Annabel thought of her father's sailing ship and the rat-droppings she used to sweep up. Her skin crawled as she remembered the day she had reached into a barrel of sea biscuits and put down her hand into a sticky, pulsating mass of bulbous warm bodies – a nest full of squeaking, hairless, stringy-tailed rats.

She had thought when she first boarded the ship that the dank vile smell of vermin was unbearable, but she had become used to it. As she was getting used to Shimoyama. It was hard to recall her life at sea. Strange as her new life was, she realised that she had never once wished herself back under Walter Smith's protection.

They were pattering over an arched stone bridge now, six lacquer shoes clicking as they started down the paved road that ran beside a wide strip of water. From the upper windows, Annabel had seen the moat that ran around the fortress, but she had not realised how wide it was nor how deeply it had been dug into the ground. It made a formidable defence. The only way across it was the bridge they had just walked over. She stopped and looked back in the direction of the delicate curved stone arch.

Fragrant dark cedars grew along the steep grassy banks of the moat. Two swans sailed on the water under the bridge, their reflections clear in the glassy black surface of the water. Towering over the scene, the many roofs of the donjon, the central keep, climbed into the sky. They were oddly angled and pitched, overlapping like the scales of a pine cone, designed so that firebombs could roll off as easily as the rain. A chilling reminder of the true nature of Shimoyama.

Annabel sighed as she turned back to the road. It curved sharply and then ran into town. The town was compact: for safety, the great stone outer walls of the fortress enclosed all the buildings. Annabel looked around her eagerly as they entered the first narrow street. She couldn't believe how clean and orderly the little town appeared. How open and colourful it was.

The shopkeepers had simply removed the rice-paper shop walls that faced the road, so that each shop front was entirely open. The grey afternoon light was fading, and most of the open fronts were brightly lit patches of colour. They walked past a shop full of straw-covered barrels. Annabel felt a thrill of delight as she deciphered the bold, black Chinese characters: Finest Sake! It was a rice wine shop. She tried to dawdle, but Mamma san kept her moving, past a green-tea shop, a shop full of strange sacks, and then a silk emporium. There was a sharp smell of the sea, and Annabel saw boxes and boxes of silvery fish, all arranged with their little tails pointing the same way.

'Stop gawking, Annabel san,' said Mamma san crossly, 'and walk elegantly. Everyone knows I've had the training of you.'

Annabel saw that the townsfolk were indeed looking at her; discreet slanting glances as they went about their business, but definitely curious. Despite the mist of spring rain pattering on the oiled paper, she lowered her umbrella a little, thinking to hide behind it, but Mamma san was already stopping outside a large, closed building. It was built in a style that reminded Annabel of the temple where she had first met Nakano. The elegant structural timbers were painted red. Black latticed screens enclosed rice-paper walls. More red timbers flanked an imposing entrance.

Mamma san and Kiku lifted the silken skirts of their kimonos and stepped off the street and on to a polished wooden ledge that ran around the building. Annabel followed suit. They pattered a few steps towards the entrance, and then stopped and took off their shoes. Their elegant lacquered footwear joined the jumble of thousands and thousands of pairs of split-toed boots, expensive shoes and worn sandals lying around the doorway.

'Will we ever find them again?' asked Annabel curiously, but she was ignored.

The toes of Mamma san's dazzling white socks twinkled beneath her kimono as she set off down the corridor. A worried-looking man with an official air rushed up to her. He bowed low in between every sentence as he whispered, 'So sorry . . . They have nearly begun . . . If you could be so kind as to enter quietly . . . This way if you please . . . The Lord Nakano is waiting . . .'

Nakano! She had nearly forgotten in the excitement of seeing the town, but now the scene around Annabel blurred and faded as she thought of him once more. She barely took in the size of the arena they entered. Her own heart drowned the hum of a thousand conversations. Her stomach lurched, but she didn't know that it was registering the smells of cooking rice crackers and snacks of pickled fish. She looked blankly at another worried-looking official, who bobbed up and began bowing low. He wanted to escort them from the back of the building, where they had entered, down towards the centre of the arena.

Annabel followed him obediently, but her confusion was destroying her ability to function. She couldn't think. She couldn't walk properly. She caught one of her white socked toes in a join in the tatami matting that covered the sloped sides of the floor and stumbled. The official sprang to take her arm. He led her tenderly through the crowds of people who sat on the floor.

The audience was sprawled around in what looked like family groups at first sight; many had food baskets, as if they were picnicking in a busy park, but a second look showed that the throng was made up of darkly clad men, with only a few gaudy women in attendance.

Now Annabel saw the wrestling ring. A circle of clay was set in the mound of earth that everyone was facing. It was brightly lit by flaring torches that smelt of tar. A tented roof arrangement hung over the ring. Great red and silver cords dangled towards the ground.

Set just before the wrestling ring, in the best position to view the fight, sat five or six men, sitting stiffly upright in formal splendour. They looked like bull seals on a beach. There was a respectful distance between their clearly defined area of sand-coloured tatami matting, and the chattering crowds of dark figures around them.

Mamma san made it easy to join the sombre group. Charming, feminine, elegant, Annabel might dislike the older woman – and she suddenly realised just how much she disliked her – but she had to admire the easy small talk and dainty gestures by which Mamma san eased them into the party. The men relaxed noticeably as she laughed and teased them. They threw off their sober air and seemed ready to be entertained.

Annabel paused uncertainly behind Mamma san's vivacious figure. Shyness made her feel large and clumsy. She did not dare move to join the party. Her mouth dried as she looked up through her lashes at Nakano. His regal figure was unmistakable. Close to him knelt the slighter figure of Hiroshi. Annabel felt heat rise to her cheeks. Had they spoken about her? Did he know that she had been intimate with his brother?

Kiku pushed past her impatiently, joining Mamma san in the round of small talk and laughter. The male figures were moving, making space for the women to join them. Annabel felt Mamma san's claw hands on her elbow and she was pushed to a position in front of the party.

She heard one of the party joke, 'The barbarian will have the best view of the sumo,' as she knelt on the soft matting. Everyone was behind her. She could hear Mamma san babbling on, Kiku's light, tinkling laugh and the deeper responses of the men, but she could see nothing.

All the skin on Annabel's back felt sensitive. Was he looking at her? She wished she could see behind her. The nape of her neck felt exposed, naked beneath her piled-up hair and the downward dip of the neck of the kimono.

A stir like the wind in a forest ran around the great arena as a small, grave figure of the master of ceremonies, his kimono sparkling in the garish lighting, stepped into the clay wrestling ring. Annabel could feel the tension and excitement in the crowd as they leant forward, arranging themselves for the best view.

The sight of the sumo wrestlers stamping into the ring distracted Annabel temporarily. She had never seen such fat men! They wore only loin-cloths, and she couldn't help but gaze at their naked, wobbling fatty buttocks as they paraded and stamped around the clay circle. The master of ceremonies had a hoarse, booming croak of a voice, and Annabel couldn't follow the unfamiliar cadences of his voice as he introduced the occasion.

There was an air of ritual about the opening ceremonies, and the wrestling itself was elaborately organised and very formal. Annabel watched two huge wrestlers bowing to one another. From their demeanour it was impossible to tell the winner from the loser.

She thought of home, and the wrestling matches her mother would have been horrified to know she had seen. But Timothy, the third groom, had dreams of winning his fortune through the sport, and so all the servants, and little Annabel, had sneaked away to watch him try his luck. The ugly brutal matches had shocked her. They were not over until one combatant had been beaten senseless, and were often continued unofficially behind the village inn. A world away from this neatly packaged, tamed and civilised violence.

A cool, hostile little voice from behind startled Annabel, and then made her wince. 'Lord Nakano was going to give you as a prize in the tournament, but not even those fatty monsters fancied a barbarian.'

Kiku! The Japanese girl was leaning forward to whisper insults under the noise of the wrestling match. Annabel itched to turn around and stare her down. Kiku was in awe of the powerful blue of her eyes, and one look was all it usually took to subdue the Japanese girl but Annabel couldn't turn around without everyone - Nakano – noticing them.

I won't let her bother me, thought Annabel, resolving to stay calm.

'You do smell,' continued the malicious soft whisper 'We Japanese are too polite to tell you so, but actually you stink like all barbarians do!'

Annabel sat statue-like, concentrating hard on the dark-skinned monster in the wrestling ring. He was bumping his enormous naked belly into the face of his rival. She wished he would do it to Kiku.

'You don't belong here. You don't fit in. Nobody wants you. Go home, Barbarian. Get back to your stinking kennel.'

Annabel shifted uneasily. She felt raw. It was true, she didn't fit in. She had been amused to discover that Japanese society was so regulated that there were clearly defined roles for even the very lowest strata of society nobody slipped through the classification net. But there wasn't even a category of social outcast for the only barbarian at Shimoyama. She was isolated as perhaps nobody else in Japan. She had never been so alone, so completely unconnected, in the world.

But if she let Kiku get through to her, she would be displaying her weakness; and the Japanese girl would use it as a weapon, Annabel had no doubt of that. Although she suspected that her neck was flushing red with anger, and so giving her away, she managed a least to keep her body as still as if nothing were wrong Until the voice began again: 'If only you could hear your accent, Barbarian! It's the next best thing to a fish speaking, it really is! What a great shame that only the lowest class of moron could be found to teach you the lowest class of Japanese language. Or perhaps it was fate, dirt finding its own level, so to speak.'

She had had enough! Hiroko's loving, delicate face

flowed into Annabel's mind, along with the memory of the many sweet hours they had spent together. Dear, loyal, patient Hiroko. She could not bear to hear her insulted.

The sibilant whisper began to spew out fresh poison: 'I've always heard that fish slime –'

Annabel spun completely round, meaning only to stare Kiku into submission. The Japanese girl gave a hateful, nervous titter and put her hand up to her mouth.

'What's going on?' asked a deep male voice.

'It's only the barbarian,' tinkled Kiku from behind her hand. 'I'm afraid she doesn't know how to behave. So sorry, but what can we expect? She's been living with a sea slug.'

Annabel's hand flew out of its own volition. It made a deeply satisfying crack as it connected with Kiku's powdered cheek. Annabel's palm stung, but she was glad to feel the pain. It took the edge off her surging, furious anger.

The Japanese girl gave a faint shriek and fell backward. Annabel tensed, expecting the Japanese girl to recover and perhaps exact her revenge. Annabel had fought very little in her life, preferring always to walk away from trouble, but it would be a pleasure to do battle now. Her blood was still boiling. Kiku had cruelly poked at all her deepest fears and sore points. It would be a relief to escape into anger, to find a physical outlet for the emotions that now surged uncomfortably around her system.

But Kiku lay shivering on the matting, covering her face with her hands. Surely I can't have hurt her so badly, thought Annabel, wondering why the Japanese girl didn't sit up, do something.

Then she became aware of the weight of many, many eyes. The arena was nightmare sea of darkness, and out of it shone the whites of a thousand, thousand shocked glances. The sumo wrestling had stopped. The wrestlers were staring her way. The master of ceremonies, who was now refereeing, had his hand in the air, halting the action, while he looked up to Lord Nakano for guidance.

Slowly, slowly, Annabel turned and met the gaze of Nakano for the first time. He was looking down at her from his considerable height. His black eyes glittered unpleasantly, and Annabel knew that she was looking into the face of a stranger.

His voice was a steely accusation. 'Fighting, Barbarian san?' he asked with ice cold calm.

Annabel was worried as she searched his eyes. She could see no memory of their intimacy softening them. She inclined her head, but remained sitting upright. 'I'm sorry we disturbed you,' she said quietly. 'I apologise for my ill manners.'

'Kiku san,' he enquired.

The Japanese girl took her hands away from her face long enough to roll over and prostrate herself upon the matting. 'Oh, oh, oh, I'm so sorry,' she cried. 'I wouldn't have had you disturbed for the world. It's the barbarian. So sorry, but she's like a wild thing. So unreliable. She attacked me without warning.'

Nakano's gaze clicked back to Annabel. He watched her quietly for some moments, but she refused to speak. She had apologised. She would not lower herself by trying to place the blame on Kiku.

Nakano looked at them both sombrely. Then he said, 'You may continue your fight.'

Kiku's breath caught on a terrified sob. Annabel gazed at him puzzled. Nakano looked away from them and gestured to the master of ceremonies. 'So sorry to interrupt the scheduled programme,' he said calmly, 'but these ladies wish to fight. Please, take them backstage and have them arrayed in a suitable costume: naked, no weapons. Their match will take place after the championship is decided.'

The referee bowed instantly. 'Of course, Lord Nakano. Will there be any prize to be announced?'

Nakano hesitated. His younger brother, Hiroshi, leant forward and said excitedly, 'Men fight for money. Women should fight for altogether more interesting stakes. My mouth waters at the prospect of a naked fight. Can you imagine anything more delicious? Anything more titillating? Well, then, let the prize be in keeping with the nature of the occasion. The winner gets to enjoy a glorious orgasm; the loser must provide it.'

Annabel looked at Hiroshi, startled. The black eyes that met hers were filled with malicious, childlike glee, but his mouth twisted with a very adult lust as he continued teasing his brother, 'Oh go on, to please me . . .'

Nakano inclined his head gravely. 'Let it be so.'

Annabel could not read his expression in the few seconds she had before she was led away. She felt sick and her palms were sweating. All the heads in the arena swayed to follow them as she and Kiku were taken around the wrestling ring and led behind some curtains.

The shadowy dressing area to the side of the stage was full of enormous naked men. They smelt of hair oil and sweat and the talcum powder they powdered their feet with. They watched with curiosity, but no surprise, as Kiku and Annabel were divested of their glorious robes. Annabel wondered if women had ever been ordered to fight before.

'I don't know the rules,' she said.

One ponderous elephant of a sumo wrestler laughed at her, but not unkindly. 'The exact rules are no good to you. It takes many years to master the subtlety of sumo.' He turned aside to confer with the referee. They quickly reached agreement. 'For you women, the match will be decided when any part of your bodies, except the soles of your feet, touches the ground, or when you step, or are pushed, out of the ring. You may use any tactics to achieve this end.'

He approached Annabel with a padded belt and a length of purple-dyed cloth. Her flesh shivered slightly as the fat man's fingers brushed her naked skin, but she submitted to his ministrations as he wrapped the fabric around her, for all the world as if she were a baby, until she was wearing a sumo-style loin-cloth.

Annabel was glad that she was not to be completely naked, but the belt would give her opponent something to grip while they were fighting. Fighting? Annabel's mouth went dry with the implication of her thoughts. Why was she going along with this charade? She glanced over at the Japanese girl. 'This whole thing is ridiculous,' she said. 'Let's refuse to fight. Why should we make fools of ourselves in public?'

Kiku was staring at her feet, restlessly playing with her fingers as she sat, well away from Annabel, in the warm stuffy area of the dressing room. 'The Lord Nakano has ordered it,' she said dully.

'Does that mean we have to obey him?' snapped Annabel.

Kiku gave her an unfathomable look. 'Barbarian,' she sighed. 'You understand nothing.'

Annabel shrugged. She had no taste for a public fight, and would have been willing to make peace, but if Kiku refused, there was nothing to be done but go through with it. And if she must fight, then she was determined to win. She tried to call back her anger, to remember all her previous grievances against the Japanese girl, but they seemed very hard to remember in the face of the coming ordeal.

The fat, naked sumo wrestlers were crowding around the curtain to watch the final match. The noise outside rose to a triumphant frenzy. One man's name was shouted over and over. The champion had been declared. Annabel tried to steady her breathing. They were next.

* * *

144

It soon became obvious that a kitten could have given Annabel a harder time than Kiku. The slender Japanese girl pawed ineffectually at the air with her small hands. Her eyes were tightly closed, and her face was screwed up in a comical mixture of resignation and determination.

Annabel took a step back and looked at the naked, doll-like figure. She could not even begin to attack someone so vulnerable, so unable to defend themselves. Guilt pierced her to the core. 'Kiku,' she whispered softly, 'let's just give this up.'

Kiku's eyes slid open. There was an anguish in them that tore at Annabel's heart. 'Lord Nakano will be very angry if we do not fight. The crowd expect it. We will humiliate him if we fail.'

Annabel was now aware of a restless surging. The smoky flares that lit the wrestling ring were so bright that behind them, where the audience sat, she could only see dim shadowy waves of movement. But she could hear a restless shuffling, and even as she listened there was a coarse shout: 'Cowards! Get on with it!'

Kiku closed her eyes again and began patting at the air. 'Please, Annabel san, you must hit me,' she said pathetically.

'Be damned if I will!' Annabel closed her own eyes for a moment, hearing the drone of the crowd in her ears, thinking rapidly. 'Let's fake it!' she whispered.

Kiku's eyes flew open and she searched Annabel's face. Her cheeks were brightly flushed and there was a question in her dark eyes. She looked ready to bolt, yet she stood there, tiny, naked, vulnerable, brave, a somehow gallant figure. Annabel forgot their previous animosity. In the face of the surging male audience, they were sisters.

'Follow my lead,' whispered Annabel urgently. 'I won't hurt you, but we'll put on a show for the crowd.'

Kiku's expression cleared from confusion to understanding, to mischievous glee. 'What shall I do?'

145

'Put your arms on mine, above the elbows and pretend to push.'

Kiku flew at her in a little rush, and Annabel smelt the subtle perfume that rose from the Japanese girl's skin as she grasped her slender bare arms. She began to push back, and the crowd roared with approval as the two naked women began to circle the ring.

Kiku put her whole soul into her performance. She flexed her creamy wheat-coloured body and bent from the waist, grunting and groaning in pretend effort. As Kiku presented her beautiful buttocks to the crowd, Annabel heard the men at the front of the ring draw in their breath sharply. Kiku wriggled in her arms. She was shaking her spread-open buttocks, which were naked save for the string of the loin-cloth, at the men. Annabel heard small gasps and murmurs of appreciation.

Annabel began to catch on to the idea. She twisted in Kiku's arms so that the men facing her could see her creamy pink-tipped breasts. All their heads turned towards her. She made a play of shaking her breasts, pretending to growl fiercely at Kiku as she did so. Annabel could sense the excitement of the audience growing. There seemed to be invisible cords of sexual tension floating in the air between her, Kiku, and the anonymous crowd. At the back of her mind, she knew that Nakano must be watching, but she was too preoccupied to turn her head and look for him.

Kiku broke their hold and took a few paces back. She was breathing heavily and a light film of perspiration shone over her skin. Her small body was perfectly formed, flawlessly proportioned with slender legs, a narrow waist, and proud high breasts with luscious dark nipples that just begged to be kissed.

Annabel remembered the sexual part of their contract and even as she had the thought, she saw Kiku's nipples harden as the Japanese girl met her eyes. Kiku drew in her breath sharply, turned away from Annabel and faced

146

the crowd, planting her tiny fists on her waist. The men roared. She bent her knees and reached behind her, straightening her loin-cloth in clever parody of the ponderous ritual movements of the sumo wrestlers. The crowd loved it. The pale heads moved backwards and forwards in laughter, and the atmosphere grew warm and exciting.

Kiku turned back to Annabel. 'Hey, Barbarian!' she yelled.

Annabel crouched and waved her fists threateningly, circling in mock aggression. 'Hey yourself!' she cried in return. 'Come over here and be pulped!'

Kiku faced the crowd once more. 'Shall I thrash the barbarian?' she screamed.

A roar that was sexual in its intensity rolled out of the crowd and into the ring. It was hot beneath the blazing lights. Annabel felt sweat start to her skin. The noise, the warmth, the dim, shadowy, excited crowd of watching men, they were all contributing to an entirely unexpected arousal. She was starting to enjoy herself. She made a lunge at Kiku, tearing the flowers out of her chignon, brandishing them in triumph before scattering the petals on the floor.

The avid multitude of watchers bellowed with one voice as Kiku's mass of blue-black hair tumbled free over her narrow shoulders. Annabel backed off and the two women circled one another, breathing heavily, very aware of the watching men. Very aware of the pact that now existed between them and against the rest of the world. Very close together.

Kiku seemed to search Annabel's face for a long moment, then she sighed and said, 'I'm so sorry, Annabel san. I was jealous of you. It made my heart black.' She looked up at the English girl with a mysteriously child-like smile. 'Can we be friends?'

Annabel's heart felt warm. 'Of course,' she murmured. She felt a sudden hot touch of skin as Kiku rushed at her. The Japanese girl hugged her fiercely for a brief second, then she threw herself back on the clay circle, her whole body touching the ground.

Annabel was a little bewildered by the speed of Kiku's capitulation, but the referee rushed out instantly, proclaiming that the barbarian was the winner. She stayed in her daze as she was paraded, as she and Kiku bowed formally to one another to signify the end of the match, and as they drew apart and faced each other once more, ready for the second part of the display.

The tension emanating from the crowd was even more intense. It was difficult to be sure because of the bright lights, but Annabel had a feeling that the audience had moved. The blurry pale circles that were faces seemed to have drawn closer, much closer to the ring, as if the men had surged forward in their anxiety to see clearly what would happen next. Her mouth was dry as she stood waiting.

Kiku stood opposite her. Her eyes held Annabel's for a long moment, the expression saying what words could not. For an instant, the two women shared a look of warm complicity, and then Kiku reached out and pulled Annabel into her arms, holding on with surprising strength when the English girl pulled back, until she had Annabel gripped so tightly by the loin-cloth, that Annabel gave up resisting.

Annabel stooped slightly, so that she could bury her head against the Japanese girl's chest. She marvelled at the softness of female breasts against her cheeks as she stood, her body rigid, in the circle of Kiku's arms. At first, she was aware of a rising and falling sensation as her fast breath lifted her chest and dropped it again. But as she stood there, sheltered in Kiku's arms, she felt her breathing slow. The bare soles of her feet seemed to draw up strength from the baked clay of the wrestling ring.

Annabel felt her body softening, slowly, subtly. She

148

sank against Kiku, warming to her touch, to the stroke of her fingers against her back. Shifting slightly, she moved her hands so that she could cradle the Japanese girl's face, tilting it close to hers. She saw a great look of longing and sadness in Kiku's eyes. The brightly lit wrestling ring fell away until there was only the two of them. Kiku's eyes blurred together as her soft mouth came closer. God help them both, thought Annabel as she lowered her mouth to just brush against the Japanese girl's gentle lips. They were going to need it.

No one had ever kissed her like this before. Every male kiss, every male intimacy, every touch, they all paled compared to the feelings that Kiku's soft womanly lips stirred within her. The cool taste of her mouth intoxicated. Her lips were coaxing and giving, so different from the hard plundering of a man's mouth. And yet her tongue demanded a response from Annabel, a response that had her melting from the pleasurable sensations that were welling up from some mysterious, primitive depths of her being.

Soft strands of black hair fell about them both. Kiku put her tiny delicate hands up to hold Annabel's face. The sensation left her reeling. And the smells: Kiku's own subtle perfume, and light female sweat, and the tangy oyster musk of a woman's arousal. The smells drowned Annabel in their potency. The sensations all rolled together, pooled within her, making her ache for more.

She had to get closer. She wrapped her arms around Kiku's delicate neck, marvelling at its warm perfumed beauty. Kiku made a sound deep in her throat, and cradled Annabel's waist, drawing her in closer along her tiny fragrant body. But it still didn't feel close enough, and Annabel let out a frustrated moan that encouraged Kiku to slide her hands over the English girl's bottom. The touch of naked skin on naked skin was delicious.

Then, somehow, the intimate triangle at the apex of

Annabel's thighs was pressing into the pubic hair of Kiku's mons. The two women stood close together for a moment, breathing in and out at the same speed, aware of the shocking intimacy of their touch, yearning for more.

Annabel released Kiku's mouth, pulling her head back as she rubbed her body against the slender oriental girl's, teasing them both, a little lost in their loving. Kiku smiled her incomparable smile and her eyes were dreamy. Annabel nipped at her lips, but when Kiku leant into her to deepen the kiss, Annabel shifted her mouth, pressing it lightly at the base of Kiku's throat, teasing them both.

A sharp whistle split the air. 'Hey! Hey! Go for it, whores!'

Annabel started at the rowdy male voice and tried to pull away from Kiku's embrace, but the Japanese girl held her tightly, pressing Annabel's head to her chest, so that the English girl could not look up to see who was abusing them.

More whistles rent the air. 'Come on! Let's see some action.' The same drunken voice, but would other men from the audience join in with his heckling?

Annabel began to shake. All her fine mood was leaking away. The adrenalin in her system was upsetting her now. Sickness soured the pit of her stomach, and she felt guilty, spoilt. She pulled away from Kiku and covered her face with her hands, so she didn't see Nakano approach, but she heard his voice clearly. 'Gentlemen, I think you should take your friend for a walk.' The command in his voice spoke more than the words.

From the nervous sounds of a hasty departure that immediately followed, Annabel knew that the problem was over. She took her hands away from her face in time to see the backs of two men as they half-dragged, half-carried a sagging male figure towards the exit. She looked up at Nakano and smiled at him warmly. He smiled back at her comfortably as he seated himself on the very edge of the clay ring. There was a distinct sexual interest dancing in the depths of his dark eyes. 'Pray continue,' he said, his voice dreamlike.

'You don't know what you're asking,' murmured Annabel. Jolted away from her sexual absorption in Kiku, she was now painfully aware of her surroundings, the flaring torches, the watching men. And yet she wanted the forbidden excitement of making love to a woman. She was going to do the unexpected, the undreamed of, and she was going to do it in public and under Nakano's interested gaze.

Kiku approached her softly, and Annabel met her gaze boldly. She wanted to touch the Japanese girl, to incorporate the danger and excitement of the situation into their lovemaking. She reached out and touched Kiku's cheek, then let her hand drift downward, to the soft swell of brown breast. Gently, she brushed the backs of her fingers against one taut brown nipple and then the other, then back to the first one. Annabel heard the faster breathing that greeted her stimulation of Kiku's breasts with satisfaction. The dark nipples looked huge, the small breasts swollen.

Kiku seemed to shiver as Annabel lifted the breast with her fingers, feeling its slight weight, feeling the silky texture of the tight skin, admiring its perfect shape. She took the dark nipple between her thumb and forefinger and tweaked it. Then Annabel bent her head to Kiku's perfect, swollen breast and engulfed the brown nipple with her lips.

A soft cry came from Kiku's throat. Surprise? Pleasure? Annabel sucked harder. The slightly salty tang of sweat was soon replaced by the natural sweetness of Kiku's flesh. Annabel's hand came up to cup the other breast, squeezing it, moulding it in her hand. Then she moved to the nipple, rubbing it, rolling it into a hard bud.

It was so nice. So warm and cosy and deliciously arousing to lick and suck at a breast. From Annabel a soft moan rose unbidden and was lost in the fragrance of the sweetly curving skin. Suddenly, Kiku pushed at her, and took a step away. Annabel staggered, and grabbed at thin air in a vain attempt to steady herself. Then she met Kiku's intent gaze. For several moments they faced each other, just shy of touching distance.

'Lie down,' said Kiku softly.

Annabel slipped down on to the crumbly warm clay. There was a stir all around as the audience pressed closer, but she put them out of her mind, although she was very aware of the watching figure of Nakano, his dark figure by the side of the ring.

Kiku lowered herself down next to Annabel. She took the pins out of Annabel's blonde hair and spread it out in a sparkling blonde cloak over the ground. The crowd murmured in appreciation. Annabel closed her eyes and a soft sigh escaped her lips.

'So perfect,' whispered the Japanese girl as she filled her hands with the creamy skin of Annabel's breasts. 'Now everyone can admire your golden yellow hair. Your colouring is so unusual, so incredible.' She looked intently at the dark dusky pink of Annabel's nipples, then she leant forward and took one tight bud in her mouth, flicking it with her tongue, suckling the tip until Annabel arched against her in sheer, wanton delight.

Then Kiku sat back and moved her hand lower, resting it on the flat of Annabel's stomach while she unloosed the sumo wrestler's handiwork with the other hand, unwinding the purple cloth until Annabel was naked for all the crowd to see.

Kiku lifted first one, then the other of Annabel's slim white legs, crooking the knees up, so that Annabel was lifted, spread wide, the open petals of her pink sex displayed for the crowd. She knew her sex-lips were wet. She could feel her arousal. She knew that everyone was looking at the wide-open readiness of her glistening engorged labia and the scented dark tunnel that opened within them.

For a moment Annabel felt disconcerted as Kiku's face, framed by its fall of long hair, slipped between her bare white thighs. She had never thought to have a woman touch her there. But at the first delicate touch, as Kiku's tongue extended to lick up the pearly beads of juice that were trembling all along the slit of the labia, Annabel fell back groaning and melting.

Her wet flower had never felt so good. She had never been sucked with such artistry and skill. As Kiku's tongue lapped around her tender flesh, Annabel parted her legs more widely to offer her better access, to increase the feelings that were storming around her body. Kiku pressed harder as Annabel's arousal grew, and yet her tongue was still gentle as it slid back and forth across the English girl's clitoris. Fresh moisture dewed the dark velvet walls of Annabel's vagina, but no male flesh came to fill it.

She looked up through her lashes at Nakano. His face was close. His eyes intent. He had moved closer to the two women. He was watching their bodies, as Kiku's dark head continued its marvellous work between Annabel's legs, but his eyes were focused on Annabel's face.

He was still watching as Annabel's eyelids fluttered closed. He was still watching as the referee began chanting overhead, seeming to call out the beats of her orgasm as Annabel felt her body writhe and coil, ready to spring loose in pleasure. Her breath was coming in pants now. She could think of nothing but the pointed red tongue that was whipping her clitoris into a frenzy.

Annabel's hips lifted. Her pleasure was breaking out into low throaty moans. Her skin was so sensitive that it was aware of the heat of Nakano's body as he moved even closer to her, absorbing the sensual nature of her cries.

She couldn't stop. She couldn't think. She was breaking up in delight. Her hips rose even higher off the ground and her shoulders rose off the clay surface, too, as she reached for Kiku in the frenzy of her orgasm.

Annabel gripped the Japanese girl's shoulders. She pressed the dark head and the busy, stimulating tongue closer and harder into the throbbing centre of her sex; digging her nails into Kiku's back she cried out aloud, her head dropping back as her orgasm exploded into fireworks and colours and a rushing, gushing sweetness that ricocheted around her body in a series of exquisite implosions that seemed to last longer than was bearable, before she let go her frantic grip on poor Kiku's shoulders – her nails had left ugly red welts in the delicate olive skin – and fell back on the dry clay of the ring.

Gasping, sweating, Annabel was suddenly painfully aware of the white smudges that were faces. Of the wall of sound that was made up of hundreds of voices, all laughing and applauding her abandon. She lay back, shutting them out; for the moment not caring for them at all, only aware of the sweet wet openness of her sex and the rightness of feeling so sweetly complete.

But now Nakano was bending over her, forcing her to look at him. She found herself hating his implacable male eyes. They were dark. They were sinister. She did not know how to meet their sexual charisma and stay calm. She sat up hastily, folding her legs to hide her private parts, shaking her hair around her to cover her breasts. A tiny smile lifted the corner of Nakano's lips. 'Stand up, Barbarian san.'

Slowly, reluctantly, she did so. She looked at her feet. The white toes were digging into the red clay of the ring. It was hard to control the nervous tremors that were rippling over her belly.

The soft command was meant for her ears only. 'Look at me.'

154

As though the effort was too much for her, she dragged her eyes to his. His expression was unreadable as he said quietly, 'I had thought that a public fight followed by public sexual congress would be a punishment for you – but you enjoyed it so much that I still feel that I owe you a lesson.'

He lifted his hands and Annabel saw that he was holding three thin black cords. Her eyes reached for him frantically as he separated the first cord from the other two. She saw something in his eyes but she wasn't sure what it was as, moving calmly, he tied the black cord around her right wrist. The gentle touch of his fingers burnt like hot heavy iron. The heat from his touch flowed through her body and slammed into Annabel's labia and she felt her sex lips engorge instantly from the hot rush of blood.

The second black cord circled her left wrist. Annabel's clitoris began throbbing in a sharp insistent rhythm. It glowed like a red jewel in the heart of her woman's place. She looked up at Nakano unhappily. She could feel blood heating her cheeks, staining a betraying pink patch of arousal on the fine pale skin above her breasts. He took the last cord and stretched it out taut between his fingers. Annabel's eyes could not leave its sinister black length.

Nakano kissed her neck tenderly and her skin melted beneath the touch of his lips. His voice was quiet, but his face was intent as he pulled back and murmured, 'I cannot teach you the lesson I have in mind until some time tomorrow. You will be taken to my apartments to wait for me. These cords will serve as a visible reminder of your submission.'

His fingers were at her throat. Annabel's arousal grew as the fine black bond slipped around her neck. Its gentle black touch was heavy with implication. Wetness pooled between her legs. Her breathing was shivery and unstable. She looked up at Nakano with arousal mixed with shame.

He reached out and flicked first one, then the other taut, crinkled pink nipple.

One touch had never affected her so strongly before. She had not known that a nipple could feel pleasure as strongly as a clitoris.

His voice was deep and sensuous. 'Will you enjoy waiting for me, Annabel san?'

She knew that he could read the answer from the stiffness of her nipples, the betraying sexual flush that stained her body red, the helpless submission of her posture. She could not answer him. She only looked at the ground, and now and then her eyelids flickered closed as she tried to hide from him.

She heard a soft laugh above her. The words were so soft she could almost have imagined them. 'I mean to insist on a true answer when I begin your punishment tomorrow.'

Nakano turned away and Annabel stared at the stiff silk wings of his formal kimono. The style of the outfit made him look large, imposing, frightening even, as he spoke to the referee, congratulating him as if the master of ceremonies had choreographed the whole thing and Kiku and Annabel were nothing.

She closed her eyes again. Her emotions roared around her body. Sexual arousal predominated. Nakano's touch had roused her to a pitch of sensuality far above normal. She was also afraid: afraid of him, afraid of the strength of her feelings.

The thin black cords burned into her naked flesh as she listened to Nakano's parting words. 'Excellent match,' he said once more. 'And remember that the barbarian is to wait in my chambers for her punishment.'

Chapter Nine

*A*nnabel was still thinking about what Nakano had said as she sat staring into space late the next afternoon. From the balcony of his austere apartment it was possible to look out over the fragile timber and rice-paper buildings of the town, out over the massive fortifications of stone and earthwork that protected all who looked to Shimoyama, and right out across space to the lines of jagged grey mountain peaks that lay in wrinkled grey folds against the soft grey sky.

So much grey! It was not actually raining, but the air was damp, warm and moist on Annabel's naked skin as she turned away from the window and cast herself on to the heap of new-smelling futons that lay in one corner of the tatami room. She had been told that the rains would finish soon, to be replaced by the heat of summer. People seemed to fear summer, but Annabel liked the warmer air that was soft on her skin as she lay in the bedding in all her naked glory.

Naked except for the thin black cord that bound her wrists and circled her neck in an overwhelming contrast of the innocent and the erotic. Annabel looked down at the fine black thongs. They were made of very thin strips of plaited material and each cord was about as thick as a whiplash. It was impossible not to feel aroused when she saw such concrete evidence of Nakano's dominance over her, and there was never a moment in the day when she didn't.

She rolled over on to her front, pushing her loosely plaited hair over one shoulder, feeling the crisp white bedding crackle beneath her. Her hands drifted down the length of her body. Her fingers twined in the springing locks of her pubic hair and just rested on the very beginning of her slit. Should she bring herself to climax once more? Last night, after the servants had left her alone in Nakano's apartments, she had been unable to resist. But masturbation did nothing to fill the incredible emptiness of her vagina, the terrible yearning for something she couldn't even name that filled her soul.

With a groan, Annabel buried her head in the pillow. The hard dry beans inside it rustled as they moved, but they could never rearrange themselves enough to be comfortable. It was hatefully foreign and unyielding. Annabel sat up and grabbed the pillow furiously. 'This country makes me so angry!' The words sprang to her lips unbidden as she hurled the horrid thing across the hay-coloured matting.

The pillow hit the ground with a dull thump just before a rice-paper screen. The screen slid open. Annabel's vision was blurred with tears, but she expected to see the startled face of a servant or guard looking in. Instead, with a shock that unbalanced her whole system, she saw the imposing figure of Nakano striding through the open shoji and penetrating into the room.

'What do you want?' she snapped. She put her hands up to her face in order to dash away the tears from her eyes, and once more she saw the black cords that bound her. The sensual heaviness nagging between her legs became hot and her knees gave way.

Nakano stepped over the pillow without looking at it.

Annabel fell back a step as he drew closer. He was wearing an achingly clean white robe. His hair was a loose midnight fall down his back. Patches of bright red bloomed on each of his high cheekbones. His skin had a warm, moist glow about it, and Annabel knew he had been bathing. He was watching her face and her eyes. She tried to gauge his expression. He was uncomfortably close. Wariness began to snake through her. She wanted to snap at him again, to keep him away from her with words, but her voice failed her, and only her light rapid breaths fell from between her parted lips.

His deep male voice was harsh and forbidding. 'Angry again, Barbarian san?'

The disturbing note in his voice made Annabel lift her arms involuntarily to cover her breasts. The black cords that bound her snaked before her eyes. She turned away so that he wouldn't see her face.

Nakano looked earnestly down at her and lowered his voice as he continued, 'You are too wild! Too ungoverned in your temper. I must curb you, restrain you for your own good.'

Annabel couldn't look at him. She wished her hair was loose so that she could hide behind it. She felt his fingers just touching her lightly where the pulse in her throat fluttered beneath the hateful black symbol of her bondage. 'You need mastering, Annabel san.'

She looked at him then, her eyes filled with hatred, but he only laughed. 'Just so do my hawks glare at me, Annabel san, but they learn to submit, just as you will.'

Annabel strove to catch her breath. His deep smoky voice made her chest ache, made her sex melt. His size and power and arrogant sureness were making heat, and fear, and love, and hatred, course around her body in confusing waves of emotion. She looked up to his dark almond eyes, shivering with apprehension. She wanted him. Her world narrowed down. She desired him fiercely. Yet as he moved so close that her nostrils flared

159

in recognition of the subtle blend of musk and testosterone that was unmistakably his, she moved back away from him, and not forward into his arms.

'What are you looking so alarmed about?' He was watching her avidly. She shook her head, wordless, and he reached out and took each one of her black circled wrists in a hard grip. Annabel's thighs felt boneless, and she trembled all over as indescribable sensations floated around her body.

His big body went behind her, his movements very fast and sure. She felt his robe brushing against her naked skin and the disturbing heat of his male body pressing into hers. The grip on her wrists increased, intensified, and then fell away, but her wrists were now bound, caught up behind her in some manner she could not see.

She was helpless with her arms pinioned behind her. The shiver of reaction that went over her in response to this realisation bemused her, because it was pleasurable. Her reactions didn't come from her mind, but from her heart.

She stood trembling and confused with her head bowed. She felt the heat of Nakano's body shift as he walked around to stand in front of her. 'Head up, shoulders back, Barbarian san,' he ordered softly.

Annabel's eyes flew open in alarm, but she obeyed him. As she lifted her head and shoulders, her naked breasts moved up and forward, pointing out at Nakano, exposed to his view, begging him to touch them. His eyes fell to examine the hard, deep pink of her nipples against the creamy white curves of her exposed flesh, but he made no move to touch them and his eyes returned to her face. 'I still owe you a punishment, Annabel san,' he said, and his voice was disturbingly thick and hoarse.

Just hearing him say that to her, and knowing that he was almost certainly going to carry out his threat, affected Annabel deeply. Invisible energy pulsated around them. All she could do was shake her head while her knees trembled beneath her and her arousal grew uncontrollably. 'No,' was all she managed to whisper softly. 'No.'

But Nakano smiled and moved so close to her that she choked with emotion. He touched her now, taking her chin in gentle fingers, lifting her face towards his. The possessive, exclusively masculine movement set Annabel's heart hurrying in her chest. A coil of heat speared her like a pain as it rose from her thighs to her stomach, spreading sharply over her breasts. She could not look at him. She looked away. Her eyes flicked over to the window. She saw that the sun was setting, casting a warm pink glow across the room.

But she could not keep her eyes away for long. The strength of Nakano's personality drew her. She had to look back at him, and as their eyes met, she knew that he was understanding the emotion in her face. He knew how she was feeling, how unnerving she found the overpowering contrast between her female vulnerability and his superior strength, and he liked it. Male triumph gleamed in the darkness of his gaze as his body, all sinew and muscle, leant forward, and his lips gently forced her mouth open. She thrilled to his masculinity as he kissed her.

'Do you love me?' he asked softly, his breath warm on her lips, moving closer to her, so close that their hot bodies melted and flowed and became one.

'Yes.' Her admission was soft in the sunset-coloured room.

The dark head bent again, burying his hard mouth on hers before he pulled back to say, 'Do you want me to punish you?'

A surge of longing so strong that she felt dizzy sabotaged Annabel's attempts to answer him rationally.

Her voice was small and shaky, tight with emotion, as she replied helplessly, 'I don't know what I feel!'

Once again, Nakano looked into her eyes, searching for the answer. Annabel was trembling, suffocating with the weight of her desire as she stood naked with her hands bound behind her back, defenceless and disabled by her passion.

Nakano's gaze narrowed speculatively. 'I think that you do,' he murmured softly, before covering her open mouth with the strength of his lips. Annabel's desire to protest sank unheeded as he delved sensuously deeper. A soft moan rose to her lips and she pressed her body to his hot strong one, acknowledging by body language what she could not bring herself to say.

For a second longer, his masculine strength crushed her blindly, then Nakano pulled away. A pleased and sensual smile lifted the corners of his lips. He nodded at her with a scorching look of desire that burnt away all Annabel's reservations. 'You shall see how right it feels,' he promised softly, and then he turned away to call for the servants.

Annabel stood trembling in the dim room as they came in. None of the scurrying figures seemed to look at her directly, but she was sure that the swiftly working servants must be soaking up every detail, and that they would relay it to others later: how the barbarian stood naked in the Lord Nakano's apartments; how her yellow-gold hair fell in a long plait down her back; how her delicate white throat was encircled by a black mark of abasement, and how her hands were tied firmly behind her as a mark of submission.

She flexed her wrists against the cords. Her pulse pounded, echoing in her head, and yet her heated flesh and quivering blood had never felt so deeply carnal, so voluptuously aroused, so deliciously right.

The servants brought in, among other things, a low table, and propped up a cushion against it. Nakano made them tie the cushion securely in place. When he was satisfied that all was as he wished it he waved them away and turned to Annabel. 'Ready?' he enquired softly.

She saw with a hot surge of panic that he was holding a thin black cane. His expression was adamant. His eyes were merciless. He looked like the conquering warlord that he was.

'No.' But the word hung in the air exposed for the lie it was. Annabel might deny her feelings aloud, but she knew what she wanted as she gazed at his approaching figure.

He came to a halt, a little distance from her. The darkly sensuous expression on his face called forth a passionate response in Annabel that surprised her, and yet seemed so right that it annihilated her rational thoughts and allowed her to sink into the here and now. To be possessed only by the moment. To allow what would happen, happen without thinking about it.

She could barely hear Nakano's voice in the shadowy twilight that now filled his room. 'I want you to walk over to that table and bend across it, presenting your buttocks to me.'

Annabel bowed her head, as if in denial, but instinctively she knew that she was going to obey him. The incredible arousal of her body's response was too strong to be denied, to be fought against in any way. Slowly, slowly, almost wishing the world would come to an end first, she forced her trembling legs to cross the room.

She came to a stop by the table and stood looking down at it. She could see that, if she were to kneel down and lean across it, the cushion would protect her soft skin from the hard edge of the table. But could she willingly submit to Nakano's demands?

An agonising shyness held her in motionless indecision above the table. Yet her knees were already bending, and she felt as if she were possessed by something beyond her control as she slowly sank, first down on to the sweet tatami matting, and then, bending, across the cool surface of the table.

Her nipples contracted where they touched the polished lacquer surface. The table was black, but so covered with fine gold pictures that it appeared to be yellow. Annabel turned her head to one side and let her cheek rest on the lacquered top. She saw her breath mist the highly polished surface as she waited, trembling, for Nakano's next move.

'Spread your buttocks,' said Nakano, sounding implacable, yet warm and sexy, too.

Her bound wrists restricted her movement, but Annabel shuffled her weight around and spread her knees more widely apart. Her belly sagged down into the softness of the cushion. She felt the purse of her sex swing free as her buttocks pointed up towards Nakano. Her body was actually more comfortable in this position, but it was hard to breathe as her feelings of vulnerability, and excitement, grew.

A faint moan of breathless protest rose to her lips. The waiting was unbearable. She could sense Nakano above her. He seemed to be just standing, looking at her as she lay spread out below him, bound, naked, waiting and helpless.

The pause was aphrodisiac. Her arousal grew into the silence. Her belly felt hot and tight. The fleshy lips of her labia were stiff and hard, so engorged with blood that they felt shiveringly heavy, twice their normal size. The humming bead of intensity that nestled between them was abnormal too; her clitoris had never been provoked into such rapturous erotic responses before. Her body took charge of her mind and banished her last feeble denials. She was all open sexuality, all waiting submissive female.

Tremors of anticipation ran over her body when she finally heard the swish of a thin cane slicing the air behind her. The sinister noise came again, and once more, warning her of what was to come, but as yet nothing touched her.

'Now your punishment begins,' said Nakano. There was a note in the caressingly deep voice that disturbed her more than the first blow, hot though that was when it fell. Her buttocks jerked under the lash. Then the anticipation began again.

After a long moment of time, the second stroke fell across her trembling flesh. She felt nothing for a second, and then, after the pressure, a hurting, burning sensation that followed the line of the second welt that now flared across her buttocks.

Sweat dewed her forehead as she waited trembling for the next blow.

As the third stroke seared her outer body, Annabel felt an inner explosion rise to meet it. She felt incredibly alive, so aware of every sensation. The red hot burning sensations spread out and coalesced, turning all the skin of her bottom into one expanse of shivering, tormented, pleasurable feeling.

'Your buttocks, so pure, so creamy,' mused a soft voice above her. 'I like to watch the colour change. I love to see your skin turn red.' His voice drifted off and he didn't say anything for a long time, he just stood behind her holding the whip.

Annabel's body trembled all over with involuntary, but conflicting movements as she lay below him. Her rational mind wanted her to leap to her feet and run for her very life, but the primitive brain that seemed to be controlling her now wanted to die; wanted to just give in and surrender, spread out her legs and offer her sex in complete capitulation to the dark figure who was mastering her so completely.

Annabel's buttocks burned and burned again. The fiery stripes hurt more now than they had when Nakano had delivered them. So why did they feel so good? She squirmed and groaned beneath him, driven beyond rational thought by the intensity of her arousal.

She felt his cool fingers drifting over her buttocks. It felt insanely good to have those burning, fiery globes touched. Her internal muscles clenched. Moisture ran the length of her dark vaginal tunnel and dripped from the opening. She could feel it slicking her thighs; smell the distinctive perfume of her own sexual secretions. Without warning, her whole bottom lifted up from the table and wriggled at Nakano in blatant invitation, offering herself for his penetration.

Annabel thought she should die from the shame of her wantonness, yet the words that drifted to the surface and drifted out over her swollen sensitive lips were, 'Please! Oh, please! I want you so!'

He was still behind her. Still running those tormenting, tantalising cool fingers over the flesh of her violated behind. And then he stopped. Time drew out in an infinity of black waiting as Annabel tensed herself, waiting for his crop to fall.

This time there was no preliminary warning swish of the cane. This time there was only the blinding heat of the blows as they fell sharply across her already burning cheeks. Now Annabel cried aloud. The pain was so severe that tears sprang to her eyes.

Nakano stopped at once.

Annabel's limbs were so heavy. Her head was so light.

Now Nakano was bending over her, fondling her with clever hands that knew exactly where to touch, how to raise the greatest pleasure. His hands slid under her body, over her breasts, raising her slightly off the table as he pinched her erect nipples. 'It hurts,' cried Annabel, and then she broke off gasping, because her words were already a lie. His hands felt incredible as they firmly coaxed and teased and nipped and aroused her. Her breasts were heavy swollen mounds. Her nipples were tightly clenched with the intensity of her feelings, the sexuality of her response.

Nakano's hot body was heavy across her back. 'Do you want me to stop?' he whispered into her hair. His mouth was everywhere tasting, provoking, torturing. His teeth nipped, skimmed, nibbled, moving from her earlobes to the skin on the nape of her back. His breath on her hairline made her shudder as she melted under his touch.

'No! Don't stop.' The words were a breathless whisper. Annabel was a helpless prisoner of her own desire. He was so expert. He had the advantage. His mouth was hard enough to make his desires known as it moved across the silken flesh of her back. He took his hands away from her breasts and slid down her body so that his warm, wet tongue could run lovingly over the red welts that burned across her buttocks.

'Ha! You moan out loud! Do you acknowledge my mastery?' he asked as his fingers thrust between her thighs with devastating confidence. He unerringly found the overheated bead of Annabel's clitoris, pressing exquisite sensations from it with lazy insistence. 'Do you surrender? Are you mine?' his hoarse voice demanded, while all the time, his sure, masculine fingers stroked her clitoris with possessive, shuddering movements.

Annabel was silent. She was so close to her orgasm that she could not reply.

Nakano pulled away.

Her orgasm hung in the edge of the air. She was suspended, but without his touch she could not come. Annabel was breathless, strung so tight with need, that she felt as if she would burst through the boundaries of sanity if Nakano didn't end this madness soon.

'Say the words,' he insisted.

Annabel hesitated for one second longer and then she felt some last reserve or hesitation snapping deep within her. 'I do. I acknowledge you. You are my master.' Tears

167

welled up in her eyes as she whispered to him, but they were the cleansing tears of a sweetly felt emotion. She felt as if large and gentle hands had taken the cares of the world away from her shoulders as his hot heavy body returned to press down firmly, crushing her bound arms into her back. His lean hands parted her thighs. Thought became unnecessary as his strong fingers took her clitoris and manipulated it with practised skill.

Annabel need only exist. Let him take her to whatever heights of sexual expression that he would. She cried out in stunned awakening as his fingers conjured forth magical sensations, not just in her body, but in her mind. Nakano had cured something lonely and raw deep within her. He had found her rhythm. He had found the key to her sexuality. The mindless waves of her orgasm took her until she jolted against the ropes that bound her wrists and went limp against the table, breathing hard, feeling her breasts, her belly, her whole body, more sensitive than ever, because she wanted more, more of him than ever.

And now she felt the kiss of cold steel against her wrists and, although the dark cords Nakano had tied about them at the wrestling match remained, the new bonds that had been holding her arms imprisoned behind her back were gone. He had cut them away with his sword.

'Sit up,' said his firm voice.

She slid back from the table and on to her knees. Then she dared to turn around and face him. He stood above her, large, dark and arrogant, still holding the sword he had released her with. She looked up at him for a long moment, and then, finally, Annabel fell slowly forward in the exquisitely graceful, but totally submissive, full bow of the Japanese.

Her naked body felt pliant and sweet as she knelt with her forehead touching the mat at his feet. She could hear his light rapid breathing above her. He made a pleased sound deep in his throat, then she felt the air stir as he stepped forward. Another light touch, and her hair was unbound. She felt gentle fingers in the blonde mass as Nakano untwisted the braid she had fastened it in that morning. Her hair had been damp when she arranged it, and once the plait was undone, it formed rippling waves as it fell loose over her kneeling form and brushed the tatami matting below her.

Annabel heard fabric rustle as Nakano's robe fluttered down his body and pooled on to the hay-coloured flooring. Then she heard a faint chink as he put away his deadly sharp sword. Her buttocks burned as she waited, and her labial lips seemed to sag heavily, stretching open the entrance to her vagina. Desire sucked and pulled at her woman's muscles, yet all her earlier urgency had vanished. She was content, now, to wait, to allow Nakano to control the speed of their lovemaking, to mastermind their intercourse.

His firm hands tangled in her hair, lifting her up to face him as he knelt before her on the tatami matting. He leant slowly forward and kissed her. She didn't pull away, but her eyes were damp when the kiss had ended. There was something so simple about it, so elemental and close to nature. Nakano pulled back and examined her expression. She felt a little tremor of excitement run through him as he recognised her capitulation, her surrender to him as a male.

His deep voice reverberated in her heart as he said, 'Lie down on your belly.'

Moving easily now, as if everything that happened was pre-ordained, Annabel lifted herself and rolled over. She lay flat on her belly, her breasts pressing into the floor. She turned her head to one side. Her cheek lay on the tatami and she smelt its summery, haylike smell.

A hot mouth and wandering tongue licked at the burning marks on her bottom. Annabel's buttocks lifted off the tatami, straining towards the source of pleasure.

A hand slid into the crack between the cheeks of her buttocks. Annabel's head flew back. She shut her eyes and felt a languorous smile lift her lips. A single finger worked itself into her anus. A shock ran over her. A thrill both unpleasant and exciting in its intensity. She suddenly stopped trembling and lay still. The crinkled oyster of her anal opening clenched around Nakano's finger, immobilising it. He stopped moving. Only Annabel's breath still moved, only her heart still pounded.

Nakano seemed to raise himself from behind her and then he shifted his body, putting his knees between her thighs, lowering his chest on to her back. His belly was hot and round. His erection pulsed in the crack between her buttocks. She could feel his lungs heaving, his body shaking.

Annabel whimpered faintly and clenched her buttocks shut, as if to deny him access. But it was too late. There was already a finger inside her anal passage and her buttock cheeks closed down on the soft hardness of his manhood as it rubbed and stroked against her.

His lips burned into the nape of her neck and she melted and swooned under the exciting brush of his mouth and the soft tremors that his breath sent coursing down her spine.

Nakano took his finger out of her. Then he put his weight on his elbows and raised his chest. Then he slid his arms under her sides, reaching eagerly for her breasts. Annabel's upper body lifted quickly to allow him to fondle her breasts, and she recognised again how much she wanted him.

Her breasts dangled into the palms of his hands. His fingers stimulated her nipples. The rosy tips were hard and swollen, and pleasure radiated out from Nakano's touch.

His cock swelled in the crack of her buttocks as it grew stiffer and longer as he touched her breasts. Annabel felt his breathing grow quicker as he rubbed himself into the space between her buttocks. The first sweat dewed them both, misting their hot skin, acting like glue to join them even closer together. She whimpered again, and her buttocks unclenched themselves. The walls of her anus felt the invading finger once more, and they did not tighten again, even when Nakano pushed hard, inserting his finger right up her back passage as far as it would go.

'Draw up your thighs, little frog,' he instructed her, his voice a soft buzz in her hair. 'Make your *ana* an open door for me.'

Before she obeyed him, Annabel turned her head over her shoulders. The room was dark, dim and shadowy, yet she could see his face. She stared intently into his eyes. She needed to know how things were between them. She saw the passion that glazed his slanting bright eyes. She saw the dark intensity that was so much a part of him. And she also saw that he understood her once more. His words confirmed it. 'This is for you, Annabel san,' he murmured. 'This could only happen between you and me.'

Reassured, Annabel let herself drift bonelessly on to the mat. She felt a moan flow over her gently parted lips as her thighs splayed out beneath her. Nakano's body felt hotter and harder against her as he raised himself on to his knees. He balanced himself on one elbow and used his free hand to guide his manhood. As the tip of his organ nestled against the dark ring of her anus, Annabel cried out, in fright or ecstasy, she didn't know. The sensations that took her were too new, too intense, too frightening in their power to be clearly definable.

But it felt good, she knew that. The hard length of his penis sank deliciously into the measureless depths of her anus. His hard fingers clutched at her hips. The fingers teased and pinched and kneaded and she felt the beat of her clitoris speed up to match the beat of her heart as it pounded out its thrilling rhythm.

171

Nakano made another thrust and this time his cock sank so deeply that she could feel his balls pressing up against the sensitive lips of her labia. Fresh delight took her and she relaxed comprehensively, sinking against him. Deep ripples shuddered sleepily over the walls of her anus. Nakano held still, and so Annabel could distinctly feel herself as she milked him.

She felt hot drops of his sweat falling on to her back. Moved by an instinct she didn't understand, she changed her position, lifting herself up from the mat and lying on her elbows. She felt the curves of her buttocks pressing into his belly. She could hear his breath, hoarse and ragged above her. She could feel her own breath. Each rise and fall of her chest seemed to inflate her excitement. She threw her head back and felt sweat slide down her neck and pool in the curve under her breasts. The exhilaration of a pure and carnal appetite was good and deep and hot inside her. Her lips lifted in a smile that bared her teeth.

And now Nakano began to move. The quality of his breathing told Annabel that he was deeply aroused, that his orgasm could not be far away. She abandoned herself to pleasure, allowing his thrusts to sink deep within her anus, accepting his strange invasion as right and natural.

Nakano's dark head bent low over hers and their locks of hair tangled in a flow of midnight black and silver moonlight. She felt air hissing from between his lips, and her buttocks slapped up into his groin as he thrust and pounded into her. And yet, thrilling as the experience was, she felt her climax eluding her.

The anal stimulation was slower, deeper than the clitoral stimulation she was used to responding to sexually. The seductive sensations that fanned out from her anus and spread out from there over her body, gave Annabel a lovely, heavy, leaden sensual feeling, as if languorous honey flowed in her veins, and trickled over her sexual organs; but she didn't feel orgasmic – until

Nakano's heavy body shifted, and with a grateful melt-ing sweetness, she felt his cool masterful fingers sinking into the longing depths of her woman's place.

Her velvety internal muscles closed hard on his fingers and the unfamiliar sensation of the penis in her back passage pushing up against the fingers in her vagina overwhelmed her and the longed-for climactic sensations approached swiftly.

Nakano kept his movements slow and steady, allow-ing Annabel to concentrate on her internal rhythms. She could feel her excitement rise. She let herself fall into the flow of the rippling, heady current Nakano's fingers were creating inside her. And then she felt her orgasm start. It began in small, fairly tame flutters at first, but the delicious wavelets of sensation grew stronger as they pressed lovingly against the brutally hard cock that invaded her back passage.

Annabel could have lingered at that point for ever, experiencing only the meltingly sweet pleasure of her first anally induced orgasm. But, as Nakano felt her begin to climax, he stepped up his own movements, plunging deeply into the open passage of her anus, grunting with each movement, sweating hard, urging her to join him with hoarse, half-muttered cries.

For a moment Annabel shrank away from the hardness of his limbs and the power of his thrusts, but then her passion burst forth to match his. Annabel felt her orgasm come back more strongly and blast into the depths of her being. She too cried out. A gorgeous muscled feeling began at the root of her vagina. It spread out with triple intensity as it wrapped around the cock in her anus and the fingers in her vagina and the hot heavy body pressed into hers. The ecstatic feeling spiralled out from her centre and rushed out to cover both her and Nakano in a hot black cloak of sensation. Their two bodies seemed to hang in mid-air, yet she could feel the balls of her feet pressing into the ground, and she was aware of her toes curling and curling into the soft matting beneath them as she pulsated and drowned against Nakano.

She felt a perfect union take their sweating naked bodies. His arms wrapped under her body and pressed her tightly all down his naked front as the waves of deliciously carnal lust tightened and let go, tightened and let go, and the searing flow of his ejaculate was matched by the hot honeyed flood of her own.

For a few moments they clung together, their breathing gradually slowing. Annabel felt cold air on her skin. She cried out as Nakano's hot body left her. He had only gone for a futon. He was back within seconds, shaking out the heavy bedding in its sparklingly white case, spreading it tenderly, encouraging Annabel to roll on to its crisp surface and into his arms.

She lay clinging to him as if she would never let him go, not for a moment nor a lifetime. Nakano gently touched her neck. His fingers were so delicate, despite their strength and hardness. Annabel pulled away a little and smiled at him. Then he slid an arm around her waist with a possessive, satisfied expression.

Annabel rested her head against his shoulder. The smell of their sex was heavy in the air. She felt soft and deliciously satiated. There was a glorious sticky sensation between her legs, and her limbs were sweetly languorous. She felt as if she had been using her body the way she was meant to. An aftershock jolted around her body and tingled in her clitoris as she closed her eyes and thought of how wonderful it had been.

Some time later, his deep voice aroused her. She blinked sleepily. Moonlight spilled through her lashes. She opened her eyes fully. The far wall of the room was open, the shoji pushed fully back. She could clearly see the big silver moon riding high in the sky over the jagged tops of the distant mountains. The sky was velvety black. The room was warm. A pile of crisp bedding lay unused next to them. She had no need of it lying within the circle of his arms. She looked up and gave him a trusting smile. 'Annabel san, Annabel san,' he said softly, looking down at her solemnly. 'I had not expected such complete capitulation from you, my little barbarian.'

Annabel's head swam dizzily as he kissed her. She snuggled her body into his, and bit him gently. 'Oh, there's plenty more fight in me,' she teased.

He looked at her in silent appreciation, smoothing her hair with absent fingers. Something in his absorbed expression worried Annabel. 'Isn't everything all right now?' she asked.

He looked rueful as he kissed her full on the lips. She strained towards him eagerly. His kiss was tender, and passionate, and there was a great sadness and longing in it, too, so that Annabel was half prepared for the words when he raised his head and sighed on a long breath, 'No, indeed. The wind will blow over many battlefields before everything will be all right.'

He looked down at her sadly and then away, towards the open shoji. Annabel waited silently, listening to her breath, feeling her pulse. She did not know what thoughts could be making his face so heavily pensive as he stared out through the gap in the rice-paper screens and over the mountains. A cock crowed lustily and then another one. At first Annabel thought they were calling at the wrong time, crying in the night as cockerels sometimes do, but then she heard the deep-toned temple bell.

Nakano stirred as if he were recalling his thoughts from a great distance. 'I must leave you soon,' he said, softly, almost sadly, but then in a louder voice he called out, 'Bring tea!'

There were faint movements in the corridor outside, and almost at once, a screen slid open and shadows flickered over the walls as a servant entered holding a candle and bearing a lacquer tray.

The servant bowed deeply before approaching. Then

she came close to where their two bodies lay tangled in the futons and placed the tray on the floor. Reflected in its black surface was an elegant teapot decorated with bamboo leaves and two matching cups. A thread of steam came from the teapot. An open fan lay on the tray. White blossoms trembled on top of the fan.

Nakano reached over to the tray and picked up one of the blossoms, handing it to Annabel to smell. Crystal beads winked on the faintly veined petals. 'It is jewelled with the morning dew,' said Nakano.

Annabel buried her nose in the cool dampness of the flower. Its perfume was faint, wild and sweet. She was aware of birds singing outside in the dark rainy dawn. Nakano blew out the candle, and as the yellow light left the room, the first grey light of dawn crept in to replace it.

Nakano's dark head bent gravely over the tray. He handed Annabel one of the delicate, handless cups. Green tea filled about two thirds of the cup: hot, steaming, bitter and utterly ambrosial. The scented liquid ran over Annabel's tongue in a delectable flow. Annabel had never really cared for green tea before, finding it thick and bitter, but now, as its tart stimulation made her feel alive and invested the morning with significance, she suddenly acquired a taste for it that was to stay with her all her life.

'Thank you for the tea,' said Annabel, staring into her cup. She said it awkwardly, almost as if she was speaking to a stranger, not her lover, but once more she was aware of the distance between them.

Nakano drained his own cup and put it on the tray. He unwound his long limbs from hers and stood up, looking down at her. 'There is a war council called for dawn,' he said more to himself than to Annabel. 'And I still do not know what answer I shall return. I had hoped that a night's delay would clarify the matter, but I am

176

still no nearer to deciding whether Yoritomo is to be trusted or not.'

'Yoritomo?' asked Annabel, sitting up and looking at him.

'You met him at the fishing village. He begs my permission to bring his army through my domain, he says to wage war upon my neighbour, but am I to trust him?'

Annabel remembered the samurai in the blue robe and his sadistic fingers picking at her breasts. She shivered. And then she thought of the traitorous members of Nakano's party and the conversation she had overheard at the bathing pools in the village.

'You do have enemies,' she said, and then stopped, recalling Hiroko's fear of reprisals. She would not wish to bring trouble upon the woman who had sheltered her, befriended her, taught her so much about Japan.

Nakano turned to Annabel, raising an eyebrow, motioning her to continue.

'I was bathing alone, at the pool in the fishing village,' began Annabel, hoping that her lie would shield Hiroko from any repercussions. Quickly she told the frowning Nakano how she had heard the men plotting, and referring to their 'real master'.

For a fraction of a second he didn't respond. He glanced down at the floor and then he looked at her sternly. 'Would you recognise them again?'

'No. I didn't really see their faces properly. I was hiding behind a rock, and there was steam rising from the pool.' She glanced up at him, worried. His eyes were full of suspicion.

Nakano's voice was stern and angry. 'It was your duty to tell me as soon as you overheard the men plotting. Why did you not do so?'

'I had not met you. I did not know if I owed you duty or not,' protested Annabel, but she was uncomfortably

177

aware that by the laws of Japan she had owed him her absolute obedience.

Nakano looked at her keenly. 'There is a lie in your eyes,' he said thoughtfully.

'No,' whispered Annabel, trying not to look at him.

She saw Nakano's eyes go hard. Then his brows drew together in a furious line. His icy voice seared her soul. 'I had thought you tamed, Barbarian, and loyal to me only.'

Annabel closed her eyes against his powerful glare. 'I am loyal to you,' she protested weakly. The tears were running down her cheeks. She could feel the weight of Nakano's gaze. His fury. She did not dare tell him about Hiroko now. She was afraid of his reaction. She could only open her eyes and gaze at him imploringly, willing him to trust her.

Nakano stood in front of her for a moment longer, holding her eyes, their gaze locked. His inspection displeased him. Annabel felt the secret she could not tell him as a barrier between them, and he sensed it too. 'It appears that your loyalties are divided,' he said eventually, half turning away. 'You shall be taken to the public cage.'

Annabel stared at him in utter amazement, unable to speak at first, and then slowly she went pale. 'The bamboo cage in the marketplace? For everyone to see? As if I were a common whore?' She felt as if one of Nakano's swords had been run through her solar plexus.

His head turned back over his shoulder and his eyes scoured her flesh. 'Naked for all to see and treated like a whore while the public look on.' His eyes were very dark. 'I think you will enjoy the experience.'

'What makes you say that?' asked Annabel, half fainting.

'The way you responded to my whipping.'

Thrills shuddered over her entire body, because she knew exactly which of her sexual responses had stirred

178

the lustful memories dancing in his eyes. 'But that was just you and me,' she reminded him. Her eyes searched his face for understanding.

'This is just for me, too,' he pronounced, his voice very deep and final. 'I will have you tamed and obedient or I will not have you at all.'

'I am true to you, I promise. There is no need to treat me so.' Unthinkingly, Annabel reached out a hand to touch him.

Nakano pulled away. 'Why not? I'll make certain that you enjoy it.'

'No!' cried Annabel.

Nakano turned his back on her pleading face and called for two guards. He would not look at her again. He turned away and pretended to busy himself with his clothing. He kept his back turned as he snapped out orders to the guards. He didn't even turn his face to Annabel when the two huge samurai grasped her upper arms and marched her out of the room.

Chapter Ten

*T*he three tawdry courtesans in the corner of the cage, who were stooped over a game played with painted shells, ignored Annabel's timid overtures of friendship. Repelled by their hostility, Annabel turned away. She moved to the back of the bamboo cage and sat down on the worn and frayed tatami that covered the floor.

The cage of the courtesans was set slightly forward, in front of the gap between a seaweed shop and a poulterer's. A large clump of growing bamboo rustled in the alleyway between the two shops. The sky was bright blue above its green leaves. The graceful stems hung over the cage at the back, giving an illusion of shelter and protection. Leaf shadows danced on the floor in the sunlight. Annabel turned her head away from the painted whores, who were squabbling over their game, and looked into the poultry shop.

Geese, ducks and hens clucked mournfully within tiny cages made of yellow bamboo. Annabel stared at the shop curiously. There had been fish, of course, in Hiroko's village, but even in Shimoyama she had never been given meat. She had thought no one in Japan ate the flesh of any animal, but this shop suggested otherwise.

At the front of the shop was a butchery area at street level. The poulterer, a cheerful-looking chap with a blue spotted scarf tied firmly around his head, was brandishing a large chopper over the neck of an unfortunate duck. Annabel winced and looked away as the chopper fell – but she still heard the thud.

The poulterer's three customers, a small boy, a bald man wearing the dark robe of a scholar over a plain kimono, and a servant carrying a basket, stood waiting patiently while the poulterer stripped the now limp duck of its feathers. They took no notice of Annabel at all, and she began to wonder if she might wait out the period of her imprisonment without further humiliation.

An old farmer trotted by, stooped under his burden of long white radishes. One of the game-playing harpies called out a derisory remark. Hot blood stung Annabel's cheeks. She was ashamed to be in such company. She was glad that the ancient countryman ignored the insults. His wrinkled face did not change, but she thought she saw a gleam of disgust in his eye as he went past.

She buried her head in her hands. Why had Nakano done this to her? They seemed to be so close, so bound by transcendental ties when they made love, but then came the separation: their different sexes, their different cultures, their different lives. She knew nothing of the politics he was embroiled in, but she knew that he had enemies, and that now he seemed to count her as one of them.

Hot salt dripped down the back of Annabel's throat as tears welled in her eyes. She put her head down on her knees and rocked miserably for a few moments. Then she sniffed hard and lifted her head, dashing the tears away. She would not despair. Being soft wouldn't help her at all. Enemies could be made into friends. She had proved that with Kiku.

The Japanese girl had been astounded when Annabel

had been dragged into Mamma san's quarters by two huge samurai. Unmoved by their size and ferocity, she had flown at them, scolding roundly, until they had let her take Annabel for a bath, comb her dishevelled hair into an elegant arrangement, and dress her in the plain yellow kimono she now wore.

There was nothing Kiku could have done that would have prevented the samurai from carrying out the Lord Nakano's orders and taking Annabel to the cage, but even as Annabel wiped away the last of her tears, a servant she recognised from the keep came pattering across the sunlit cobbled square of the town, carrying a lacquer tray.

'From Miss Kiku,' said the little maid brightly as Annabel rose to meet her. The tray would not slide between the bars of the cage, but the maid passed in the bowls of food, one by one. Annabel lifted the lacquered lids. Her mouth watered as she saw a fluffy mound of soft white rice, a divine-smelling miso soup with clam shells rattling in the bottom of the dish, a selection of pickled vegetables and a sweet pink rice cake. There was even a flask of boiling green tea.

Annabel picked up her chopsticks with a much lighter heart. 'Thank Miss Kiku,' she said warmly. 'Please tell her how very happy her gift has made me.'

The maid nodded. Black eyes twinkled over her rosy cheeks. 'Yes, honourable Barbarian,' she said. 'I will tell Miss Kiku your message.' She skipped off across the cobbled square, swinging her tray gaily in the sunshine.

Annabel took the first mouthful. Salty fish eggs exploded on her tongue. Her belly growled, and she began eating quickly. She attacked the sour pickles eagerly and then drained her soup. The sun was very high in the clear blue sky. It must be nearly midday, and she hadn't eaten properly since midday of the day before. Through nerves, she had been unable to eat the food provided while she waited for Nakano after the sumo match. Now she was starving.

She finished up the last grain of sticky white rice, then stacked the bowls neatly by the edge of the cage before sitting down again, choosing the cleanest spot on the worn matting. Her tender buttocks flared as she put her weight on them and an aftershock zinged over her. She was still sore from the whipping. Her body felt liquid and sensual when she thought of the man who had marked her.

It was warm. Annabel lifted the fan Kiku had given her and wafted it idly, enjoying the air movement. Insects shrilled soporifically in the bamboo behind her. The rustling shadows danced in hypnotic leaf patterns before her eyes. Annabel was asleep.

A heavy thump followed by raucous cries awoke her. The insects still shrilled and the air was still warm, but the bamboo-patterned shadows had moved quite a distance over the floor of the cage. The hard sunlight had softened and mellowed, so that Annabel knew it was late afternoon.

'Hey, hey, my little pussy-cats,' yodelled a cheeky male voice. 'The rich banker Takatoshi is having a party. He commands us to fetch him some plump little dovies. Who's coming to his party?'

The whores squealed in delight and began scrabbling for their combs, purses, fans. Annabel sat up. Two rough, well-muscled characters with tattoos on their backs and shoulders stood laughing by the bars of the cage. They wore loin-cloths and head-cloths and nothing else. Behind them was a very plain palanquin, suspended from a long bamboo pole so that they could carry it between them.

'Hey! hey!' shouted one of them when he saw Annabel lurking at the back of the cage. 'Are you coming to the party, my little actress?'

Ice-cold blood thumped into her heart. Was this what

being in the cage meant? That any who wished to satisfy their carnal lusts could send for her, and that she had to go?

'Don't be an idiot!' snapped one of the whores. 'This is no actress. It is the Lord Nakano's barbarian. He is said to be angry with her, but we don't know yet if he has cast her off. You would be a fool to meddle with her.'

Annabel nearly fainted with relief. She was safe then, for a little while longer.

'A real barbarian!' Both men pressed against the cage, lifting their faces to see better. 'Nobody told us, and we've just come from the temple. It's like a barracks at the moment, there's so many men camping there. I can't believe those horny samurai don't know there's a barbarian in the cage.'

'Barbarians are ugly and boring,' snapped the oldest of the prostitutes, scrambling through the now-open door of the cage and down to street level.

'Why look at the savage when you've real women to deal with?' added another, patting her hair as she descended.

'And a fare to make,' remarked the third, tapping one still-staring porter on his shoulder with her fan. 'I don't think you weaklings are up to carrying three women between you. Far better we send for another chair.'

The porters turned away from Annabel at once. 'What? And split banker Takatoshi's fare?'

Satisfied to have the attention returned to them, the women piled into the chair, pushing and giggling as they squeezed on to the shabby check cushions. Annabel could see a butterfly sash poking out of one side of the chair, and an arm holding a fan out of another. The three elaborately coiffed heads bent closely together, then fell apart in a fresh burst of giggles.

The porters grunted, balanced the pole on their shoulders, grunted again and straightened their knees, lifting the laden chair from the ground. Their walk was not quite straight as they strained under the heavy chair, labouring towards the outskirts of the town.

It was very peaceful when they had gone. Annabel sat in the warm afternoon sun, listening to the trilling insects, the rustling bamboo and the crooning of the poor doomed poultry. The shops were still open, but it was obviously a quiet time of day. Few customers were about. Few people stirred, yet Annabel was not surprised when only an hour later, the first pair of soldiers appeared outside the cage.

They stared up at her as if she were a caged tiger: unusual, fascinating, possibly deadly, and with no human understanding whatsoever. A few more samurai drifted up to join the first two. Annabel sat quietly, her eyes closed as if she were meditating, just peeping at them through her lashes. She thought that perhaps if she did nothing, they would grow bored and move away, but the samurai pushed and jostled in front of the cage, staring at her, and a few more men appeared to join them.

'It's fake, that gold hair. Made out of straw or some such,' pronounced one samurai with great authority. 'I said, when they told me about a so-called barbarian wrestling at the sumo, it will be fake, I said. Look at that hair! Straw! No doubt about it.'

'What about its skin, then?' demanded another man. 'Look how pure and white it is. That's not fake skin.'

'It's sick,' offered a third. 'Or it's a freak of nature. I saw a rat that was born white once, red eyes it had, like little rubies.'

'You make things up, you do. No, the thing is too big to be a sick woman. I reckon as it's a fella, dressed up. Like them Kabuki actors.'

'Here, let me find a stick. I'll poke it. Wake it up, like.'

'Yes, and then you'll see its eyes and you'll know I'm right.'

'Hear it yelp in a man's voice, you mean. Where's a blasted stick?'

'Have a few stones instead. That will shake it up.'

Annabel's eyes flew open. She had no idea what she could do or say, but anything was better than sitting still while they stoned her. She rose to her feet and moved gracefully to the front of the cage. 'Good evening, gentlemen.'

They fell back astounded. The numbers had grown. There were perhaps twenty men now, exclaiming:

'Blue eyes!'

'Round! Round eyes! Did you ever see the like?'

'It's a woman, all right.'

'A gaijin. An outside person.'

'Where do you think it's from?'

Annabel now saw that these soldiers looked nothing like Nakano's smooth and matching guard. They wore garments of different hues. Some were faded, patched. Many had bare places on their kimono, where the insignia showing which lord they served had been torn away. They were all neatly groomed, though, and smelt of soap and discipline.

Fragments of information flew into place, and she knew that these men, although samurai, were masterless, and so without an income. They roamed the country, getting their living as they may, sleeping where they could.

'Are you hoping to join the Lord Nakano's army?' she asked.

The samurai at the back of the crowd pushed and shoved, asking each other, 'What did it say?'

'Don't be silly!' joked a few more. 'Barbarians don't talk! They grunt.'

But a young man standing very close to the bars of the cage, raised his proud open face towards Annabel and answered her quickly. 'Why yes. We hear that he is

186

planning a campaign. Do you know how many men he might be needing?'

The young samurai's cheekbones were sharp in his face, and looking at the slenderness of his neck and wrists, Annabel guessed times had been lean for him recently. She raised her fan to her face. 'I cannot tell you my Lord Nakano's plans,' she said sweetly.

'But you know something?' questioned the young man eagerly.

Annabel peeped at him over the top of her fan. His slanting black eyes locked with hers. She could see a tiny reflection of herself in one dark pupil. Her eyes were very sparkling, round, blue and bright. She gave him a mysterious feminine smile. She knew nothing, less than these men, probably, about Nakano's plans, but no way was she going to admit it. She now had a possible way to control the situation, and she was quick to exploit it.

'I can tell you nothing of my lord's plans,' she said again. 'But perhaps I could tell him about any fine soldiers I might happen to meet.'

The young man's eyes blazed with hope and exultation as he looked at her. 'Oh, my sweet lady –' he began, but behind him a loud voice broke in:

'Hey! I hear there's a foreign tart in the cage! Let's get its clothes off! I've always wanted to see one of these gaijin whores naked.'

The biggest samurai Annabel had yet seen pushed to the front of the cage. There were about fifteen men following the leader of the pack. They looked as if they had seen better times, just as the other masterless samurai did, but they also looked well-fed, in a rough, lawless, kind of way, and Annabel remembered that some were said to have taken to robbery in order to survive.

They terrified her. She knew instinctively that these men could not be managed, twisted around her feminine wiles. Too much of their humanity had been stripped away as they fought to survive. They had the flat black eyes of ocean sharks. Merciless, predatory thugs.

The soldiers pressing around the cage gave way to the newcomers without argument, except the slim young man who had been talking to Annabel. He refused to fall back. He turned to face the newcomer, and bowed to him politely. 'This is the first time we have met,' he said formally.

The big man was still for a moment, and Annabel was suddenly worried. Swords glinted in the sunshine. She could sense wariness all around her, and hear faint movements as all the watching men instinctively shifted their stance or rearranged their clothing so that their weapons could be drawn instantly. But then the big man bowed, and completed the ritual. 'This is indeed the first time we have met.'

Annabel saw the evil in the thug's eyes as he raised his head, and she wanted to scream a warning to the young man who stood so bravely protecting her, but nothing showed on her face. She felt her heart thudding in her chest, and a drop of ice water trickled down her spine. The bamboo bars looked so fragile. The door wasn't even locked. The bamboo cage was a symbolic enclosure rather than a real one. It offered no protection.

Annabel saw the thug's eyes go blank as he enquired politely, but very dangerously, 'Are you establishing a prior claim on the barbarian, young man? Because I must tell you, that now I have seen how fabulous she is, the desire to see her naked overwhelms me.'

Annabel's protector bowed low. 'Excuse me, honourable sir, perhaps you were not aware that this is the Lord Nakano's barbarian.' He spoke calmly, but Annabel could see how quickly his chest rose and fell.

A faint glimmer of contempt enlivened the outlaw's flat eyes. 'And so you hope to curry favour? Well, I've had enough of the fine lords and their promises. I no longer feed at the hands of the rich.' He paused though, and Annabel could see that for all his bluster, the name of Nakano had shaken him.

But she could also see that it was too late now. The giant samurai had taken a stand, and if he were to back down, then he would lose face in the eyes of his men. He would fight and die willingly rather than lose face, all samurai would. She bit her lip and chewed frantically, trying to think of some way out of this impasse.

The huge man continued, 'Oh, Nakano may be playing some sexy game, but if he's thrown his mistress into the common cage, then, technically, she becomes common property. I am free to act as I want. And what I want is to see the fabulous barbarian's naked body.'

Time seemed to stretch out as Annabel glanced around. The crowd had swelled, but it was very clear that none of them would interfere. In fact, they were moving back out of the way as the eyes of her young protector and the huge outlaw samurai met each other with an almost audible click. They were doing battle with their minds before drawing their swords, psyching up the atmosphere so that the air around them seemed to glow and flex with hostility.

Annabel's mind worked swiftly. The outlaw samurai leader had only expressed a wish to see her naked. If she granted him that, then his honour would be satisfied, and he could back down without the situation exploding into violence.

'Wait!' she said clearly. It was nearly too late. The two warriors were so deep in their mental combat that she had to call them again to get their attention.

Annabel half-turned her back on the men, smiling flirtatiously at them over her shoulder, because she knew that the Japanese male considered the nape of the neck the sexiest part of the human body, and, at the back, the neckline of her primrose-coloured kimono dipped low to expose the pale skin there.

'If you'll stop being so silly,' she called to the outlaw,

'I might, just might, consent to show you a little of what you fancy.' Her voice shook, and there was a horrible trembling in her knees. She had never felt less seductive in her life, but she pouted her lips and whispered sexily to the big man, 'I thought you said you wanted to see my naked body?'

It was working. The danger was fading away. He was on leave, in between battles. His mind was hungry for love rather than war. He turned away from the young man, bowed to Annabel and said, 'More than ever, now that I hear you speak! Most fabulous of barbarians, might I not see you naked?'

His flat black eyes met hers, and she saw that he understood very well what she was up to, and that he had decided to accept her proposal. Yet she was still unsure enough of her reading of the Japanese mind to check their understanding. She whispered to him softly, privately, 'And if I strip for you, you'll return to your quarters? Seek satisfaction elsewhere?'

He bowed low once more. 'I had presumed no further,' he said.

Annabel relaxed. The danger of violence was over. She had won that battle. But she now had to keep her side of the bargain, and the crowd was growing.

More soldiers were arriving every minute. Informed by some telepathic sense that the time had come to hawk their wares, peasants selling sake and rice crackers were working the crowd. Annabel saw a few merchants, a gaily dressed courtesan or two, and three or four soldiers in Nakano's livery, but most of the fifty or so people who now pressed against the cage were masterless samurai.

The only way she could deal with the watching men was by blocking them out. At some level, part of her mind would always know that the samurai were there, hungering for her. She could hear their faint restless movements as their cocks hardened into pistons beneath

190

their robes as they watched her. She could smell the musk of their arousal as pheromones evaporated into the air. She could feel their eyes burning her skin. Eyes that were greedy and covetous; loving and longing; lustful and admiring; so many eyes.

She could never be unaware of the heady brew of emotions that emanated from the men who pressed forward so eagerly, yet she forced herself to ignore it. She pretended that she was alone, at home in England, preparing to climb into the oak four-poster bed that she had always slept in.

But then she decided that she was not quite alone. If Annabel had to give a striptease performance, she was feminine enough to want it to be a good one. She pressed her hands over her eyes for a moment, calming her mind, going more deeply into fantasy.

It would be dull to be alone in the bedroom she was picturing so clearly in her mind. No, somebody special was watching her. She imagined a window and a dark figure outside it. A man who had risked much to be there, but dared all because she was worth it.

Despite knowing that eyes were upon her, Annabel didn't worry about what she looked like, or about being sexy. A faint, and totally delicious warmth, was bursting softly in the glowing heart of her clitoris. The warmth imploded gently, and then spilled outward, rippling through her body. She concentrated on her own feelings and sensations. She abandoned herself so deeply to the spell of erotic pleasure that she was weaving, that no reaction from the crowd of watching men could break her sensual trance. No movement or sound could destroy the mood of sexual abandon that was upon her.

Annabel lifted languid white arms up to her hair. Kiku had lovingly arranged the blonde locks into an elaborate, formal, Japanese-style arrangement. Moving slowly, gracefully, deliberately, Annabel unpinned the flowers she found there.

She was moving as if she were fathoms deep under water as she lifted the half-open spray of white flowers to her lips and kissed it gently. A heady perfume rose from the warm blossoms. She didn't know what the flowers were called, but their waxy, half-open petals smiled up at her like the lips of lovers with secrets, and her own lips curved up in a dreamy answering smile.

She inhaled the wild, sweet perfume deeply once more, before tossing away the spray of blossoms. She heard a scuffle as the samurai fought for the flowers from her hair, but she blocked the noise out, and the bamboo bars of the cage solidified to become – in her mind – the walls of an English bedchamber. Yet despite her powerful illusion of aloneness, her nipples hardened and a tingle between her legs answered the erotic reality of her watchers.

Annabel tipped her head back, exposing the length of her throat and neck, in a graceful swanlike movement. She swallowed, and felt all the muscles move there. She parted her soft pink lips and opened them wide, swallowing again, imagining that a long length of penis pulsated between them. Her tongue came out and touched her lips in a reflex reaction to that erotic fantasy.

A tender, delicious ecstasy of excitement woke between her legs. Her woman's place melted, and the welts on her buttocks burned, reminding her that, soon, all would see the evidence of Nakano's carnal attentions.

Annabel retreated further into the abstract space and enclosed quietness of her mind. She lifted her white arms to the top of her head once more. The yellow silk of her kimono sleeves slid down her tender skin, exposing her bare arms, the soft curls of yellow hair that nestled in her armpits.

With deliberate, graceful movements, she inclined her head, first to the left, then to the right, teasing out the ivory combs that held her hair in place. There were three of these combs. Annabel ran gentle fingers along their

192

smooth surface, tracing the carvings that indented the backs of the combs. The carvings were ornate, realistic and yet highly stylised.

The first showed a dragonfly. Its jewelled eyes were filled with daytime dreams as it basked on a rock in the midday sun. Annabel raised the comb to her mouth and touched the pale surface with a kiss. The ivory was warm under her lips. Then she tossed the wonderful comb into the crowd. She was so deep in her dream that she hardly heard the resulting scuffle, or the shout of triumph from the outlaw.

The next comb depicted a frog. The carving had caught the beast at the moment of leaping into a water lily pond. Annabel kissed the comb, tracing the pattern of carved water drops with the tip of her tongue, before tossing it into the crowd. The hair ornament seemed to move through the air in slow motion, curving around to where the upstretched arms of her young champion waited.

And the last comb depicted a number of cranes, flying stretched out across an autumn sky. As Annabel threw the trinket out of the cage, she imagined Nakano flying towards her. She would magically sprout wings with fine pale feathers, and he would sweep her away over the wild and lonely mountains, and they would fly until they broke through the clouds and reached the round silver moon together.

His image brought a tender smile to her lips. As her blonde hair came loose and cascaded over her shoulders, she would have swopped the fifty or more full-throated male sounds of appreciation she heard outside the cage for just one – Nakano's.

But Annabel would not let her longing for Nakano unnerve her. Instead, she wove him into the fantasy she was spinning. She was the virginal maiden, innocently disrobing in her bedchamber. He was the dark invader, watching at her window. And she determined to please him.

Annabel ran her fingers through her blonde hair, combing it out with her bare hands. She lifted the heavy golden mass and let it fall again and again, knowing that, in Japan, her fine blonde hair was as unbelievable as her round blue eyes and pale skin. She made the most of its erotic attraction. The flaxen ripples tumbled over her shoulders. Annabel stroked and preened her soft hair with rhythmic movements, falling deeper into the illusion that she was displaying herself to only one man.

Moving with lingering sweetness, she ran her gentle fingers down to her waist, which was bound with a stiffly tied obi. Kiku had tied the yellow kimono with a sash of spring green. The yellow kimono was a simple cotton one, and the sash was knotted in an appropriately modest bow. Annabel had no difficulty in reaching behind her to untie it.

She undid the butterfly twist of green fabric very slowly. Then she repeatedly ran the willow-green fabric through the palms of her hands, examining the weave as closely as if there were poetry written on it, before finally smoothing the length of green material into a neat coil. She turned away from her audience to stow the discarded obi safely on the worn tatami matting of the cage.

But when she turned back to them, her kimono was now free of its bonds and falling loosely open by her sides. Annabel swayed gracefully, teasing, knowing that flashes of her creamy-limbed body were visible as she twisted and turned, dancing a few steps as she moved. Her feet brushed over the worn matting as she took a step back, one to the left, a step forward, one to the right.

The gentle swaying movements increased her feeling of being in a trance. Subtle feelings of expansion ran through her whole body as her sexual responsiveness grew. Still moving as if she were in a dream, erotic feelings of floating and lightness drifting over the surface of her skin, Annabel lifted her bare arms and slid the first layer of kimono over her shoulders and down to the floor. The primrose fabric lay crumpled on the rice straw surface.

Annabel stooped to her knees, aware of her diaphanous undergarment trailing loosely behind her. The fabric was so sheer that the flesh tints of her body must be clearly visible as she knelt over her lovely yellow kimono, patting it into shape, folding it as carefully as if she were a lady's maid.

As she bent, the cheeks of her buttocks burned in sharp and sensual flares. This morning, as she bathed, she had slipped her hands behind her and run the pads of her fingertips over the welts that slashed her backside. The lines of swollen flesh had felt oddly pleasurable under her gentle exploration. But she knew that her buttocks must be livid with savage crimson stripes.

Liquid gushed in the dark spaces of her vagina as she remembered how Nakano had marked her as his own. The material that was draped over her kneeling form was so thin that, by now, every single one of the watching men must be aware that Nakano had punished her last night. But then she wanted them to know. She wanted to show every man there that she was Nakano's.

The stinging of her buttocks made her feel gloriously alive. Her body was relaxed and comfortable. She was deliciously aware, moment to moment, of her muscles, her nerve endings, her skin. She was sensationally aware of her responses; how sexy she felt.

A wicked and saucy impulse made her alter her balance, tilting her buttocks out as she did so. The gossamer-fine fabric tightened over her cheeks and, from the sharply drawn breaths behind her, she knew that it had been most effective.

She rose to her feet again, keeping her back to the watchers. Slowly, oh so slowly, she slipped the fine gauzy layer of her undergarment over her shoulders, lifting first one shoulder-blade and then the other. The skin of her back was a creamy unblemished expanse, until it reached the sharp contrast of the red welts left by Nakano's lash.

She stood, exposed so, for a long moment. Then, gathering up the slipping spider webs of fabric over her breasts, she turned to face the spot where, in her fantasy, the dark watcher lurked behind her bedroom window. Her smile was dreamy as she teasingly rearranged the almost transparent cloth, still keeping her breasts hidden under the soft brush of fabric.

Every cell in her body was fresh and aroused. She let her eyes roll shut and her head tip back, exposing the length of her white throat. She closed her legs, rubbing her thighs together, trapping and intensifying the great good feelings that circled there. As she swayed in pleasure, fine shivers running over her body, anguished shouts broke out in the crowd:

'The barbarian orgasms!'

'She's going! She's going!'

'Oh! Beautiful sight.'

'How can I stand it? I must go with her!'

The voices were sympathetic, filled with passion and the longing to share her bodily experiences, but Annabel stopped moving. She lifted her head and stared at the samurai. Her illusion rippled and faded away. Dear God! There must be nearly a hundred people out there. She was struck by their alien faces and eyes, the uniformity of their difference from her. She was the foreigner here, the odd one out, and they were all watching her.

Annabel's breath caught in her throat and she felt a sour taste in her mouth as it dried. She was terrified. If only she hadn't looked at them. Her knees shivered beneath her. She gripped the fine gauze that floated over her pale shoulders with such trembling hands that it slipped and wafted to the floor, leaving her completely naked. Her heart fluttered and heaved, trying to escape out of her body along with her breath. She shook her head sharply and retreated behind her curtain of glossy blonde hair.

Her eyelids slid closed. Annabel wanted to retreat into the velvety blackness behind them and hide there for ever. But then courage came back to her. She would not hide. They were calling to her in appreciation. She was proud. Proud to be exactly the shape and size and race she was.

She tossed back the concealing veil of hair and lifted her chin. She lifted her pale white arms proudly above her head. She pulled in the sweet curve of her belly and pushed out her backside. Her ribs stood out sharply over her slim waist as she posed, naked and unashamed, the pink of her nipples thrusting in triumphant peaks towards the watching samurai.

A fierce exultation ran through her body. She lifted her arms even higher, and turned slowly above the crowd. She wanted them to see how tall she was, taller than any man save Nakano. She wanted to display her bright sapphire eyes and have everyone notice how open and round they were. She flaunted the impossible colour of her long yellow hair, the pinkness of her lips and nipples, and every inch of the pale bare skin that made her different. 'Here I am!' she cried loudly. 'I am the barbarian! I am naked and unafraid.'

Annabel felt her abdomen tighten and her buttocks clench. A subtle, non-specific flow of delicately sensual feelings ebbed and flowed around her body. She abandoned herself to their gentle pull. Her breath came quickly between her parted lips as she experienced the sweet sexual stirring. The waves of pleasure came faster now: rising and sinking, re-forming and tightening, before fading away, only to return with even greater insistence.

In those last few seconds before her orgasm, Annabel's

hands drifted into her slit, feeling between the blonde curls of pubic hair for the magic button of her clitoris. Her touch was shallow and fast, almost butterfly light. Chemical currents flowed around her body. Her belly twisted and tightened. Her knees bent dizzily as she swayed heavily.

All her deep, loose, easy feelings of pleasure swept up into a tight and viciously pleasurable hot knot of delight. Her breath rasped in her ears and she heard it whoosh out between her lips as the catherine wheel of her orgasm spun her into ecstasy.

Annabel let her body hang limply, and shudders ran over her as she slowly came back from the experience. Then a soft blow touched her flank. She flinched and trembled. An object grazed her bare arm. She struggled to understand: they were throwing things at her.

Another blow touched the curve of one breast. Her hands flew up to protect herself, and the next missile that whizzed towards her naked breasts went straight between her open hands, as if it had been aimed at them. She caught it reflexively, clasping her hands tight, then opening them wide to see what she had caught.

A crumpled red spot lay on one of her shaking palms. She trembled, the object moved, and with the shift in perspective, she recognised the round crimson shape for what it was: the perfect waxy bloom of a camellia.

They were throwing flowers at her. Flowers buffeted her slender body with soft little impacts. Flowers pattered to the ground around her feet. Flowers perfumed the air around her. Annabel plucked a yellow spring flower from the air and twisted it between her shaking fingers. She dropped her head to look at the bloom. Its fragile beauty blurred as she tried to concentrate on the dainty petals. Shouts beat in her ear: her own name, compliments, extravagant claims for her beauty.

'Hurrah for Annabel san.'

'Number one in Japan!'

'I go where the barbarian goes!'

'Annabel san! I worship your beauty.'

She lifted her head and smoothed back her flowing blonde hair. There were silver rivers of tears on her cheeks as she looked out at the cheering dark faces. Their warm emotion rolled towards her. 'I thank you, gentlemen,' she said with a shy smile.

'Annabel san! Look at me, I beg you. Just for a moment let our eyes touch.'

'Say the word and I'll die for you.'

'Live for ever in my heart!'

Annabel watched the shouting men for a long moment. Then she waved. Then, still hearing their cries in her ears, she stooped and retrieved her clothes. She retreated under the bamboo bush to dress, slipping on first the gauzy undergarment, then the primrose-yellow kimono, then the willow-green sash. She kept her head down as she worked. She could not tie a ceremonial bow behind her, and so she just wrapped the length of spring green around her slender waist and tucked the ends under, out of the way.

As she tucked the last sash end in place, and turned to face the crowd of eager men who waited at the front of the cage, she noticed that dusk was falling. An apricot glow spilled out from the seaweed shop. As her feet brushed over the matting and she turned to walk to the front of the cage, the poulterer came out carrying flares to light up his shop. The sky behind the waiting faces was indigo now, and the air had chilled.

She could not put Japanese words to the tangle of emotions that choked her, so she stood silently, smiling shyly out at the samurai who clustered about her. Their cries grew plaintive.

'Won't you look at us?'

'Darling Barbarian! Speak to us!'

Emotion made her lips tremble, but Annabel's voice

was sweet and steady as she replied, 'With great pleasure.'

She bent gracefully, seating herself on the worn flooring of the cage. To her surprise, all the samurai followed suit, seating themselves on the ground outside the cage, so that her eyes were only a few inches above their eyes. The ranks of massed soldiers sat like good children waiting for a story, while the flower-seller took her empty sacks home and the sake-seller hurried up with a new straw barrel full of fragrant rice wine.

Annabel scanned the ring of intent faces. The big outlaw was standing at the back, just about to leave with his band of followers. He met Annabel's eyes and bowed to her gravely before taking the road that the whores had taken. She felt as if a restriction had been lifted. She was glad he had gone. She was now free to meet the eyes of her young champion. He smiled eagerly at her from his position right at the front of the cage. She returned his smile and nodded, acknowledging him. His eyes blazed with hero-worship.

The other men gazed at the young samurai enviously, breathing hard in their awe, waiting to see what Annabel would say. She picked up her fan and peeped mischievously over the top of it. Her single pair of sparkling blue eyes was reflected back to her from a hundred dark ones, but she was not afraid now, for she had made them hers.

'Now, as military men, you will understand that I can say nothing about Lord Nakano's plans,' she began clearly.

Heads nodded. 'Of course that's right!'

'Discretion is all in matters of war.'

'She understands very well, that one.'

The samurai approved of her. The big men sat in the palm of her hand. As she waited for the murmurs to quieten, Annabel's fan wafted the fresh evening air over her sensitive cheeks. Her body was slowly folding itself down, like the petals of a night-blooming flower. She was moving from the intensely sensual state of her earlier striptease and orgasm – where her body had taken over – to this calmer situation where her mind would be in control.

As the streak of lambent red that had been colouring the horizon faded, a few silver stars glowed in the navy-blue sky. A mosquito whined past Annabel's cheek. A harbinger of the warmer summer weather that was on its way.

The men were quiet now, and Annabel smiled warmly at the thin young samurai as she continued, 'The Lord Nakano, however, is bound to be interested in what I can tell him of the abilities of the soldiers who are in town. You were about to tell me what battles you have fought in, what adventures you have had . . .'

Chapter Eleven

*A*nnabel was so absorbed in trying to decipher one of the many poems that had been arriving at the cage all morning that she did not hear a palanquin stop, nor someone important get out. It was not until a familiar male cough broke into her concentration that she looked up. 'Oh, you poor thing!' came a male voice. 'I was never more shocked in my life!'

Annabel put down a sheaf of rice paper covered in exquisite calligraphy and turned to face the speaker. 'Hiroshi!'

'I came as soon as I heard! I'm sorry it took me so long; midday of the second day already! My dear, was it so awful? But never mind that now. I've come to take you away. You must be longing for a bath.'

'Thank you. You are most thoughtful, but Kiku and her maid kindly escorted me to the bathing place this morning.' And washed every inch of me and supplied me with this dainty blue kimono and combed up my hair into the arrangement you now see, continued Annabel silently. They are my true friends. Are you?

She looked searchingly at Hiroshi. Compared with the rough honesty of the masterless samurai she had been talking to, he looked overdressed and foppish. His mouth was a bloodless slit as he urged her, 'Come on, do! Throw away that rubbish and come with me.'

'It's not rubbish!' objected Annabel.

She looked around at the colourful piles of flowers. The single heads and stems that had been thrown last night were still sweetly scented, but their heads were drooping now. Even though most of the soldiers had brought fairly restrained bouquets in the Japanese style – a few spears of gold and azure iris in a tall vase, some mountain magnolias delicately arranged – so many of them had brought her tributes that the bamboo cage was packed full of fresh flowers. Others had sent her the poems she was now poring over.

Annabel held out a cream-coloured scrap of paper towards Hiroshi. 'I was just trying to read this poem. What does the third line say?'

He took it from her as if the piece of paper were dirty and screwed up his mouth as he read:

> 'Under the moon
> The radiant barbarian
> Shedding her own light.'

'That's so pretty!' Annabel cried, offering Hiroshi another paper scroll shadowed with pink. 'Here's another one I had trouble with. I love this elegant way of writing, but all the curves and swirls make it hard to read.'

'No good poem was ever written on paper decorated with cherry blossoms,' sneered Hiroshi, brushing it away. 'It shows a coarseness of mind; as does the derivative trash in the first poem.'

'Oh, do you think so?' asked Annabel, feeling bruised. 'Only, no one ever wrote me poems before. I can't help being thrilled.'

'We're wasting time,' said Hiroshi pettishly. His eyes

caught the noonday sun in a hard glare. 'Will you come along!'

Annabel's body did not want to move. 'But ought I not wait until the Lord Nakano sends for me?' she protested.

Hiroshi gave an exasperated sigh. 'Even a barbarian should be able to understand that he will never do that. Do you want to stay in the whore's cage until the novelty wears off and you are treated like a common or garden prostitute?'

Annabel's voice cracked and she could barely ask, 'Why do you say that Nakano will not send for me?'

Hiroshi's expression was pitying; there was a hint of exasperation there too, and, below the surface of his eyes, lurked other emotions that Annabel could not read.

'How long do you think my brother keeps his consorts?' asked Hiroshi. There was a trace of venom in his voice. 'He is, after all, the mighty warlord. Any woman would count it an honour to pillow with him. He may take his choice, and he may change his choice as often as he pleases.'

Annabel stood up and brushed down her sky-blue kimono. How happy it had made her to put it on that morning. She walked across the cage to stare between the bamboo bars. The view of the town square was suddenly bleak. As bleak as her life now looked.

Hiroshi shook his head and met Annabel's gaze squarely, as he continued, 'Japanese women, however, know how to behave when cast off. Their families come for them, and they return home happily enough, or they kill themselves with the maximum of drama. Either way, the business is easily settled. You, however, my little barbarian, pose my brother a problem. One I have taken upon myself to resolve.'

Her eyes never wavered from his. 'How? How will you solve the problem I seem to have become?'

'I shall take it upon myself to remove you from the cage.'

How bleak her heart was. Annabel's head drooped and her shoulders sagged. 'I still think I should wait for him.'

'My blasted brother!' spat Hiroshi, unveiling an anger and bitterness she had not seen before. 'Why do you persist in your dream? How does he arouse such loyalty?' He spun on his heel and turned his back to the cage.

Annabel stared at Hiroshi's back. He was wearing a magnificent ceremonial robe. The chestnut silk gleamed in the sun. The crane insignia was clearly visible. She thought of being left, for ever unclaimed in the cage, and her courage failed her. She thought she would go with Hiroshi, but when she saw the anger in his eyes when he turned around, she changed her mind again.

'I don't know,' she said despairingly. 'I don't understand the rules, or know what I should be doing for the best.'

Hiroshi looked at her with urgency. 'I can't hang about here,' he said. 'I don't have the time to argue with you. You can stay here and descend into whoredom, or you can come with me now.' He saw the uncertainty in her eyes and added, 'And who knows, when you are safely in the castle and wearing delicious clothing, maybe Nakano will change his mind and send for you again. I couldn't stop him, you know. I'm only the younger brother.'

'I will come with you,' said Annabel quickly. Her decision felt wrong to her, but what else could she do? Hiroshi was hurrying her, applying too much pressure, yet she could not resist the bait that he offered. 'Maybe it will be as you say and Lord Nakano will send for me again,' she said. But her eyes held little hope as she lowered herself out of the cage and into her waiting shoes, ready to follow Hiroshi back to the castle.

* * *

'What magnificent quarters!' said Annabel, following Hiroshi into his apartment.

'A few peasants' rooms in the keep,' he replied bitterly. 'Only my brother, the mighty warlord, is allowed to sleep in the tower of the donjon.'

Now Annabel looked more closely, she could see that the gold-coloured metal that gilded the squared screens of the room was tarnished. The colours of the painted frieze that ran along the bottom of one wall had darkened. It was difficult to make out the clouds and mountains hovering over the battles that were pictured below. 'This room is still charming,' said Annabel. 'It looks very peaceful and antique. Like an old castle at home.'

She took a few steps into the dimly shadowed room. Her feet brushed over the very thickest and finest of tatami matting. Its summery haylike smell hung so heavy in the air that it made her eyes smart. 'May I open a shoji?' she asked. She began moving towards a rice-paper screen that, from the faint glow that illuminated it, looked as if it might open out on to the outside world.

But Hiroshi said sharply: 'No. Don't open it.'

Annabel's hand froze in the act of reaching for the screen and she looked at him surprised.

'It's boring out there,' he said petulantly, 'and the light fades my paintings.'

'Paintings?'

He came forward eagerly, went past Annabel, and stooped down to a wooden chest with three drawers. The wood looked well-handled and gleamed with polish. 'Made from the wood of the foxglove tree,' Hiroshi told her, carefully opening one drawer. 'This is where I keep my collection of, shall we say, the more exotic representations of the pillow arts.'

Annabel leant forward curiously. Colours swam before her eyes in the dim light as she looked at a picture of the seashore. In the background was a heavily stylised ocean of green covered with the white foaming caps of sea horses. A nude figure with skin the colour of pearls lay in the foreground. A naked woman, lying on her back in an ecstasy of abandonment, her hair streaming loose around her. Her face showed only delight.

But, looking more closely, Annabel could now see that the reddish limbs that entwined her nude body belonged not to a human, but to a large octopus. Its tentacles clasped the orgasming woman firmly. Her sex was gathered up into the sea-monster's mouth. Its eyes were fixed upon her enjoyment as the lurid act of cunnilingus took place.

'I can't believe that!' gasped Annabel, falling back quickly.

Hiroshi chuckled. 'No? My little innocent. Perhaps it is time your education was extended. Please, tell me what you think of this one?'

Annabel pushed the proffered sheet of paper away. 'I'd rather not,' she said stiffly. The paper smelt musty, as if it was rarely disturbed from its dark hiding place in Hiroshi's apartment, and she wished that she could not smell it.

'Oh? Well, if you like the first of my little pictures so much . . .'

There was an age-old look in his eyes that made Annabel feel wary. 'I don't like it!' she said firmly.

Hiroshi moved closer. His body was hot. His breath smelt sour. He stretched his arms around her and fumbled with the knot of her sash behind her back. The sky-blue obi dropped away with a soft brushing sound. It lay on the floor in an abandoned curl of blue silk. Annabel's kimono brushed across her skin as it began to untuck itself, fall free without the restraining influence of the sash.

Annabel clutched at the folds of fabric, trying to prevent them from slipping open. 'What?' she said, looking at Hiroshi, shaking her head, trying to understand him.

His eyes were hot and slimy. His voice shook a little as he enquired softly, 'Resistance, Annabel san? You do surprise me. Have you no gratitude?'

'Gratitude for what?' asked Annabel, but a cold sinking in her belly told her that, at some level, she understood him very well.

Hiroshi tossed his head. 'You cannot have truly understood what I saved you from, otherwise, you wouldn't mind acknowledging your indebtedness to me.'

'I don't remember that we struck any bargains!' protested Annabel.

'What did you think would happen?'

'That I would go back to Mamma san, I suppose.'

'And so you probably will. But what difference does that make to us now?'

Even as he spoke, Annabel remembered how the older woman had fawned over the warlord's brother; how Mamma san had insisted that she take his penis into her mouth and pleasure him. Too late now, to wish that she had not succumbed to Hiroshi's urging, to wish that she had stayed in the cage.

A hand snaked between the folds of her vivid blue kimono and gripped the top of her thigh. 'Was it so very unpleasant, fellating me?' Hiroshi enquired in a silky voice. 'I said to you then, and I'll repeat it now, I don't need to take any woman by force. After all, I am the warlord's brother. Any service you render to me, you render to him.'

The hand gripped Annabel's thigh more tightly, and then began to stroke it in a gentle, rhythmic motion. She looked down at Hiroshi, startled. 'You mean that if I please you, then I please Nakano?'

The stroking hesitated for a second and then continued. 'That's exactly what I mean,' said Hiroshi, his voice filled with softness and sincerity.

Annabel could feel the stroking intensely. Soft fingers brushed over and over the sensitive skin of the top of her thigh. Her breasts felt full and heavy. A dark excitement began to gather in her woman's place. Liquid gushed deep within her and flowed softly around the entrance to her vagina.

Hiroshi's questing fingers slipped into the springing yellow curls of her pubic hair. Then his whole body went still. Then he withdrew his fingers. He looked down at them frowning. They were wet and shiny with love dew. Annabel could smell the ocean smell of her own arousal. Hiroshi wrinkled his nose. 'Disgusting,' he said. 'A vagina that is too wet and large will never do.'

Annabel was startled by the revulsion she saw in his face. 'How so?' she protested. 'The lubrication that comes with arousal is a true sign that a woman is ready and willing to love.'

'It makes me think of the other men who have had you.' Hiroshi stepped back, shouted for a servant to bring hot water, and then crossed the room to slide open the large cupboard that took up one entire wall at the end of the room. He reached into the dark and frowsty interior, rummaged around, and returned holding a pestle and mortar made of marble.

As he began grinding, Annabel wrinkled her nose. 'What a smell!' It was sharp, aromatic.

'These herbs will make your vagina so wonderful, that no man could ever bear to leave it,' promised Hiroshi.

'Is it a love potion?' asked Annabel wonderingly, drawing her loose kimono around her as a servant crept in with a bowl of hot water.

Hiroshi ground vigorously. The air was redolent with the smell of leaves, roots and bark. 'From China,' he said, his eyes gleaming. 'They know how to make a vagina so tight and so dry, that you will feel like a virgin when I penetrate you.'

'But you know that I'm not!' said Annabel logically.

Hiroshi ignored her remark. His eyes were half-closed and his mouth pursed as if he were conjuring up erotic

pictures in his mind. 'That delicious struggle to penetrate! The ultimate friction on my heavenly member!'

He ground more vigorously. As the herbs disinte-
grated into powder, dark clouds puffed up into the air.
Hiroshi sneezed, and said joyously, 'They are ready.
That sneeze is the sign.' He held out the marble bowl to
Annabel.

'What do I do with it?' she asked, looking into the eyes
that were so lustful now.

'First you must wash inside your woman's place with
hot water. Then you must remove those loathsome
secretions with a finger, wipe out your vagina with a
cloth, then you must insert this powder.'

Annabel was looking at him, thinking about what he
had said, the significance of what he was asking her to
do. 'Do you truly dislike love dew so much?'

Hiroshi's mouth screwed up tightly. 'Fucking a wet
woman is like swimming in the muddy waters of the
yellow Yangtze river! A morally healthy woman would
be dry naturally, but you of course are a loose barbarian,
and so I must use the powders.'

He stared at her for an instant, then his eyes blazed
with impatient lust. 'Get your clothes off and begin,' he
ordered.

Slowly, doubtfully, Annabel slipped out of the protective folds of her kimono. Hiroshi made no move to touch
her or let down her hair; he just stood watching, still
fully dressed, as she hesitantly knelt by the bowl of hot
water and dabbled her fingers in it, delaying.

'You act as if your private places are unknown to you,'
jeered Hiroshi.

Annabel looked down at her mound as if she was
surprised to see the curls that sprang from it, but at last
she reached down and touched herself. The hot water
felt so pure and so natural, that it was a pleasure to
trickle it over the lips and folds of her sex, despite the
watching man.

Warm sensations flowed gently around her body as she dabbled and washed the outer folds of her labia. Her blonde bush twisted into damp curls that were darker than usual. A few diamonds of water gleamed on them.

Annabel ran her hands over the tender skin of her inner thighs, pressing gently, feeling an answering heaviness inside her. Then she lifted herself off her knees so that she could reach up inside the strange dark spaces of her vagina.

She felt the warm, wet muscles suck at the finger she had inserted. She ran the finger around the walls, feeling the familiar, and yet also unknown folds of hot flesh closing around her finger in a friendly embrace. When she removed her wet hand, the finger that had been inside her was coated in white pearly moisture.

Annabel regarded the pearl drops of love dew for a long moment. Then she touched her finger to her lips. Her own sweet smell touched her nostrils, and her tongue confirmed her other senses: her moisture was sweet, fragrant, utterly natural and right. But now she must do as Hiroshi commanded, and wipe every trace of her natural lubrication away.

He threw her a towel when she had finished. 'Dry yourself thoroughly with that, inside as well as out.'

Annabel felt strange as the towelling touched her inside. The concept of dry sex was difficult for her to grasp, but Hiroshi's eyes combed her face as if daring her to object, and she leant forward and dipped a finger into the gritty powder that lay in the small marble bowl of the pestle and mortar.

Then she spread open her thighs and reached inside her, holding the lips of her sex open with one hand, while she slipped the drying potion inside her vagina with the other hand. The Chinese concoction felt coarse and hot as it touched the delicate membranes of her sex, but she scooped up the powder and patted it inside her until all the walls of her vagina were coated with the mixture.

A cool dry tickling started high up inside her vagina. Annabel looked at Hiroshi uncertainly. 'I'm not sure about this,' she said.

His eyes were like small black stones. 'A woman should define her satisfaction in relation to the pleasure she gives a man,' he told her.

His body moved close to hers in the dim shadowy apartment. His hand snaked between the lips of her sex and pushed fruitlessly at the now tightly closed entrance to her vagina. 'Oh! Ecstasy! Not even a finger will penetrate!' he moaned.

Annabel fell backward on to the softly yielding surface of the tatami matting. Her legs opened wide. Hiroshi rubbed his body up against her. She could feel one of his fingers pushing at the crinkled dry hole that the entrance to her vagina had become. It seemed to excite him. His breath came hard and fast.

He reared up so that he could rip open his kimono. His erection poked out through the opening in the chestnut robe. Annabel looked at the gnarled club of his cock warily. The whole length of his organ was swollen, and the tip was crimson and bloated. As he threw himself impatiently down on her, Annabel saw that his face had turned the same dark crimson colour as the tip of his cock. There was no understanding in his eyes, only a hard and selfish lust. As Annabel registered the lack of connection between them, her body shivered and grew cool.

It was as if desire had drained away with the secretions from her vagina. She felt no warmth towards the dark head that pushed into her breasts, no urge to caress the twitching shoulders under the brown silk robe that he had not bothered to discard. She was glad that the thick penis slithering over her belly had no chance of penetrating. She didn't want him inside her.

Hiroshi reached down and prised her thighs apart, but the reddish-purple head of his bulbous cock thrust against the parted lips of her sex without gaining entry. A finger probed between the folds of Annabel's labia, hunting for the entrance to her vagina. She whimpered softly as he found it, then winced as the tip of his finger curled and pushed a fraction of an inch into her dry and unresponsive hole.

Grunting in excitement, Hiroshi thrust his cock towards her as if he were aiming for the tiny opening he had created. You're not coming inside me! thought Annabel, shuddering at the idea of his sperm discharging in her delicate spaces. She reached up her hands and grasped his organ.

She heard Hiroshi give a muffled cry of protest, but she ignored him and jerked and pulled at his ramrod hard penis. She felt it flex and twitch in her grasp. Hiroshi arched his back and shuddered violently. Mingled sounds of pleasure and anger burst out through his clenched teeth. Annabel felt a hot pattering on her belly as white strings of his sperm landed on her skin in hot spurts that dribbled down the curve of her stomach to pool wetly below her.

Hiroshi cursed and rolled over on his back. 'You ruined that, you stupid barbarian!' he shouted.

'Oh, please excuse me. I'm so sorry you are not happy, Mr Hiroshi,' said Annabel sweetly. She arranged her face to express nothing but tender concern. If nothing else, she had learnt the art of duplicity from Mamma san.

Hiroshi's voice was tight with frustration and anger. 'A rat off the rubbish tip would know more of the pillow arts than you do!' His eyes were black and angry, but he didn't look as if he suspected that her actions had been deliberate.

Annabel bowed her head as if in shame. 'Please excuse my clumsiness. Perhaps I had better go back to my training,' she suggested meekly.

Hiroshi rolled over on to his front, stood up, and began straightening his clothing with sharp, angry movements. 'Go on then, you useless bitch,' he snapped. 'But I'll have you again – and next time you'll get it right.'

'So sorry, Master Hiroshi. Please forgive the poor barbarian,' chanted Annabel sweetly. Inside she was raging. She picked up her discarded kimono and shook it out, but she didn't put it on. She didn't want it to touch the slime on her belly. Too angry to care whether anyone saw her stalking bare-skinned through the corridors of Shimoyama or not, she held the blue silk away from her as she pushed open the screen and stepped naked out of the foul room.

The corridor was bright and light after the dimness of Hiroshi's den. The cool fresh air of outside was a balm on her naked skin. Annabel's stomach churned as she visualised his unnatural desires. Part of her wished that she had followed her primitive instincts and screamed her disgust at him; but she knew it had been sensible to dissemble. Her situation was precarious enough without making an enemy out of the warlord's brother.

She went up several flights of stairs and hurried along a long corridor until she was well away from Hiroshi's room. Then she found a window embrasure and stopped next to it. The window, although delicate and soaring, was built so that it could double as a station for an archer. Heavy, iron-covered shutters could be swung shut against attackers. Annabel stood for a long time, her cheek against the cool plaster of the opening, staring out over the huddled roofs of the town. Sunlight glinted off their shapely tiled curves. Beyond them Mount Fuji was a magical outline against the sky. The heat of her anger faded. It may have been sensible to dissemble, but she was ashamed of herself.

She looked down. The steep walls of the keep fell away below her and dropped into the moat. She thought fleetingly of leaping, but she quickly dismissed the image from her mind. Her mind drifted back to the scene in Hiroshi's room. Instead of being depressed by it, in an odd, wonderful way she now felt free. Her dislike of Hiroshi had taught her a lesson. She knew, now, what she wanted.

She had been drifting, surviving, making the best of things rather than following her heart. She felt a warm glow of joy as she thought of the man she wanted, the man she would cherish for a lifetime. She wasn't going to lie, or pretend any more about who she was and what she wanted, and she was going to find Nakano and tell him so.

But she did not feel able to go to him just yet. She flinched from the contamination she perceived on her skin. Her courage faded for a moment as she looked at her soft body. She felt vulnerable in her nakedness. Fear of the unknown future came close to paralysing her. She felt her aloneness as a pain deep within her, but she found courage there too, and she stepped away from the embrasure and looked around her, getting her bearings.

Annabel knew there were hot springs underneath the castle. She had been to them once or twice, and she thought she could find her way to them from this point of the keep. Her skin yearned to be scrubbed all over and then eased into deep, hot, steaming water that would wash away every trace of her contact with Hiroshi.

'I'll do that,' she whispered, the words a soft promise to herself. 'After a bath I will be better able to face Nakano.'

Chapter Twelve

The caverns under the keep were empty. Annabel looked about her nervously before she waded out into the water. A green and ghostly phosphorescence hung about the pools of the hot spring. She felt very alone. The sulphur-scented water touched her skin with a hot bite as she let her shoulders slide under the surface. Water trickled and gushed in the background, falling into the stone basins where she had just washed thoroughly. Water drip, drip, dripped from the roof as steam gathered there and condensed; falling back down to the shiny wet stone floor with an endless plink, plink, plink.

The silence behind the watery sounds of the underground cavern made Annabel jittery. The only candle that she had been able to find made wavering shadows and cast little light in the dark misty atmosphere. She had taken it down to the water's edge with her, and then dripped a little wax on to the rock and fastened the candle in place. As she looked at its feeble glow, she wished for a good English candle. One made from beeswax that gave a fine yellow light. These Japanese wax-tree things were a poor substitute. Annabel pushed away homesickness and concentrated on the here and now.

The hot water caressed her limbs, but it did little to soothe her aching tension. Each splash she made in the sulphur-scented water echoed oddly in the confined space of the cave. Annabel ignored the sounds. She refused to be spooked. Dark shadows moved all around her. Her skin furred with gooseflesh. She peered at the dim forms uncertainly. It was just a trick of the shadows, wasn't it?

The light from her candle flickered and went out.

A sudden flurry of splashes right next to her. Real sounds. Annabel turned her head quickly; felt a kick over her heart. Real men approaching. The sharp frightening pain of fear knocked all the blood in her body into a hammering motion.

Her hands flew up to prevent her terrified heart from battering its way out of the rib-cage, but otherwise, she stood there rigid, like a sacrificial lamb, unable either to move forward or run away, as the dark shadows flickered out of the mist and raced towards her.

Water splashed just behind her. Annabel whipped around. A dark figure looming over her.

Her paralysis finally broke. Her blood slammed in heavy painful strokes in her chest, her throat. She opened her mouth to scream.

A dark figure jumped.

Hands pulled at her brutally. Hands grabbed her upper arms, her waist, her thighs. One efficient hand came down hard over her mouth.

She struggled. She fought. The hot water dragged at her legs. She could hear splashes, her heart thudding, the hissing breath of her assailants. Two of them? Three? The pressure of their hands was hurting her. Her ribs, held in a hard embrace, felt as if they were cracking.

'Give it up!' A hot and vicious voice in her ear. The pressure increased. Breath was impossible. They were killing her. Annabel stopped fighting and went slack. Straight away, the cruelty of the hands that were gripping her eased off – but she was still very much a prisoner.

'Don't struggle, and we won't hurt you. Our orders are to take you somewhere.' A thick, slushy voice, muffled as if its owner were disguising it.

Orders? thought Annabel dizzily as she hung limply beneath the alien hands that lifted her out of the water. Her head tipped back. The only light was the faint glow from the water. She could see only the dark wet rock of the roof. She heard water moving as her captors waded through it. Four men at least. Who would send four men with orders to capture her? It made no sense. Her brain was dizzy. Her body jolted beneath her.

'Put me down,' she gasped unsteadily. 'I'll walk.'

Her answer was a slurred, but authoritative, 'No noise.'

The darkness grew more intense as they moved away from the pool. Darkness like hot velvet pressing down on her throat. Her captors' feet made the faintest of brushing sounds on the rock floor. Barefoot then. Men dressed in black. Noiseless. Under orders. But not orders to kill her, it seemed.

The dark disoriented her, as did the sensation of movement beneath her. As she was carried along, high in the air and close to the top of the cave, black shadows seemed to jump out at her. Annabel kept ducking her head. She was afraid that a dip in the unseen stone ceiling of the rocky passageway would crash into her and knock her out.

The jolting and jouncing that her body was receiving made it hard to think. She wished that the men who were carrying her would put her down, but she was also afraid that they would drop her.

It was a relief when they finally stopped. It was still dark. Annabel could clearly hear each man breathing in the silence of the cave. Hands let her go. She slid over the bony ridge of a strange man's shoulder. Her feet touched bare wet rock. Her knees crumpled a little, and she sagged back against a smooth cool wall. She must think, do something!

One man spoke to another: a quick, hissing interchange that she could not follow. Rock grated against rock. She was pulled upright. Pushed hard. She was catapulted into the darkness. One step. Two. Three. Rock met her outstretched hands. Her palms stung with the impact. She crumpled against the stone wall that had stopped her flight through the darkness and tried to choke down the throttling knot of fear in her throat.

Rock grated against rock again. She was alone. Imprisoned in the cool damp dark of an underground tomb.

It took an age to calm her breathing, to fight down panic, to take stock of her surroundings. There was water in the cave. A steady trickle that sounded loud in the darkness. In one corner, fresh water oozed down the rock wall and trickled out of the cave. The water exited through a hole too small for a cat. No hope of escape that way. But at least she could relieve herself. And the water from above was clean enough to drink.

She dashed some water over her face and eyes, hoping it would help her think. The water was cold on her face. A few drops on her breast made her shiver. She was naked, and while the cave was not exactly cold, the air was nowhere near warm. It remained the same steady, even temperature. She would have to move around to keep warm if she were to be locked in this underground dungeon for long.

I don't need to keep warm! I need to escape, thought Annabel frantically. Once more she had to struggle to push down the panic that seemed to close in on her with the walls of the cave. She forced herself to run the palms of her hands over the uneven surface of the rock. She wanted to know how big her prison was.

Not very big. Three steps in one direction, five in another, then three, then four, and she was back at the uneven line where the entrance to the cave was. Perhaps she could chip a way out along the already-made opening where the door was? Annabel dropped to her hands and knees and began brushing her fingers along the moist, cool surface of the cave floor, hoping to find a loose rock that she could use to batter her way out.

There were no rocks. But her questing fingertips brushed against the wooden surface of the type of light wooden box in which the Japanese carried food for picnics, or the midday meal for those who were away from home. There seemed to be a pile of them. She ran her fingertips over the surface of the boxes several times, counting them. There were twenty-five boxes. She didn't want to think about why she had been provided with twenty-five boxes of food. She didn't want to think about that at all.

She would eat. And when she felt calmer, she would think. As she unwrapped the food, she could smell tart pickled vegetables. Her mouth watered as she identified smoked fish. There was rice too, shaped into a ball with a morsel of flavouring at its heart and wrapped up in seaweed that smelt of the ocean. She would eat, and then she would think. There must be a way out.

Annabel had eaten thirteen of the boxed meals when a slight scraping at the door of the cave sent her cowering back against the far wall of her prison. Her mouth dried with fear. She had no idea who or what to expect.

As the rock swung back, a brilliant glow illuminated the darkness. Annabel blinked. Her eyes watered. A black figure, one that appeared to have a dark aura due to a trick of the glowing light, hovered uncertainly, stooping under the low entrance. 'Annabel?' demanded a familiar voice.

'Hiroshi!'

Indecision kept Annabel pressed against the rock. Was this her mysterious enemy?

'Oh, you poor child!' He came further into the cave. Annabel turned her head away from the glare of the candle in his hand, but his soft words were already allaying her fears. 'Really, my dear,' he continued, 'you are going to have to be more careful! One day I won't be here to get you out of these scrapes that you seem to specialise in.'

Annabel's lips parted, and hope flickered in her heart. 'Get me out?' she questioned softly.

The dark figure halted, as if astonished. 'Well, of course, my dear. What did you think I had come for?'

'I don't know.'

A warm, moist hand closed on her upper arm, urging her to her feet. 'I rescued you last time and I'll rescue you this time.'

He smelt of soap and perfume; a heavy musky fragrance with something medicinal and not entirely pleasant lurking underneath. As Annabel struggled to her feet, the silk robe of his kimono brushed her cheek and she smelt the cleanness of fabric that had dried in the sun. 'Thank you!' she cried, her whole heart in her voice. 'Oh! Please take me out of here, do!'

Hiroshi began guiding her towards the entrance. He waved aside the samurai clustering around the entrance and continued to guide Annabel himself. His hand was placed high enough on her arm so that with the back of his hand he could touch her naked breasts.

Annabel stumbled three or four times and her tender feet were scoured by the rough passage that Hiroshi led her along. She didn't ask the men to slow down. She wanted to keep moving, to get out of this terrible place. Her hair hung in a tangled mass down her back and around her face. She kept pushing it back with her long, delicate fingers. Her skin felt dirty, and as if it had shrivelled up.

Words flowed to her lips and spilled out as she tried to compensate for the dark aloneness of her time in the prison. 'It was so dark ... I thought I would die there ... how long I was there I don't know ... it was so cold ...'

Hiroshi hurried her along. 'Don't try to talk now.'

Her voice was just a croak in her throat as she blurted out the question that had troubled her above all as she lay alone, naked in the darkness: 'What about Nakano? Did he not miss me? Ask for me?'

'Hush now,' said Hiroshi, pointing to the robed back of the samurai who trod solidly in front of them. Hiroshi lifted his candle and looked down at Annabel. When she winced and shrank away from the light, he passed the candle to one of his men and motioned him to walk on ahead. Then he put another warm, moist hand on her arm and brought his face close to hers. She smelt sourness on his breath as he said very quietly, 'You should not ask about Nakano! It is he who had you imprisoned.'

The bitterness of hearing her darkest fears put into words reduced her voice to a powerless whisper. 'Why? Why should he do that to me?'

'I told you that you posed him a problem. He wants you dead, and seeing as you will not commit suicide as his last discarded mistress did ...'

'No! I won't believe it.'

He sounded very amused as he said to her, 'It's true, I do assure you. Sat right in front of the war council where no one could possibly miss her and slit her throat open with a knife. No one behind her to finish her off, either. Messy business.'

'I didn't mean –' Annabel broke off. Her heart would not believe that Nakano wanted her dead. Her memories of their lovemaking were too sharp, too significant to be discounted. But she was also remembering how angry Hiroshi became each time she expressed loyalty to Nakano. She had best be silent now, and keep her true thoughts hidden.

She looked at him seriously. 'If the warlord wants me dead, then what am I to do?' she asked practically. 'Surely there is no way to withstand him?'

She was abnormally sensitive not only to light, but also to nuances in voices. Dry satisfaction rustled in Hiroshi's as he replied, 'I have thought of that: the most exciting news arrived while you were missing. How would you like to go home, Annabel? Under the protection of your father?'

'My father?' She stumbled over her feet, unbalanced by the news. 'He is dead. My father died at sea.'

'Oh no he didn't! He was washed ashore, further down the coast.'

She forced herself to be calm, to deal with the incredible news but, when she spoke to him again, her voice shook terribly. 'Did any more people survive?'

'A few,' said Hiroshi indifferently. Then real excitement lit up his voice. 'But the cargo survived! Guns! Lovely, lovely muskets, cases of them, and powder and ball, too!'

His hand tugged at Annabel's arm, urging her along the dark corridor. She followed him. 'Why did no one hear of this?'

He bent close to whisper. His hair brushed over her cheek and neck. His voice buzzed unpleasantly in her ear. 'Plots, my dear, and deadly dealings. The people who found him wanted to keep the weaponry to themselves.'

Annabel pulled away. Truth and lies were mixed in his voice. Hiroshi gripped her arm harder and pulled her back. 'We have a very good understanding, your father and I,' he hissed. 'I have paid him handsomely for his weapons, and he has promised to return with more for me.'

'For you?'

Hiroshi shook her arm. 'For Nakano, I mean. Did you think I meant to set up against my brother?'

'I don't know what to think,' said Annabel honestly as they approached the end of the tunnel. 'Oh! I can smell earth; and green growing things and wet air.'

She had to cover her face with her hands, so intense was the light outside, but she peeped through her fingers and saw that they had come out into a formal temple-style garden on one side of the keep. The humid air was as warm as a blanket on her skin. The cicadas had never shrilled so sweetly. She paused for a moment to breathe in her freedom, but Hiroshi began to pull her away from the massive stone tower of the donjon. Annabel dug in her bare heels and said, 'No! I won't go!'

'Don't be a fool! Your father is waiting at Okitsu, the staging post on the Tokaido road. You are to travel with him to the port of Yokohama, and there a Portuguese ship will take you home.'

Her father was nothing to her now, he was still dead in her mind; and Annabel was tired of being pushed into decisions that felt wrong. She took a deep breath and faced Hiroshi. 'I will not leave without seeing Nakano again.'

He looked at her angrily, and she could see frustration and spite lurking in his eyes, negating his soft voice. 'My dear, you are not thinking straight,' he cooed. 'You are tired after your terrible ordeal.'

'I am also naked,' said Annabel, temporising. If she could delay long enough, maybe Nakano would come. 'And I am desperate for a bath. Surely it will take some time to prepare for the journey to Okitsu? Can I not at least return to my apartment for a few minutes?'

Hiroshi glared at her, but then seemed to come to a decision. 'Just for a few minutes then.' He sent half of his men scurrying off to the stables with orders to get the horses ready, and then turned towards the tower, still keeping a tight hold on Annabel's upper arm.

Her eyes were adjusting to the light. The cool stone passageways seemed quite comfortably lit as they hurried towards her little room. 'You can't stay long,' warned Hiroshi. 'It could be dangerous for you if Nakano finds out you're here.'

'I can't believe that I could be in any danger from Nakano,' said Annabel, pushing open the screen of her room.

It was cold and alien after her long absence. The room was dark and shadowy. Discarded clothing lay in a bundle on the floor. Flies buzzed in the corners of the room. A thick unpleasant smell hung in the air.

Annabel began to say, 'No one has been in to clean –' And then her voice broke off in a sharp gasp. She could see, all too clearly now, that it was not just clothing that lay on the floor. The ominously stiff, still, outline of a person lay motionless inside the forlorn bundle.

She had taken too many shocks that day. A faint, high buzzing began in her ears, but otherwise she couldn't feel any natural emotion at all. She seemed to be watching Hiroshi cross the room to examine the corpse from behind a sheet of thick ice that insulated her from the scene. Hiroshi bent down, pulled aside a fold of cloth using the tips of his fingers, and then let it fall again. 'Kiku san,' he said briefly.

When he turned back to Annabel, she could see that he was furious. 'How could this happen?' he demanded. 'How could anyone mistake little Kiku san for you? Does a Japanese girl resemble a great hulking barbarian?'

He was so angry that flecks of foam appeared at the corners of his mouth. His face was suffused with crimson blood as he bellowed for his samurai. They stood trembling before him as he continued with his tirade, finishing, 'Of all the stupid mistakes! Heads will roll for this! Go now, I command you, and find out who killed little Kiku in mistake for the barbarian!'

Still naked, standing alone and forgotten, Annabel could hardly believe she had understood him. 'In mistake for me?' she questioned.

225

'Of course for you!' He looked grim as he answered. 'Why else is there a dead body in your apartment? I told you Nakano wanted you dead. How much more proof do you want? You must come with me now, just as you are. You can change at an inn on the way, but you must come now. It is too dangerous to stay here any longer.'

Dazed and confused, Annabel allowed him to urge her out of the room and away from Shimoyama.

Just before they reached Okitsu, Annabel had to dismount from her horse to be sick.

'How is your headache?' asked Hiroshi, approaching her with a mixture of impatience and sympathy in his face.

'It's easing,' lied Annabel. Her head was pounding harder than it ever had before. Daylight darted cruel spears of light into her eyes. Her whole body ached from the unaccustomed exercise of riding a horse; and now the sour taste of vomit burned her nose and throat, adding to the misery of her raw and throbbing feet. Her stomach churned, and she yearned to be through with this whole miserable journey.

'Not much further,' said Hiroshi, pushing her back on to her horse. 'In fact, you can see the roofs of the inn from here. There will be a bath, and hot food, and your father is waiting for us. What could be more charming?'

But as they approached a guest bungalow that was set to one side of the inn, Annabel was nearly sick again. 'I never smelt anything so vile,' she gasped. 'There must be a dead rat under the floor. Let's go back to the main building.'

She looked at Hiroshi, expecting him to turn away, but he was looking at the low, thatched quarters they were approaching. Disgust was plain in his eyes. 'It is very bad, I agree. I had thought you would want to be near your father, but I suppose I can arrange for you to stay in the main inn.'

'My ... my father?' said Annabel stupidly. Saliva flooded her mouth as the reek of corruption grew stronger. They stepped up on to the wooden veranda that ran around the thatched building. Dark shadows moved behind the rice-paper screens. There were people staying in that stench? Then Annabel saw that the shadows had European silhouettes and her heart began to thump painfully as one of them slid open a screen and gestured to them to enter by the opening he had created.

As Annabel looked up at the waiting figure she could no longer avoid thinking about the forthcoming meeting with her father. How would he greet her? She couldn't see him clearly. She hesitated, waiting for him to make the first move. His voice was choked with emotion. 'My little girl!'

Tears filled her eyes at the sound of the English language, and, momentarily forgetting the smell, she moved forward with her hands held out. 'Oh, Papa! Is it really you?' But as she drew closer to the waiting figure of her father, Annabel's heart was gripped by pain and confusion. Her awareness of the smell returned. The stench that rose from his stooped and wasted figure was so pungent, so deeply foul and malodorous that she could almost taste it. Annabel closed her mouth and tried to breathe in through her nose as her father reached out to embrace her.

His touch was unfamiliar. His light frame and stringy arms stirred no memories of the past, for they had rarely touched. Annabel broke free as soon as she could. She swallowed saliva that tasted as if it were polluted by the body odour that hung in the air like a miasma, and stepped back to look at her father.

She was startled to see that he was crying. Tears trickled from her red-rimmed eyes. Then she saw that he was holding a bottle and realised that they were the easy tears of the drunk. 'Come in!' cried Walter Smith, waving the bottle. 'You too, Hiro, you old sod! It's grand to see you.'

Annabel ducked away from the arm he stretched out and nipped into the room unaided. It was like being in the lair of a jungle carnivore; one that lived on rotten corpses and entrails. 'Leave the screen open,' she pleaded. The English words came stiffly to her lips.

'You're as bad as them bloody Jap monkeys,' grumbled her father. 'Always wanting to sit by open windows and such. Bloody crazy if you ask me.'

But he left the screen half open, and, breathing shallowly, Annabel looked around by the light that came through it.

The cook, a couple of seamen, and her father. The only four souls saved from the shipwreck. She nodded at them, but they appeared to be too drunk to take any interest in her. There was no sign of big jolly Peter, but she had mourned for him during the long months in the fishing village, and his absence did not disturb her now.

'I've no chair to offer you, Annabel girl,' said her father. 'But here! Have some rice wine. It's bloody good!' He took a long swallow and offered her the bottle. 'Go on! Sit on the ground. We all do.'

Annabel refused the wine with an unhappy shake of her head. She stared out of the open screen for a long moment before turning back to say, 'I'll stand, thank you.'

The room had been provided with tatami matting, but it was ripped and littered with food scraps and rubbish. Her father and the sailors were lounging around in clothes that had obviously come from Portugal, including boots, and she could not bring herself to sit where their filthy feet had been. Hiroshi, too, remained standing.

'Friend Hiro!' Her father addressed Hiroshi in Japanese so villainous that it took Annabel a few moments to understand him. 'You like big bang-bangs, eh? I get you plenty bang-bangs from England.'

Hiroshi bowed slightly. 'And I will give you plenty of money,' he said clearly to Walter Smith, then he turned to Annabel. 'You would be doing me a great favour, Annabel san, if you would kindly translate for your father and me. It is always as well to double-check these little business arrangements, don't you think? Misunderstandings are so unpleasant.'

In fact, Hiroshi and her father were in perfect agreement about every detail of their weaponry deal. As they finished, Walter Smith turned to Annabel and said approvingly, 'He's a good lad, for a heathen foreigner, this Hiro chap.'

Understanding only the tone of the Englishman's words, and satisfied that his business was done, Hiroshi seized the opportunity to back out of the malodorous room and retreat to the main part of the inn. Annabel knew that he planned to spend the night there and return to Shimoyama in the morning. She felt surprisingly bereft, left alone with her father. How would it be, to cross the ocean in such doubtful company? To return to England with no security or role to fulfil?

'By the time I get back with a second load of guns,' continued Walter Smith, 'he'll be in charge, and a good thing too, I say.'

'In charge?' asked Annabel.

Her father turned a woozy, heavily veined face to her. Annabel's body jerked in disgusted reaction as she saw lice crawling in his sparse grey hair. It was hard to meet the eyes that were so sharp and crafty, and believe that they belonged to her kin. Her father tapped the side of his nose and said, 'That's what he wanted my guns for. Oh, he's a fly one all right. This pal of his, Yoritomo, is it? Well, he's making his way through the province, right? With all his army. Soon as he gets into position – bang! Old Hiroshi chops off his brother's head. Them samurai what are loyal to him cut up the others, and there you are, king of the castle.'

'Did he tell you all this?' she cried sharply.

Her father closed one eye in a knowing wink. The debased expression on his face tore at her heart. She felt the last shreds of her loyalty to him flake away. How could he approve of such treachery and double-dealing, she wondered as he continued, 'Not in so many words, like, but Walter Smith's no fool. I can draw me own conclusions from what's been said and done.'

Annabel's heart told her that her father's deductions were right. All the pieces of information that had come her way fell into place – the plotting samurai she had overheard at the village; Yoritomo's request to march through Nakano's kingdom; the secrecy surrounding Hiroshi's purchase of the guns – and the whole plan was clear. The only question was, what should she do about it?

For a long time she stood looking out into the darkness that was falling over the Tokaido road. Her father, completely unaware of her mood, boasted about the money he had already made and rambled on about how wonderfully he would restore their fortunes with the shiploads of guns that he would return with to Japan. Every second spent in his company made Annabel realise how impossible it was that she should ever return to England. Her future lay here in Japan.

As her thoughts moved slowly towards her final, inevitable decision, Annabel's heart felt lighter. She would not stay here. She would slip away at the first opportunity, and take her chance with Nakano. She shook her head miserably as she thought of the warlord. Somehow, she seemed to have lost his trust and, when she returned to Shimoyama, there was a chance that he might not even give her a chance to speak.

But she would have to risk it, because she couldn't do without him; couldn't bear to live without him.

Chapter Thirteen

*A*nnabel and the thin young samurai accompanying her came to a stop in front of the massive wooden doors that barred their way. Two huge samurai stood on guard in front of the doors. The guards stared over their heads with a look of blank indifference.

'This is where I must leave you, Annabel san,' said her companion. 'I have no authority to allow you into the heart of Shimoyama.'

'No matter,' she said, smiling into the adoring eyes of the thin young samurai who had escorted her this far. 'I will ask one of these guards to send word of my coming to the warlord.' The guards did not stir, so she raised her voice and added loudly and distinctly, 'Lord Nakano will want to know at once that his barbarian is outside.'

The samurai guards still did not look at her, but they seemed to come to some silent agreement, because one of them hurried away from his post. Annabel hoped that he was going in search of Nakano. She shrugged. There was nothing more she could do. She turned to the young samurai. 'It was so lucky that you, of all people, should be guarding the way into Shimoyama, and have the authority to bring me this far.'

The young man blushed and stared at the floor. 'But without you, sweet lady, I would not have permission to move within Shimoyama. I knew at once that it was your doing when the Lord Nakano took me into his service.'

Annabel returned his bow, but then she clasped his hands briefly before standing back to watch him return to his duties. Was it just coincidence? Or had Nakano taken the young man on because she had singled him out while she was in the cage? It would be a good sign, if so, but it seemed impossible, and she had better not start inventing good omens.

Annabel pushed back her tangled hair with shaking hands. She wished fervently that she had been able to tidy up. She smoothed down her travel-stained kimono as the jingle of metal alerted her to the return of the guard.

He still did not look at her, but he bowed respectfully before announcing: 'Follow me!'

Annabel clasped her shaking hands behind her back and tried to walk serenely. Her mouth dried as he took an unfamiliar turn. Was she following him to prison? Suddenly it was hard to breathe, and the dark corners of the stone passageway seemed to close in on her. Her nerves almost overwhelmed her as they stopped at a carved wooden door.

The guard bowed, opened the door and bowed again. 'Enter!' he commanded, and gestured her through, closing the door behind her.

Annabel felt cool, polished wooden boards under her bare feet. She looked down astonished. Then she felt ashamed. Her feet were dirty and bloodstained. She took one hesitant step forward, and heard the boards sing under her feet. The nightingale room! No one could cross it in silence.

She stopped and looked across the expanse of gleaming polished wood. Soft orange light from the lamps that burned high up at ceiling level illuminated the scene.

Walls made of white-plastered panels opened out before her. Her eyes went to the only item of furniture in the room: a carved wooden frame holding a panel of patterned brocade fabric.

In front of this screen, motionless, gorgeous in his ceremonial robes, sat Nakano. A stringed musical instrument, a shamisen, lay to one side of him, as if he had been playing it and just laid it aside. There was something so deeply unhappy about his silent posture, that Annabel moved towards him impulsively. The floor began to sing under her feet, but Nakano did not move. 'Nakano! Oh, Nakano!' she cried. Her little voice was almost lost in the sound of the nightingale floor, but now Nakano looked up slowly.

'Welcome back,' he said quietly as she walked up to him.

Annabel's throat was so choked that she couldn't speak, not yet, nor could she find the words to say what was in her heart; so she dropped gracefully to her knees and bowed low in complete and silent homage to the man who sat so quietly above her.

Nakano sighed long and hard. 'I do not understand why you have returned. What could you possibly want of me?' Annabel lifted her head to look at him. His voice was stern, but his eyes were full of pain.

Annabel wanted to hold him close to her, to make up for all the bad things that were happening to him, but the dreadful tidings she had for him inhibited her. 'Nothing, my lord.' She was crying as she said the words. 'I want nothing from you, but I have sad news that I must tell you.'

'I think I do not want to hear this news of yours, Annabel san,' said Nakano. Despite his sadness there was resignation in his eyes. Annabel had a feeling that he knew very well what she must tell him, but she waited for him to give her permission to continue.

She sat silently for a long time, staring at the smooth

wooden floor, breathing in the cool, waxy smell of the polish. Finally she heard Nakano shift slightly, as if he were bracing himself, and say, 'Well . . .'

She could hardly bear to say it, but she knew she had to. 'The men I heard plotting are loyal to Hiroshi. He has bought guns from my father and plans an assault with Yoritomo.'

'I already knew it.' Nakano spoke with a smile, but his voice was unsurprisingly bitter.

Annabel looked up at him surprised. 'Then . . . then I need not have told you?'

He glanced at her briefly, and then looked away. 'I knew it in my heart, but I had no proof.'

'I am sorry to be the one who brings you that proof.'

'I am not; for until this moment, I was uncertain what your feelings for me were.'

Annabel kept her eyes on the polished floor. She ran her fingertips over the warm boards, and marvelled when they responded to the light pressure with a faint whisper. She took her fingertips away and the silence grew unbearable. Then at last she looked up at him. 'I love you,' she admitted softly, in a little voice that pierced the silence of the dimly glowing room. Tears filled her eyes in an emotional rush.

'I had not dared to think so,' said Nakano, his voice filled with tenderness and regret. 'Perhaps I should have acted other than I did.'

She smiled at him through her tears. 'How could you doubt me?' she whispered.

Nakano looked at her with eyes that were old and wise and loving. A sympathetic cry rose to Annabel's lips, because she saw in his expression the shadow of distant disloyalties, and the raw new pain of his brother's betrayal. For an instant, they shared that pain, and then Nakano stood up. 'I see you understand me,' he said softly.

Annabel bowed her head low. 'I do understand, and

I'm sorry,' was all she could say for the tears that choked her.

Nakano touched her hand softly, pulling her away from her thoughts. 'I must leave you now, for I have many matters to arrange.' Childlike amusement lit his eyes for a moment. 'Including payment for that horse you stole. Do they not hang horse thieves in England?'

Annabel turned to him with a smile. The salt water in her eyes shattered into rainbow prisms as she dashed it away. 'Why yes. And I had not meant to steal a horse at all, but it was standing there unguarded as I crept out of the inn and I was in such haste to reach you . . .' Her voice trailed away. 'It was not for my comfort that I stole it,' she added, looking down at her stained and grubby kimono ruefully.

She was suddenly aware of her body. Her muscles were shaking with fatigue and soreness. She did not dare look at the skin of her thighs, but the chafing pain between them told her that it would be many days before they were smooth and white again. She pushed back the maddening tangle of her hair once more and said, 'I'm sorry, but I came to you directly. I've had no time to repair the damages of the journey.'

Nakano's eyes were kind. 'I appreciate what you have done for me, Annabel san.' He hesitated, and a boyish shyness that melted Annabel's heart crept into his voice. 'I must leave you now . . . and after I have seen to the traitors within the keep, I must ride out against Yoritomo . . . but, I think we'll have time to . . . Before I go, that is . . . I would be most honoured if you would partake of the tea ceremony with me.'

Careless of her less than formal gown, Annabel bowed low. 'I would be honoured to join you.'

A slight frown furrowed Nakano's brow. 'You will not wish to return to your apartments.' He had not made it a question, but Annabel shook her head fervently, thinking of Kiku, little Kiku and her sadly luckless end. She could never return to those rooms again. Nakano completed his train of thought. 'Then you had best go back to Mamma san.'

'No!' The word burst out with such force that Annabel felt obliged to soften it. 'That is, I'd much rather not.' Nakano still raised an eyebrow. Annabel hurried on, 'Now is not the time, but later, if you please, perhaps after the tea ceremony, I wish we could talk. I could explain my reasons to you then.'

His lips gently brushed her forehead. An ache rose deep within her in response to his maleness. 'It shall be as you wish,' he said with a tiny smile. 'You shall have three of my guards, faithful men who I am certain are true, and your own samurai friend.' He gave a small laugh. 'No need to worry about his loyalty. I never saw a man so smitten. They will accompany you to my chambers and wait there with you. You can bathe, and rest – I still cannot believe how quickly you rode from Okitsu! You must be in sore need of sleep and refreshment.'

Annabel slept around the clock before he returned to her. She had not been awake long, but she had eaten and was dressed. Her kimono was the colour of snow on a grey mountain glacier and was embroidered with the dancing cranes of Hokkaido. Her red obi symbolised the rising sun. A few inches of the black underkimono peeped out, acting as a contrasting frame for the glorious pattern.

Nakano stood silently next to the open rice-paper screen for a moment, just looking at her. His face was tired, but his eyes lit up in appreciation. 'Peerless, Annabel san,' he said softly, looking at the silver ice of her kimono. 'I have prepared the tea house for us. It would be a great honour if you would accompany me there.'

Annabel dipped her head low. The ritual formality of

the Japanese expressions seemed very right and natural between them. 'You do me too much honour,' she replied correctly.

She followed him out of the room, stooping to put on the shoes that waited for her in the corridor, aware of the brush of soft silk over her bare legs. Nakano seemed content, but very remote as she paced slowly alongside him. His winged chestnut kimono was simple, but immaculate, and he had obviously bathed and prepared for this meeting. He smelt of fresh linen and sandalwood, and his thick black hair was bound up in a formal arrangement. Annabel glanced at him from time to time but was silent. She did not know how to ask what she wanted to know. 'Hiroshi?' she finally questioned.

Nakano sighed a little. 'All is in order,' he said quietly.

The finality of his tone sent a chill over her. Her voice trembled as she asked, 'And the samurai who were plotting?'

'They, too, have taken the honourable path to death.'

Then Hiroshi was dead. 'He did have me imprisoned,' she murmured softly, as if trying to convince herself that his fate was merited.

Nakano stirred beside her. 'Oh no! That was I.' She looked at him startled. 'It was to keep you safe,' he explained. 'I suspected that the conspirators were closing in. I can only regret that poor Kiku san fell into the snare that was laid for you.'

Sadness misted Annabel's eyes. 'I shall grieve for her.' Her shoes echoed sadly on the stone steps beneath her feet, then crunched over the gravel of the courtyard they were crossing. Warm air caressed Annabel's skin. She looked at the light grey clouds that drifted across the sky and felt disoriented. From the angle of the sun, she judged it to be late afternoon. She had only been awake for a few hours. How divorced she had become from the normal rhythms of life. The weight of the plots and betrayals around her was iron in her throat. 'And Yoritomo?' she questioned.

'Messengers have been sent. I do not know if he will continue with his attack now that Hiroshi is dead. But he is strong and arrogant. He must be discouraged from continuing with his aggression. I shall ride to meet him tomorrow.'

Annabel looked up at Nakano and he answered the last question; the one she had not dared to ask.

'I allowed your father to return to England.'

Her heart was light as they walked towards a wooden gate set into a wall made of cream plaster. A long roof of ridge tiles sat on top of it. A wall with its own narrow roof looked strange to Annabel. She thought of the coping stones used to top a wall in England. It seemed very far away.

The gate swung open noiselessly, and Annabel passed through silently. The moment did not feel right yet, to say all that she had to say. A perfumed summer's breeze swept across the garden, and, as she looked around its green simplicity, she realised that she was beginning to appreciate the Japanese style.

The garden had been sprinkled with water very recently. It smelt fresh, and wet flagstones gleamed beneath her feet. More drops of water hung from the branches of the stiff pom-pom trees. It was not dark, but Nakano moved around the winding path that followed the tiny boundaries of the garden, putting a taper to the oil lamps that swung from the trees.

The insects stopped shrilling as Nakano passed, and then began again. Although it was daylight, the flickering oil lamps made the green trees look greener. Annabel could smell moss and hear water trickling peacefully as she followed Nakano towards the simple pavilion that seemed to grow out of the ground in one corner of the garden. It was set on pilings of wood and raised a foot or so above a carpet of pure white sand. She had to stoop to follow Nakano through the low, curtained doorway.

Inside the tea house, Annabel felt a great sense of harmony as she settled herself on to the impeccable tatami matting. She arranged the ice-grey skirts of her kimono into a delicate pattern with unconscious care. The light of a candle shone from within a paper and bamboo flower that hung from the cedar rafters. It illuminated the meticulously placed bundles of thatch and reed that made up the ceiling.

The craftsmanship in the tiny building was a pleasure to look at. Every piece of smoothly polished timber was punctiliously joined to the next one. All was peace and order and tranquillity. Nakano moved quietly into a tiny kitchen annexe. Annabel heard his faint movements as he prepared the tea. She was content to sit quietly, drinking in the atmosphere as she waited for him. The perfume of cedar wood surrounded them. Small pieces of aromatic wood smoked in a small charcoal brazier to keep away the mosquitoes that would come out shortly, as the sun was beginning to set.

In one dim corner, a vase of stunning pink and purple azaleas perfumed the air. A few fallen blooms lay on the floor below in an artistic scatter of pollen. In the centre of the room, below a copper chimney, a black kettle boiled with a tiny singing noise. As Annabel gazed into the red heart of the fire of black charcoal that was laid out on an area of white sand beneath the kettle, she wondered if even the sticks of charcoal had been measured, counted and arranged in order, so strong was the impression of precision in all the arrangements of the tea house.

Nakano returned, holding a lacquer tray. As he offered it to Annabel, she saw that each item was arranged in perfect harmony. She bowed low before accepting it. She took up her chopsticks carefully and took each exquisite morsel of food so that the pattern remained balanced.

She felt Nakano's approval. When she had finished eating, she again bowed low to him.

Nakano now took up a bamboo whisk and began to beat the green tea until it was perfect. Before pouring it, he offered Annabel a choice of cups. She selected a brown earthenware glaze that spoke to her of mountains and permanence, perhaps because that was what she yearned for: permanence and a commitment from Nakano. She watched Nakano pouring the tea and, as she took her cup from him, she smiled questioningly. 'I thought the Japanese drank tea before they ate?'

He bowed slightly. The lamplight illuminated the crane symbol embroidered on his kimono. 'I had heard that you disliked the custom.'

Annabel returned his bow. She felt her heart lift because of his thoughtfulness, his willingness to change the old customs to please her. 'I am touched by your concern.'

A comfortable silence fell. As Annabel sipped the bitter green tea, she stared at the glowing sticks of charcoal in the fire. Beautiful peonies with flame petals seemed to bloom and crumble as she watched. The atmosphere of the tea ceremony, the dedicated light-filled atmosphere, and the heady seriousness of the ritual held her entranced. Feeling very close to Nakano, she remained silent for a long, significant moment after she finished the last sip of tea.

They sat quietly together, keenly aware of the beauty of their surroundings. The tiny fire burned with a sweet wooden smell. It seemed to glow brighter as dusk gathered in the corners. A cricket chirped in the rafters, sounding very loud in the silence. A gentle breeze rustled the thatch of the roof. Still they sat. All the poetry in Annabel's nature rose in answer to the moment that Nakano had created.

A great ecstasy of happiness fell upon her as she sat quietly in the gathering dusk, listening to the hollowthroated frogs singing of love as they courted in the rush-lined pools and the glittering streams that ran through the stiff, formal, asymmetrically charming garden outside.

She did not turn to Nakano until she felt him stir. A sweet melancholy flowed over her as the spell he had woven released her. He did not have to tell her that the tea ceremony was over. She could feel the enchanted moment slipping away. 'That was so beautiful,' she whispered softly. 'I felt as if we touched eternity.'

Nakano bowed low. The look in his eyes touched her deeply. 'It is you who do me honour.' His voice was gruff but loving. 'You have given me an exquisite memory to take into battle with me.'

The hiss of the kettle was very loud in Annabel's ears. Her heart drummed dangerously. The moment had come to speak. She tried to make her voice sound confident. 'I want to come with you.'

He looked cool and professional. 'Women have no place in the war zone.'

Annabel felt desperate as she looked at his formal exterior. The gathering dusk made it hard to read his expression. The soft glow of the oil lamp threw as many shadows as it did patches of illumination, and there was a forbidding shadow on the wall behind him. The stiff wings of his kimono seemed to grow larger as she faced him, crying passionately, 'I'm not a courtesan! I'm a barbarian, and there is no place for me at Shimoyama without you. I'll die if you shut me up with the women, waiting for you to spare me a few minutes.' A lump seemed to swell up in her chest and choke her as the silence around them grew.

Nakano reached over and touched one cheek with gentle fingers. She was surprised when his hand came away wet. She had not known she was crying. 'My Annabel,' he said softly. 'Your heart was in your eyes as you spoke. I should have known that a woman who came to me over the oceans of the world would not take kindly to captivity. But, strong as you are, I cannot believe that a woman could suffer the rigours of a campaign. You will not mind the deprivations?'

She was quick to shake her head. 'Not me! I'm tough! I'm strong!'

He smiled at the earnestness of her reply. 'For now, anyway. You are young, and free of the encumbrances of womanhood. Later we shall see, but even now, I don't know.'

He shifted his weight slightly. Something about the angle of his head told Annabel that he was going to make a pronouncement and she held her breath. He shook his head very slightly before beginning. She had to stop him. Annabel's pent-up breath came out in a whoosh of frantic air. 'I can't bear it! Don't leave me behind, mewed up with the women!'

He was watching her face and her eyes. 'You have not completed your geisha training.'

Annabel looked into the heart of the glowing fire before saying unhappily, 'You cannot force me into that mould.'

His tone was only half-serious. 'I must love you as you are?'

Her head bowed. 'I cannot be otherwise.'

The shadows gathered around them. The frogs sang. The bamboo clumps outside rustled in the breeze. Annabel wondered what emotions lay concealed within Nakano's kneeling form. The stiff wings of his kimono threw a giant-shouldered shadow on the wooden wall behind him. His outer aspect was so forbidding, that it was a surprise when he said to her gently, 'Then you may accompany me.'

She looked up at him, thrilled, and he smiled at her expression. 'I may even send you to negotiate with Yoritomo,' he teased.

Annabel's heart danced in her chest. 'I'd deal with him like that!' she said and snapped her fingers.

Nakano laughed out loud as he gestured to her to rise and took her arm. 'I believe you would, my little barbarian,' he said, as he led her out of the wooden pavilion of the tea house. 'But actually, I'm short of a good cook, and so I must make use of your other talents.' They were both laughing now, as they paced through the perfection of the lamp-lit garden.

'Very well, Master Warlord,' said Annabel, pretending to be very serious. 'I can cook lovely barbarian dishes for your samurai. Ha! Roast frog and wriggly worms . . .'

Nakano reared up in feigned outrage. 'What, and make my soldiers sick? That would be sabotage! I thought you were loyal to me?'

Annabel faced him as they reached the gate, and now she was serious. A lantern swung in the branches above them, illuminating his face, the dark pools of his eyes. 'I am yours,' she promised softly. Her words vanished into the winds and the night shadows. 'Now and for ever.'

Nakano leant towards her and took her hands in his, and then he kissed her gently. 'And I am your servant,' he promised simply. 'Now and for ever.' And there was a dedication in his kiss that had not been there before. Annabel felt all her passion rise up within her like a flame as she returned his fervent embrace.

'Shall we love?' he whispered softly. There was a flush on his cheeks and a radiance in his eyes that transfigured him. A chord in his deep voice triggered sensual responses in Annabel. She smiled at him warmly and an answering blush rose to her own cheeks. He nodded in reply to her unvoiced answer, pulling her even closer to him. 'We have had matters of great gravity to discuss and settle, my Annabel san, but now we shall be a simple man and woman together.' He rested his cheek against hers. 'I know a willow grove, not far from here, where the moss grows in soft pillows. Will you spend the night in my arms there?'

As he lifted his dark, soft, loving eyes to Annabel, it seemed to her as if the doors and windows of heaven were suddenly opened. It was one of the supreme moments of her life. 'Anywhere, my lord,' she whispered, and touched him gently with her lips.

They passed through the gate and left the tea house behind. Samurai waited under the dark velvet sky, their armour glinting in the star light. Nakano sent some of them running for servants, others he sent to the barracks to check on the preparations for tomorrow's march.

Annabel stood back a little and watched him proudly, and with anticipation. An erotic shiver ran through her. It was hard to believe that the mighty warlord who was now making such efficient arrangements for battle would shortly be lying naked in her arms. As she stood watching him, the knowledge was a secret delight blossoming between her legs.

The first servant arrived bearing a paper lantern that cast a pink light. Others arrived. Lanterns of peach, amber and yellow joined the procession that Nakano led towards a gardened corner of Shimoyama. The garden stood on a rise of land. The servants tied the lanterns on to the branches of the softly rustling willow trees. The willow leaves blew white in a sudden breeze as a sleeping area was prepared in the lush sprouting grass.

Nakano took Annabel's arm. The silk of their garments brushed together as they walked a few steps. The breeze shook the outer silk of Annabel's glacier-grey kimono, showing the beginnings of the dark underkimono as she walked. The dark bulk of the fortress was a warm shadow at their backs as they stood together on top of the rise, so close together that Annabel could feel the heat of Nakano's body through the soft, warm silk of his kimono. A deep and steady joy burned in her heart as she looked out over the interlocking keeps and moats, lesser castles, towers and bridges that ran down to the huddle of town buildings that served Shimoyama.

There was no moon, but the stars blazed high in the heavens. They shone like trembling diamonds sewn on to black velvet. A soft breeze, cooler now, as the evening turned into night, blew up from the distant mountains and patted Annabel's cheek. Below them, she could hear rather than see the preparations going on in the barracks: men shouted, wheels rumbled and a horse whinnied loudly. Pungent smoke rose from the cooking fires that glowed orange here and there.

'All is in order,' said Nakano, nodding a little grimly. 'We march with the dawn tomorrow.' He turned to Annabel and ran a gentle finger over her jawline. 'If you come with us, tonight could be your last night on this sweet earth.'

She met his gaze honestly. 'The dangers of battle are nothing to me if I may be with you.'

Nakano smiled tenderly at her and caressed her cheek. 'Now you live as samurai. When life and death are the same, the fear of death vanishes, and so a man – or a woman – lives with true appreciation of life – and its pleasures.'

Annabel caught his hand and kissed his open palm. She felt more alive than she had ever done.

Nakano's voice was husky. 'The servants are gone.'

His warm body moved against hers. Annabel followed him to where the white of spread futons was a bright patch on the dark grass. She could see the dim shadows of samurai on guard, but by now she was so used to Nakano's permanent escort that she could ignore their presence. Erotic desire rose in her, and she knew it was strong in Nakano too. She could see it, feel it, sense it in his closeness, in his shallow breathing.

The multi-coloured lanterns bobbed in the high trees. Fireflies pulsed and danced in the lower branches of the trees, festooning the tender greenery with strings of glowing lights. A bird trilled in the bushes. A nightingale? Or a day bird woken by the unusual lights? Annabel didn't know, but she was aware of liquid warbling notes making the air beautiful as Nakano kissed the silken length of her neck beneath one ear. 'I want you,' she murmured huskily.

'What I want –' Nakano's eyes darkened as he raised one of her white hands to his lips, kissing her fingers so that his words were a warm murmur against her skin '– what I want, my precious barbarian, is you.' He pulled her closer, enclosing her in his arms. 'Naked on those futons, next to me.' He lowered his head and nibbled her earlobe. 'With the sweet spaces of your woman's flower open to me.'

Annabel looked up at him for a long warm moment before speaking. 'And I want you, naked, above me, with your manhood inside me.' She felt his quivering response to her bold words.

'My passion for you is so strong,' he murmured, looking at her with love. Annabel felt that no one had ever looked at her with such tenderness in their eyes, until a faint memory awoke of being a much-loved and cherished child. She smiled at the memory and nestled against the protective strength of his body as he continued, 'It has been so since I first saw you. Alone, proud, so beautiful, so unique in your wildness.'

He kissed her lips and drew back, sighing deeply. 'I thought you were lost to me. That you would return over the oceans to your fabulous island home.' He paused and shook his head. 'I grieved more than a samurai should; and I dreamed ceaselessly of holding you, of touching you, of kissing you like this.'

He bent to kiss her again, and the taste of his kiss on her lips was powerful and exciting. He kissed her again. 'Oh, Annabel san, how I've dreamed of us being together once more.'

'I, too, have dreamed of you,' she murmured.

He buried his hands in her hair, disturbing the elaborate formality of the arrangement. He carefully removed the combs that held it, and ran his fingers through the blonde mass as it fell to her shoulders. 'Gold,' he murmured, laughing openly at the play on words. 'True gold, like your heart, and as precious.' He drew Annabel to him and she sighed as he covered her lips with his, kissing her with all the power and passion of his warrior's heart.

Annabel relished the feel of his hot, masculine body pressing against hers. She moulded her body to fit his. His lips played with hers, coaxed them open, then captured them with his sweet strength. She kissed him back openly, matching his passion, his vigour, his hunger for life.

His hands dropped to her shoulders, massaging them lightly, then rubbing them with gentle erotic strokes. She melted against him, soft, and limp, and so willing to know his strength. Her breasts pushed against the silk of her kimono, and she longed to feel his sweet skin against her inflamed flesh and aching nipples. She wanted nothing between them. She wanted heated bare skin to touch heated bare skin. She wanted nothing to act as a barrier to their love.

She raised her hands to her neck and parted the silk of her kimono, trying to bare her breasts for him, but the fabric would not yield. With a sound of impatience, she turned her back to him, presenting the intricate folds of her obi for him to untie. She felt his fingers moving surely over the red butterfly knot of her sash, and then a feeling of release as it fell away and lay on the ground in a slash of crimson.

She turned back to face him and he kissed her once more, fully, deeply, his tongue plunging into the dark velvet of her mouth, seeking and giving a taste of the erotic pleasures that awaited them both. His hands reached into the open folds of her ice-coloured kimono and played along her backbone, pressing against her skin, moulding her to him. His fingers aroused her powerfully as they roamed over her sensitive skin.

When his hands reached her lower back, he spread his fingers over her buttocks, stroking their luscious curves, pulling her to him, running his fingers over the place where he had once marked her. An instinct older than both of them – way beyond Annabel's control – made her lift her hips and push her mons into Nakano's rock-hard body, urging them closer together with a suggestive, bumping, grinding motion that made her passion obvious.

He released her, and she could hear the strain of his breathing. 'Annabel san,' he breathed, and he snaked his arms around her and lifted her effortlessly into his arms.

She looped her slim white arms around his neck, rejoicing in his size and sturdiness. She planted a kiss on his jawline, then another and another, moving from his lips to under his ear. The cool night air touched her skin, and the stars shone brightly behind him, seeming to laugh out of the dark sky.

His heart beat in his chest with a steady, regular rhythm as he walked slowly to where the white bedding awaited them on the green grass of the grove. The smell of the crushed vegetation below the futons rose in a herby, aromatic and pungent cloud. The futons gave crisply below the weight of her body as Nakano slowly lowered her into the fresh embrace of the bedding.

His shadow was large and dark above her. She could feel him, but not really see him. The outline of his samurai hair was foreign. His black eyes were unreadable slits above his high cheekbones. Annabel gave a little shiver. His dark outline was erotic, but unsettling. The series of warm, friendly, moist kisses he planted along her neck reassured her. This man was her true mate. Her lover for all time.

She could feel his breath sighing over her breasts as

his capable hands reached behind her to ease her shoulders out of the open kimono. The silvery-grey fabric appeared white in the starlight. As Nakano pulled the garment free, his kisses continued down into her cleavage. The white folds of the crane-patterned kimono slid over Annabel's sensitive skin in a slither of sensuous silk. Nakano tossed it aside and reached for her again. The dark undergarments followed, and when she fell back into the pillows, she was naked.

He was kneeling above her fully dressed. Annabel lifted her white arms and reached for the sash of his obi. It fell apart sweetly in her hands, as did the folds of his kimono. His shadow grew flapping wings for a moment as he floated the layers of silk over his head, and then he became a mortal man once more, naked and simple, facing her in the starlight.

His body fell on top of her. She felt her whole body tremble with the excitement and the ecstasy of the thrill that swept over her. His hard body touched her soft one. His male muscles covered her female curves. He put his mouth on hers and pulled her so close that they were one person.

His kisses were warm, his caresses were hot. His manhood was warm and hard against her flanks as his impassioned lips covered hers. His firm chest was hard against the softness of her breasts. The feel of his hard body against her skin thrilled her. Annabel's whole being melted under his embrace. She twisted and moaned. 'I want you,' she whispered, but there was no need for her to say the words aloud. The erotic movements of her body told Nakano all he needed to know.

His hard muscled legs were between hers, forcing them open. The touch of his fingers on her clitoris sent a shiver of pleasure flooding over her. She knew she was wet, and she knew that he liked it. She heard him grunt softly as he touched the sweetness of the honey dew that pooled over his fingers. He moved his body swiftly, and the hardness of his cock was inside her.

She said his name aloud: 'Nakano!' repeating it in surprise and pleasure as she felt the size of his manhood and his hard desire. 'Nakano! Nakano!' His dark head was buried in her shoulders. He was moving quickly and she caught his urgency. There was no place for restraint here. A thousand million years of evolution told Annabel that she was safe in the arms of a man who would die to protect her; she could abandon all fear and restraint.

Annabel flung her arms around Nakano and clung to him, heedless of skill or technique. The sheer naturalness of their coupling was bliss. All she wanted was to feel his cock moving inside her. He seemed to feel the same. His powerful body rammed into her freely. Each powerful stroke sank further inside her. She could feel the sweetness of his balls against her vulva. Sweat sprang out and joined their naked, heaving bodies. As all the pores of their skin opened, a lovely musky fragrance surrounded them.

It was too sweet, too intense to last, this wild impassioned coupling under the stars. All their passion seemed to come together in a single moment of abandon and they clung together even more tightly as their two separate earthly bodies shared a single heavenly orgasm.

They lay peacefully in each other's arms long after it was over, feeling the sweetness ebb away, feeling the sweat dry on their bodies. Then Nakano lifted himself on one elbow and looked down at Annabel in tired pleasure. 'Sleep now, my sweet barbarian,' he said to her.

'I think I'm too happy to sleep,' she murmured, smiling trustingly up at him.

He leaned over and kissed her and she smiled as he said, 'If you are to follow the drum you must behave as samurai on campaign: eat and sleep while you may, for who knows what tomorrow's battle will bring.'

Nakano reached over and pulled a snowy-white futon over their naked bodies. The cotton was crisp, and cold from lying on the grass. The trilling bird sang from a willow tree. Fireflies pulsed and flickered among the dark leaves. Annabel yawned as she snuggled under the futon and rested her head on Nakano's shoulder. He smoothed her hair like a child's, his movements growing slow and drowsy as he drifted off to sleep.

Annabel lay quietly for a few moments. She felt him grow heavy against her. Then she turned her head slightly to look at his handsome shadowed face. There was the suggestion of a smile on his mouth and his long lashes cast lovely shadows on his cheeks. 'Sleep tight.' She whispered the words in English, but he was already fast asleep in her arms and dreaming. He was breathing softly, but Annabel seemed to hear the distant thunder of horses' hooves and see sunlight winking on the spears and banners of his army, and she thought he was dreaming of war.

The night breeze grew cooler yet. It blew softly over her face and lifted her curls, teasing them. The starlight fell on Nakano's head and arms and shoulders as he slept in her arms, making his skin shine with some mysterious light. Annabel rejoiced in the muscled beauty of his body, the strength and warmth that rose from him, but it was the inner man that she embraced as she lay there.

She lay sleepless, looking into the sky. Directly above them, one great planet burnt with a diamond flicker. The moon rose as she lay watching, and she found that its light was in her mind and spirit. The darkness of her previous existence had been taken from her.

Moving carefully, so as not to disturb Nakano, Annabel propped herself up on a couple of stiff, rustling pea-filled pillows. Their strangeness no longer troubled her.

Now she could see over the huddle of black rooftops to the rows of jagged mountains. Far away, just above the top of the distant volcanic cone of Mount Fuji, two white birds were in gentle flight. The white curve of their wings identified them as cranes. They soared and sank again, infinitely graceful and lovely. The silver moonlight touched their wings and breasts. Then they soared once more and were lost in the ever-increasing moonlight.

Annabel told herself that she must be mistaken. No cranes flew as high as that, nor did she think they flew in that manner, yet as she held Nakano's sweetly breathing body in her arms and followed the path of the flying cranes with her eyes, the sense of harmony and peace that she had been looking for all her life flowed sweetly through her veins and she was content at last.

LOOK OUT FOR THE ALL-NEW BLACK LACE BOOKS – AVAILABLE NOW!

All books priced £7.99 in the UK. Please note publication dates apply to the UK only. For other territories, please contact your retailer.

OFFICE PERKS
Monica Belle
ISBN 0 352 33939 X

This is the story of Lucy Doyle, a red-haired and hot-tempered London Irish girl with her eyes on the prize – and young men's trousers. Her family have got her a job in a Parochial House in North London for the summer, between leaving school and going to university, but she is sacked on her first day for doing something she shouldn't with the groundsman. Determined to stay in London she signs up as an office temp, faking her references and chancing her luck. Along with fellow recruits – the ladylike but filthy Bobbie and the completely dirty Sophie – this cheeky 'flower of Erin' carves a swathe of debauchery through London's office land, collecting lovers, outraging her bosses and drinking far too much as she causes havoc in the way only a bad girl can. **A wildly entertaining XXX-rated story of girls on the pull, causing mayhem and loving it!**

UNDRESSING THE DEVIL
Angel Strand
ISBN 0 352 33938 1

It's the 1930s. Hitler and Mussolini are building their war machine and Europe is a hotbed of political tension. Cia, a young, Anglo-Italian woman, escapes the mayhem, returning to England only to become embroiled in a web of sexual adventures. Her Italian lover has disappeared along with her clothes, lost somewhere between Florence and the Isle of Wight. Her British friends are carrying on in the manner to which they are accustomed: sailing their yachts and partying. However, this serene façade hides rivalries and forbidden pleasures. It's only a matter of time before Cia's two worlds collide. **Literary erotica at its best, in this story of bright young things on the edge.**

THE BARBARIAN GEISHA
Charlotte Royal
ISBN 0 352 33267 0

When Annabel Smith jumps overboard from her father's sailing vessel she expects to die – but is instead washed up on the shores of feudal Japan and into the hands of the brutal warlord, Lord Nakano. Enchanted by her naked blonde beauty, Nakano takes her to Shimoyama, his fortress home. There Mamma San teaches Annabel the arts of sensual pleasure. Shimoyama is a world of political intrigue and Nakano's brother warns Annabel of the dangers that surround her. Will she ever be accepted as a barbarian geisha? **Unusual story of arcane erotic ritual in a hidden society.**

MS BEHAVIOUR
Mini Lee
ISBN O 352 33962 4

Santa is a university student with a wonderful new boyfriend and bright future. However, she's also a bad girl with a wild streak who cultivates an illicit and obsessive relationship with her law professor. The older Professor MacLean's attractions are too numerous and beguiling to avoid and Santa cannot stop herself from teasing him and rousing his ire with her saucy behaviour – in and out of class. Caught up in this dangerous game, she is neglecting her studies but honing her sexual skills, driving all the men around her to distraction. When MacLean sets Santa a defence assignment that mirrors their own highly charged situation, the sexual tension reaches boiling point and threatens to spill over into something far more dangerous. **A sizzling hot story of forbidden lust with a modern twist.**

FRENCH MANNERS
Olivia Christie
ISBN O 352 33214 X

Gilles de la Trave persuades Colette, a young and beautiful peasant girl from one of his estates, to become his mistress and live the life of a Parisian courtesan. However, it is his son Victor that she loves and expects to marry. In a moment of passion and curiosity she confesses her sins to the local priest, unaware that the curé has his own agenda: one which involves himself *and* Victor. Shocked, Colette takes the only sensible option for a young girl from the provinces: she flees to Paris to immerse herself in a life of wild indulgence and luxury! **An erotic and beautifully written story charting a rural young girl's journey into adulthood and sophistication.**

Also available

THE BLACK LACE SEXY QUIZ BOOK
Maddie Saxon
ISBN 0 352 33884 9

- What sexual personality type are you?
- Have you ever faked it because that was easier than explaining what you wanted?
- What kind of fantasy figures turn you on – and does your partner know?
- What sexual signals are you giving out right now?

Today's image-conscious dating scene is a tough call. Our sexual expectations are cranked up to the max, and the sexes seem to have become highly critical of each other in terms of appearance and performance in the bedroom. But even though guys have ditched their nasty Y-fronts and girls are more babe-licious than ever, a huge number of us are still being let down sexually. Sex therapist Maddie Saxon thinks this is because we are finding it harder to relax and let our true sexual selves shine through.

The Black Lace Sexy Quiz Book will help you negotiate the minefield of modern relationships. Through a series of fun, revealing quizzes, you will be able to rate your sexual needs honestly and get what you really want from your partner. The quizzes will get you thinking about and discussing your desires in ways you haven't previously considered. Unlock the mysteries of your sexual psyche in this fun, revealing quiz book designed with today's sex-savvy woman in mind.

Black Lace Booklist

Information is correct at time of printing. To avoid disappointment check availability before ordering. Go to www.blacklace-books.co.uk. All books are priced £6.99 unless another price is given.

BLACK LACE BOOKS WITH A CONTEMPORARY SETTING

☐ SHAMELESS Stella Black	ISBN 0 352 33485 1	£5.99
☐ INTENSE BLUE Lyn Wood	ISBN 0 352 33496 7	£5.99
☐ A SPORTING CHANCE Susie Raymond	ISBN 0 352 33501 7	£5.99
☐ TAKING LIBERTIES Susie Raymond	ISBN 0 352 33357 X	£5.99
☐ ON THE EDGE Laura Hamilton	ISBN 0 352 33534 3	£5.99
☐ LURED BY LUST Tania Picarda	ISBN 0 352 33533 5	£5.99
☐ THE NINETY DAYS OF GENEVIEVE Lucinda Carrington	ISBN 0 352 33070 8	£5.99
☐ DREAMING SPIRES Juliet Hastings	ISBN 0 352 33584 X	
☐ THE TRANSFORMATION Natasha Rostova	ISBN 0 352 33311 1	
☐ SIN.NET Helena Ravenscroft	ISBN 0 352 33598 X	
☐ TWO WEEKS IN TANGIER Annabel Lee	ISBN 0 352 33599 8	
☐ PLAYING HARD Tina Troy	ISBN 0 352 33617 X	
☐ SYMPHONY X Jasmine Stone	ISBN 0 352 33629 3	
☐ SUMMER FEVER Anna Ricci	ISBN 0 352 33625 0	
☐ CONTINUUM Portia Da Costa	ISBN 0 352 33120 8	
☐ FULL STEAM AHEAD Tabitha Flyte	ISBN 0 352 33637 4	
☐ A SECRET PLACE Ella Broussard	ISBN 0 352 33307 3	
☐ GAME FOR ANYTHING Lyn Wood	ISBN 0 352 33639 0	
☐ CHEAP TRICK Astrid Fox	ISBN 0 352 33640 4	
☐ THE GIFT OF SHAME Sara Hope-Walker	ISBN 0 352 29935 1	
☐ COMING UP ROSES Crystalle Valentino	ISBN 0 352 33658 7	
☐ GOING TOO FAR Laura Hamilton	ISBN 0 352 33657 9	
☐ THE STALLION Georgina Brown	ISBN 0 352 33005 8	
☐ DOWN UNDER Juliet Hastings	ISBN 0 352 33663 3	
☐ ODALISQUE Fleur Reynolds	ISBN 0 352 32887 8	
☐ SWEET THING Alison Tyler	ISBN 0 352 33682 X	
☐ TIGER LILY Kimberly Dean	ISBN 0 352 33685 4	

☐ RISKY BUSINESS Lisette Allen	ISBNO 352 33280 8	£7.99
☐ OFFICE PERKS Monica Belle	ISBNO 352 33939 X	£7.99
☐ UNDRESSING THE DEVIL Angel Strand	ISBNO 352 33938 1	£7.99

BLACK LACE BOOKS WITH AN HISTORICAL SETTING

☐ PRIMAL SKIN Leona Benkt Rhys	ISBN 0 352 33500 9	£5.99
☐ DARKER THAN LOVE Kristina Lloyd	ISBN 0 352 33279 4	
☐ THE CAPTIVATION Natasha Rostova	ISBN 0 352 33234 4	
☐ MINX Megan Blythe	ISBN 0 352 33638 2	
☐ DIVINE TORMENT Janine Ashbless	ISBN 0 352 33719 2	
☐ SATAN'S ANGEL Melissa MacNeal	ISBN 0 352 33726 5	
☐ THE INTIMATE EYE Georgia Angelis	ISBN 0 352 33004 X	
☐ SILKEN CHAINS Jodi Nicol	ISBN 0 352 33143 7	
☐ THE LION LOVER Mercedes Kelly	ISBN 0 352 33162 3	
☐ THE AMULET Lisette Allen	ISBN 0 352 33019 8	
☐ WHITE ROSE ENSNARED Juliet Hastings	ISBN 0 352 33052 X	
☐ UNHALLOWED RITES Martine Marquand	ISBN 0 352 33222 0	
☐ LA BASQUAISE Angel Strand	ISBN 0 352 32988 2	
☐ THE HAND OF AMUN Juliet Hastings	ISBN 0 352 33144 5	
☐ THE SENSES BEJEWELLED Cleo Cordell	ISBN 0 352 32904 1	

BLACK LACE ANTHOLOGIES

☐ WICKED WORDS Various	ISBN 0 352 33363 4
☐ MORE WICKED WORDS Various	ISBN 0 352 33487 8
☐ WICKED WORDS 3 Various	ISBN 0 352 33522 X
☐ WICKED WORDS 4 Various	ISBN 0 352 33603 X
☐ WICKED WORDS 5 Various	ISBN 0 352 33642 0
☐ WICKED WORDS 6 Various	ISBN 0 352 33690 0
☐ WICKED WORDS 7 Various	ISBN 0 352 33743 5
☐ WICKED WORDS 8 Various	ISBN 0 352 33787 7
☐ WICKED WORDS 9 Various	ISBN 0 352 33860 1
☐ WICKED WORDS 10 Various	ISBN 0 352 33893 8
☐ THE BEST OF BLACK LACE 2 Various	ISBN 0 352 33718 4

BLACK LACE NON-FICTION

☐ THE BLACK LACE BOOK OF WOMEN'S SEXUAL   ISBN O 352 33793 1
    FANTASIES Ed. Kerri Sharp

☐ THE BLACK LACE SEXY QUIZ BOOK Maddie Saxon   ISBN O 352 33884 9

To find out the latest information about Black Lace titles, check out the website: www.blacklace-books.co.uk or send for a booklist with complete synopses by writing to:

> Black Lace Booklist, Virgin Books Ltd
> Thames Wharf Studios
> Rainville Road
> London W6 9HA

Please include an SAE of decent size. Please note only British stamps are valid.

Our privacy policy
We will not disclose information you supply us to any other parties. We will not disclose any information which identifies you personally to any person without your express consent.

From time to time we may send out information about Black Lace books and special offers. Please tick here if you do not wish to receive Black Lace information.   ☐

Please send me the books I have ticked above.

Name ....

Address ....

....

....

....

Post Code ....

Send to: Virgin Books Cash Sales, Thames Wharf Studios, Rainville Road, London W6 9HA.

US customers: for prices and details of how to order books for delivery by mail, call 1-800-343-4499.

Please enclose a cheque or postal order, made payable to Virgin Books Ltd, to the value of the books you have ordered plus postage and packing costs as follows:

UK and BFPO – £1.00 for the first book, 50p for each subsequent book.

Overseas (including Republic of Ireland) – £2.00 for the first book, £1.00 for each subsequent book.

If you would prefer to pay by VISA, ACCESS/MASTERCARD, DINERS CLUB, AMEX or SWITCH, please write your card number and expiry date here:

....

Signature ....

Please allow up to 28 days for delivery.

A PUFFIN BOOK

PROPERTY OF

_____

_____